WINNIPEG

WITHDRAWN

DEC 0 1 2010

PUBLIC LIBRARY

D1006273

Quest for a Killer

a&b

Quest for a Killer

A Rose McQuinn Mystery

ALANNA KNIGHT

First published in Great Britain in 2010 by
Allison & Busby Limited
13 Charlotte Mews
London W1T 4EJ
www.allisonandbusby.com

Copyright © 2010 by ALANNA KNIGHT

The moral right of the author has been asserted.

All characters and events in this publication,
other than those clearly in the public domain,
are fictitious and any resemblance to actual persons,
living or dead, is purely coincidental.

This book is sold subject to the conditions that it shall not,
by way of trade or otherwise, be lent, resold, hired out or
otherwise circulated without the publisher's prior
written consent in any form of binding or cover other than
that in which it is published and without a similar condition
being imposed upon the subsequent
purchaser.

A CIP catalogue record for this book is available from
the British Library.

10 9 8 7 6 5 4 3 2 1

13-ISBN 978-0-7490-0738-6

Typeset in 13/16 pt Adobe Garamond Pro by
Allison & Busby Ltd.

Paper used in this publication is from sustainably managed sources.
All of the wood used is procured from legal sources and is fully traceable.
The producing mill uses schemes such as ISO 14001
to monitor environmental impact.

Printed and bound in the UK by
CPI Mackays, Chatham ME5 8TD

ALANNA KNIGHT has written more than fifty books in an impressive writing career that has spanned forty years. She is a founding member of the Scottish Association of Writers, Honorary President of the Edinburgh Writers' Club, and Convener of the Scottish Chapter of the Crime Writers' Association. Born and educated in Tyneside, Alanna now lives in Edinburgh.

www.alannaknight.com

Available from

ALLISON & BUSBY

The Rose McQuinn series

The Inspector's Daughter
Dangerous Pursuits
An Orkney Murder
Ghost Walk
Destroying Angel

The Inspector Faro series

Murder in Paradise

The Tam Eildor series

The Gowrie Conspiracy
The Stuart Sapphire

In memory of Alistair,
husband, best friend and enabler.

CHAPTER ONE

Autumn 1899

That sunny morning, as I stood at my kitchen door in Solomon's Tower, surveying the peaceful little garden, the swallows had left their ancient nesting places and another sound obliterated the raucous cries of corbies, eerie black shapes forever haunting the lofty crown of Arthur's Seat.

The distant strains of a pipe band marching our gallant soldiers, the Black Watch, to Waverley Station on the first stage of that long sea journey to South Africa – ready to fight and die for queen and country.

Britain was at war. There was a lull in the resumption of hostilities while Boers waited for the spring grass to maintain the horses and oxen of their commandos; the British, meanwhile, awaited urgent reinforcements of imperial troops.

This state of affairs did not please everyone. In the initial stages of trouble brewing, William Buller, the brilliant outspoken commander-in-chief in Cape Colony, had declared British policies were foolish and did what he could to avert an Anglo-Boer war, which he believed would be a calamity. Damned as a pro-Boer and recalled for his efforts, he became in his own words 'the best abused man in England'.

My arrival in Edinburgh four years ago saw constant unrest and bloodshed in the distant outposts of the British Empire, but on a more personal level, concerning the distress of an old school friend, I was plunged into investigating the behaviour of a husband with murderous tendencies. This was my first case; I solved it successfully. Not without considerable danger; it set the pattern for a career as a Lady Investigator, Discretion Guaranteed, my life's secret ambition – to follow in the footsteps of my father, Chief Inspector Jeremy Faro.

The financial status of my career has improved considerably by taking on those anxious to keep their skeletons firmly locked in the family cupboards, afraid that their shameful secrets would be made public by laying them before the prying eyes of the police.

My clients are mostly the well-to-do: the labouring class could not afford the services of a private detective even if they knew such amiable creatures existed to sort out their troubles. Sadly, often in despair they resort to more violent and permanent solutions which result in prison, transportation and even death by hanging.

And thus I have had cause to learn much about the hierarchy of Edinburgh society and have gained a remarkable insight into the sanctity of middle-class life, where the qualities of respectability and law-abidingness are taken for granted. Frauds, thieving servants, sexual transgressions, husbands (particularly those addicted to the lure of comely housemaids), wives with blackmailing lovers and even, on several occasions, already recorded in my logbooks...

Murder!

Not that my investigations began that way. A distressed client entered with a list of suspicious facts to be investigated. Not until I was enmeshed in the web of intrigue did realisation dawn that this case was more suited to the police than a private detective, a fact which my client, for now obvious and frequently sinister reasons, had been most anxious to conceal, revelations that came too late to avert the looming catastrophe.

I owed my life on more than one occasion to the presence of Thane, the strange deerhound who originates from somewhere in the depths of Edinburgh's extinct volcano, Arthur's Seat (one baffling mystery I have failed to solve). It took the arrival of a very much flesh-and-blood creature, Sergeant Jack Macmerry of the Edinburgh City Police who also saw Thane, to convince me that my sanity was not in doubt.

Jack and I became lovers and would have married, indeed we were on the very threshold two years ago. There was only one impediment. Determined to become a detective inspector of the calibre of my father, a legend in his own lifetime, Jack realised that my chosen career might well inhibit all his chances of promotion.

And so we parted company; my permanent excuse that I was not officially a widow – my husband, Danny McQuinn, merely classed as missing in the state of Arizona – continued to aggravate Jack.

He guessed it was only an excuse and, to be honest, so did I. I did not want to remarry, but without this commitment, my ambitious lover (who longed to see me in the traditional role of a picture book housewife) finally accepted the truth.

He knew in his heart that I did not love him enough and so he went elsewhere for comfort, and the silence of almost two years suggests that he has found the love of his life and is doubtlessly happily married. Much as I still miss his companionship, his warmth and humour, the sacrifice he demanded was too great, one that could not have made either of us easy in a marital relationship.

A difficult choice but my father's daughter indeed: the dream of a domestic life, of a home with a husband and children, was somehow lost on me. I had become addicted to puzzling evidence, and the search for clues; even personal danger did not deter me from solving a case. Among my clients an occasional attractive and eligible gentleman of means, but a few meetings, dinner and a concert were sufficient pointers to recognise that gleam in the masculine eye and the knowledge of what was on offer. Alas, a position in middle-class society held no temptations to abandon my chosen career.

As well as logbooks of every case, I now have five more extensive accounts of those apparently innocent investigations which had sinister hidden agendas and almost cost me my life. And along with the march of progress I now own a bicycle and, recently, a typewriting machine. A gift from my stepbrother Dr

Vince Laurie, it sits in idle splendour in the great hall, one more challenge I have yet to tackle.

In one respect it seems that I have never learnt. Alongside those essential skills for a private detective, of observation and deduction, I was aware of one ingredient in short supply: I was not ruthless enough. Deep-rooted in my personality was a highly developed social sense, with an unfortunate tendency to seek out the goodness in humanity. And that included bloodthirsty renegade Indians in Arizona, and now in South Africa those Boer farmers who refused to give up fighting for suzerainty over the Transvaal while the British retaliated by burning their farms and herding them into concentration camps.

The sound of bagpipes faded to be replaced by the honking of wild geese in steady formation as they flew high over Arthur's Seat to their feeding grounds on St Margaret's Loch, and less distant, the faint babble of voices intermingled with fiddle music, hammering and high activity.

I sniffed the air. A faint jungle-like smell drifting on the breeze whispered 'wild animals'.

The circus had come to town!

This event should have been full of joyous anticipation but its advent heralded a sorrowful anniversary, a reminder that the first time I had heard these sounds coincided with my arrival from Arizona, certain then that I would not be alone for long, confident that Danny McQuinn would come home again.

Alas, gone are the days when I lived in hourly

expectation of a door opening and my missing husband standing on the threshold, smiling, with arms outstretched, ready to clasp me to his heart. I have now accepted that Danny is dead, lost to me for ever, lying in some unmarked grave among the red rocks of the Arizona desert, where he disappeared during his detective activities five long years ago.

Far below in Queen's Park, the sounds of activity gained momentum. At my side the deerhound froze. Thane had sensed something else, well out of my range.

I put my hand on his head. 'What is it?'

I knew he didn't like the circus or the animals and was frowning in that almost human way.

The circus was an annual springtime event. This was an additional visit. Posters advertised it everywhere. Hengels Circus was paying Edinburgh a visit 'for a short season' after a well-publicised command performance for Her Majesty Queen Victoria at Balmoral Castle and before returning to their winter quarters on the outskirts of Glasgow. This extra appearance, with the additional thrills of merry-go-rounds and swingboats, was pleasantly anticipated by the children. And for the more mature in age, in addition to a fortune-teller and a shooting range, there would be daring sideshows, featuring seriously underclad ladies who, according to lurid posters, rashly promised to make 'old men young and young men ambitious'.

The greatest delight, however, for children of all ages, was the clowns. In particular their leader Joey – an unending source of wonder, with his tricks and nonsense guaranteed to raise a smile on even the sober countenances of the more aged and respectable citizens of Edinburgh. Although I did not class myself among the latter, I must confess to a weakness for the circus. The smoking fires, roast potatoes, the smell of horses and crushed grass all added to a way of life that harked back to pioneering days in Arizona — exhilarating and dangerous in a quite different way to my present existence.

This time the circus was destined to be less innocent, more fraught with sinister happenings. Its arrival coincided with a local bank robbery a mile away, where one of the clerks had been killed and, nearby, two girls had committed suicide within hours of each other.

Were the three deaths linked? Were the suicides also to be classed as murder?

CHAPTER TWO

The facts under investigation by the police were that the girls, unmarried and at present unemployed, had met death by hanging themselves from ropes attached to the drying racks on their kitchen ceilings. This had happened within hours of each other in the same tenement in St Leonard's, just a short distance from the scene of the bank robbery in Newington Road.

These tragic events raised many intriguing questions, sadly far outside my field as a private detective, especially as sensational newspaper reports hinted at foul play, a killer at large, firmly dismissed by more sober editorials as 'base rumours set about to terrorise the good citizens of Edinburgh'.

Nevertheless, my interest deepened. In my experience there was, to quote a well-worn cliché, 'no smoke without fire'. According to the terrified surviving bank clerk interviewed by the police, the man seen running from the tenement in the direction of Queen's Park at the time of the suicides bore a remarkable resemblance to the robber who had brutally killed his senior colleague, leaving a widow and four young bairns fatherless.

There had also been a series of local burglaries. One at Newington House close by Sheridan Place, my childhood home, long since vacated by my father, who now in his retirement travelled the world with his companion, the Irish writer, Imogen Crowe.

Coincidences maybe, but the possibility of a connection could not be dismissed. Perhaps it was even encouraged as there was little crime in Edinburgh, with headlines devoted to the Boer War, although it seemed too remote except for those with sons, fathers or sweethearts in the Black Watch regiment. Names listed as 'missing' or 'killed in action' made melancholy reading.

I knew all about danger and violent death, having had first-hand experience sharing the hazards of Danny McQuinn's daily life with Pinkerton's and the Bureau of Indian Affairs. Ten years of encounters with Apache raiders, Mexican bandits, and lawless white men, witnessing sudden death at close quarters, and though it grieves me to say, often enough with my own hand on the rifle. I was in a better position to understand the dreadful reality of Her Majesty Queen Victoria's war against the Boers, to be followed at a safe distance by eager readers, where murder at home seemed almost a novelty.

According to newspaper reports, based on somewhat reluctant interviews with neighbours, the girls' last brief employment was at a laundry, locally known as 'the steamie' in Newington. They appeared to be happy, cheerful lasses; indeed, Amy was courting and expecting to be married as soon as her fiancé's ship returned to Britain.

As for the other suicide, Belle was devoted to a disabled grandfather, a veteran of the Crimean wars. She would never have abandoned him. This was duly confirmed in yet another painful newspaper interview, which at least aroused the public concern and beseeched a subscription to ensure the bereaved grandfather's future care.

Studying these reports, the closest I could hope to get in such matters, one fact emerged strongly. There had been no reason for suicide in either case apart from the identical manner the two friends had chosen within hours of each other.

A sinister alternative to a strange suicide pact was the man seen rushing from the scene, which suggested that the Newington bank robber had claimed two other victims.

The search for a killer had no immediate result which was hardly surprising in such baffling circumstances. A scapegoat was urgently needed while the police made their initial investigations and rumour was swift to point to the newly arrived circus with its motley crew of humanity. And this included the inevitable gravitation of the tinker clans to the site, as they moved nearer towns to set up their settlements away from the harsh snows of the Highland winters.

And so the evening performances at the circus were destined to be overshadowed by fear. One of Joey the Clown's comic antics which always raised howls of laughter was a pursuing clown in the guise of a policeman, at whom Joey points a gun, yelling: 'Bang, bang!' The policeman obligingly falls down dead but the gun, instead of emitting a shot, throws out a string of sausages. The scene continues with more police clowns milling round, then a weeping Joey takes out an enormous loop of rope and pretends to hang himself.

This did not raise quite as many laughs as usual; the applause was thinner for Joey's antics, tainted with the whisper of true events, of real life beyond the canvas walls of the tent, where the safety of lights ceased to penetrate. Above the circus loomed the heavy mass of Arthur's Seat with its hidden caves and lost hiding places, and uneasy thoughts drifted inevitably to what lurked beyond the darkness, a killer with a lust for blood waiting, perhaps already stalking his next victim.

The night held unseen dangers to be faced and young females unaccompanied would cling together, giggling nervously as they left the safety of the crowds behind them and hurried through the night to their destinations. The servant girls took extra care to make sure that they locked and bolted the master's kitchen door securely, the flame of their flickering candles casting scary shadows as they crept up to their attic rooms.

As for the killer, he could have come from any stratum of society. From the fetid ill-smelling closes, the ghettos of the High Street with their poverty, their often criminal humanity, or – dare one whisper such sacrilege – from the upper classes. Some monstrous creature hiding terrible evil behind a mask of respectability and affluence, of the kind Mr RL Stevenson had brought to life in *Dr Jekyll and Mr Hyde*, a story, with sensational success, of a killer not for gain but to satisfy some hideous impulse to destroy.

Such was the reasoned apprehension, and rumour persisted that all three deaths – the bank robbery and suicides – had coincided with the arrival of the circus. The work of setting up the arena had begun two days before the show opened. The canvas structure of the tent had been erected, and within it, the trapezes and high wires were hoisted into position. And the most hazardous of all preparations for the townsfolk; the cages of the wild animals – including the lions and leopards – were moved into place.

Thoughtful minds now leant heavily towards another link and the finger of suspicion pointed in the direction of the tinkers, always a likely target for any misdeeds. They swarmed like flies upon fairs and circuses. As well as women telling fortunes, selling clothes pegs and occasionally lifting washing from the drying greens (for their more unscrupulous menfolk), there was opportunity for clever tricksters adept at extracting money from the unwary, as well as wallets and pocket watches. Until the tinkers and circus left, it followed that any burglary in the south side of Edinburgh, Newington, the Grange and Morningside would be laid at their caravan doors.

This supposition provided unexpected benefits for the killer. It gave him the advantage of gaining time, covering his tracks, and irritated the police by diverting their attention to lesser evils, petty crimes at the Queen's Park encampment.

Murder investigations involving the police were not for me. As an outsider I must remain content to watch events regardless of my own suspicions and conclusions.

Such was the situation shortly after my new friend, Elma Miles Rice, and I had become acquainted.

CHAPTER THREE

Thane and I were out walking on the hill; it was a fine, sunny, brisk morning. Once the church bells had finished pealing, an air of tranquillity filled the air. There were no sounds from the circus, who respected the traditions of an Edinburgh Sabbath day.

Suddenly Thane stopped in his tracks. Listening, I heard far off the faint sound of a dog barking.

Normally that would not have been a cause for Thane's behaviour: dogs frequently barked when out with their owners on Arthur's Seat – there were rabbits in plenty, and exciting canine chases – but this was different. Thane's imploring look in my direction was one I had learnt to recognise and respect: danger ahead. His instinct, as always, was well ahead of humans.

The barking he drew attention to was an animal in distress.

He led the way and I followed. The sound grew nearer, more urgent, and materialised as a fierce, small, white, Highland terrier that did not seem pleased in the least to see Thane. He was being held on a lead by someone invisible behind a boulder.

We went closer; the dog now bared his teeth, and growled ferociously. Thane ignored him completely and gave him the equivalent of a contemptuous human shrug, much to the dog's anger; the barking got fiercer until it was quelled by a woman's voice calling faintly, 'Oh, do desist, for heaven's sake, Rufus. If you can't do something useful, do stop barking. That is no help at all.'

The voice sounded querulous, pained. I shouted, 'Hello there,' and, walking carefully around the other side of the boulder to avoid the dog, discovered a lady sitting on the ground, nursing her ankle.

I did not ask, 'Are you hurt?' So much was evident.

She looked up at me and smiled wanly. 'I think it is broken. I don't know *how* I'm to get down the hill again. I can't walk.'

All this was obvious too.

'Perhaps *I* can help you. Do you think you could stand up?'

She sighed deeply. 'With your assistance, miss, I will do my best.' As she held out her hands, I grasped them and set her upright, not without considerable effort as I am under five feet tall and, although slender, she topped my small frame by some four inches and several pounds in weight.

Leaning against the boulder, she gave a whimper as her injured foot touched the ground.

Handing over the dog's lead she said, 'Hang on to him, miss, if you please, or he'll be off like a shot.'

Rufus did not care for this changeover; he stared at me suspiciously when I said, 'Good dog,' to which the lady added sternly, '*Behave*, Rufus!' At this he devoted himself to darting Thane angry looks and menacing growls, to which Thane remained blissfully oblivious.

Still holding on to me, the lady looked around despairingly; the terrain was empty of all but heath and boulder with its distant view of Edinburgh's spires.

She groaned. 'Oh dear, I suppose we're absolutely miles from anywhere.'

'Not *quite* miles. I live over there,' I said whilst pointing. 'My house is just out of sight down the hill.'

'*Down* the hill,' she repeated tearfully. 'How on *earth* am I going to get down there?' she added with another groan.

'I'm sure Thane and I will manage that.'

She gave an apprehensive glance at Thane. 'He's very big but I hardly think—'

Anticipating that comment, I said reassuringly, 'He is also very strong.' And as the lady looked alarmed, I added hastily, 'I don't expect you to ride on his back, but if you put one hand on his shoulder and the other around my waist...' I demonstrated, 'like so – then I think we shall make a decent job of getting you to the Tower.'

'The Tower?' was the faint echo. She sounded alarmed.

'Yes, Solomon's Tower. That's where I live...'

She stared at me wide-eyed. 'How extraordinary,' she whispered.

What on earth did she expect? But this was no

time for explanations. 'And while you are having a reviving cup of tea, I'll go along the road towards St Leonard's and see if I can find a hiring cab to take you home.'

'You're very kind,' she murmured. 'I live in the Grange.'

I had already guessed by her clothes, her accent and demeanour that the Grange or Morningside might be her home.

As we made our unsteady, painful, hopping progress, I observed her more closely. Even twisted in pain, a well-shaped mouth turned down at the corners could not mask outstanding looks. The eyes anxiously regarding the terrain were deep blue, large, long-lashed. She had a porcelain complexion with honey-coloured curls escaping from under her bonnet. Here was a classical beauty indeed, the kind artists dream of painting.

'I am so grateful to you, miss,' she said. 'I might have lain there until darkness, probably all night and frozen to death, if you had not come along. It doesn't bear thinking about,' she added with a shudder. 'I can't ever express my gratitude.'

I smiled and didn't tell her that Thane had been her saviour. I doubted from that distance if a dog barking would have raised feelings of alarm or indicated that its owner was lying injured. It would have suggested nothing worthier of investigation than someone having a Sunday morning walk on Arthur's Seat with his dog who had spotted a rabbit.

Certainly Rufus did not share his owner's feelings

on her survival. He continued to growl menacingly at
Thane and did not approve of his beloved mistress's
hand on the deerhound's shoulder. No sense of gratitude
whatsoever. Thane continued to ignore him completely
as if the little white dog did not exist.

Elma – I later learnt that was her name – needed
all her breath for the last part of the steep descent and
she was almost sobbing with exhaustion by the time we
reached the garden gate of the Tower.

The sight of a kettle on the hob was a blessed relief
to her and she brightened visibly. My kitchen was a
large and hospitable place and I kept a fire going as
soon as the weather turned chilly: the Tower could
be cold in winter and was not helped by fierce winds
finding their way through every crack in its three-
hundred-year-old stone walls.

Taking a seat she continued to nurse her ankle;
stretching it out gently, we both knew it was not
broken. As she sipped her tea I wrung out a towel in
cold water, a commodity always easily accessible.

Handing it to her, I said, 'You were very fortunate.
Twisted as you fell, a bad wrench, but this will help
the swelling and ease the pain meanwhile. Do this
at home and get your doctor to have a look at it
tomorrow.'

Removing her boot she applied the cold compress
gratefully.

'That's better already!' she sighed. 'So painful,
though, and *such* an idiotic thing to happen.'

She had my sympathy. It had often happened to
me and I saw that her delicate and doubtlessly very

expensive boots were totally inadequate for one who walked on the hill every day.

'Regardless of the weather, daily exercise is so important,' she said sternly.

Rufus had lapsed into sullen silence and flopped down by her feet with a groan. She touched him tenderly. 'Poor wee soul, he is such a good dog, so loyal and protective. His bark really is worse than his bite.'

'Of that I am heartily glad. He sounded very fierce indeed.'

'At least in these difficult times I do feel quite safe with him.'

I had already noticed the wedding ring and her elegant attire which fairly shouted Jenners Mantle Department; her conversation and the Grange suggested where she fitted into Edinburgh society. The only odd thing was, that unless a widow like myself, why walk alone? Did she not have a personal maid? And surely an affluent anxious husband would have insisted that she be accompanied on a long, lonely stretch of Arthur's Seat each day.

I considered her jewellery: even for a morning stroll there were earrings and diamond rings, which I guessed were worth a fortune. This suggested a foolish notion when walking on a lonely hill – especially with tinkers and a circus in the vicinity.

Insisting that she was feeling much better after the cup of tea and was ready to go in search of a hiring cab, she stood up gallantly, wobbling a bit, but said firmly, 'If you will lend me your arm once more, perhaps you have a walking stick somewhere, rather than your dog.' She added, 'Since Rufus *will* persist in being so disagreeable.'

I didn't have a stick. The best I could provide was a gentleman's large umbrella, left and never reclaimed by some male client.

She tested it against the floor. 'This will do admirably. I am sure we will manage splendidly.'

And so we set off down the road together. She was oddly silent during that short walk and I concluded that her strained expression indicated that her ankle pained her more than she pretended.

As we reached St Leonard's Station luck was on our side as a cab was just depositing a passenger.

Turning, she held out her hand. 'I can never thank you enough for all you have done. I do hope we will meet again, miss. What is your name, by the way?' she added.

I answered and watched as the cab departed, carrying her and her bad-tempered little dog to the Grange.

Walking back to Solomon's Tower the rain that had been threatening for the past half hour began in earnest and I wondered if I would ever see Mrs Elma Rice again, or my umbrella which she had used to assist her into the cab.

Too bad. A sturdy umbrella in Edinburgh's uncertain weather is an absolute necessity, particularly on the days, when not riding my bicycle, there is a dismal prospect of a drenching.

However, I need not have been concerned. At midday the next morning a smart carriage stopped outside my garden gate.

CHAPTER FOUR

Mrs Rice emerged from the carriage and, seeing me at the door, she held out the umbrella apologetically.

'Sorry about that. I was so agitated at getting Rufus settled I didn't realise. I trust you did not get too wet.'

It was a grey dreary morning and I was glad of a visitor. Inviting her in, she said, 'That is kind of you.' And looking over her shoulder she called to the coachman to wait. 'I shall not be long.'

She was limping only slightly, but gladly accepted the offer of my arm. 'Our doctor had a look at it, assured me that you were right, just a bad sprain. It is all bandaged up now so I am quite comfortable as long as I don't put too much weight on it.'

I thought that unlikely as I gently led the way to the kitchen via what had once been the great hall, now sadly neglected from lack of use and lack of purpose since I preferred the warmth of the kitchen.

In truth, I felt lonely and rather foolish sitting at one end of the seventeenth-century dining table, surrounded by previous owners' deep and rather uncomfortable Jacobean chairs which had passed their days of grandeur, velvet and brocade worn and shabby, overshadowed by ancient tapestries on the stone walls depicting biblical scenes and battles long ago, with once vivid colours long since faded.

Elma halted, looked around and sighed deeply. 'What a *marvellous* room. You are fortunate to live in such a place. So impressive!'

I smiled. 'I'm afraid that is rather lost on me. This room is distinctly chilly even on a summer's day and winter is quite intolerable. I scarcely ever use it, I long ago decided to retreat to the kitchen with its warm stove and sunny aspect.'

'But surely it could be kept comfortably warm too – such a vast fireplace?'

'Indeed; it is large enough to roast an ox, which it very probably did in days gone by. Alas, it is now quite inadequate for modern-day coal supplies. Or to keep at bay the draughts seeping in through every crack in those stone walls. And as Arthur's Seat is devoid of trees, not much hope of cheery log fires.'

Her eyes narrowed. 'But I can just imagine those tapestries coming to life on windy evenings.' Laughing, she clasped her hands together. 'Oh, wouldn't I just brave anything, even the cold, to live in the lap of such history?' Then, shaking her head sadly, 'My home is quite modern, not yet thirty years old. A kind of monstrous mini-Balmoral Castle, complete with turrets and so forth. Everyone, it seems, wants to follow the fashion set by our dear Queen. So ostentatious and quite ridiculous, don't you think, for a suburb in Edinburgh?'

I had to agree, but before I could say so, she continued: 'If *I* lived in such a place as *your* Tower, I would do so much to preserve its history.'

I smiled tolerantly. A worthwhile ambition but I had neither time nor money nor, I might add, inclination to resurrect the splendid home she envisaged. On my return to Edinburgh to find that my family home had been sold, I was glad to accept this ruinous tower which my stepbrother Vince had inherited from its eccentric previous owner.

I thought, with silent amusement, how shocked this genteel lady would be if she knew the truth of the ten years I had spent in the pioneering towns of Arizona: living rough with Danny McQuinn, often sleeping under the stars when we had no home and frequently at the mercy of Indian uprisings, bandits and cattle thieves when we had one.

In the shack towns of the Wild West, guns were more readily on display than fancy ornaments, and the feathers of scantily clad saloon girls smoking their cheroots as they displayed their wares for clients would have shocked middle-class Edinburgh matrons into the vapours.

I led the way into the kitchen and the warmth of a steadily burning fire. The tea I offered was readily accepted. The talk today was of trivialities and I realised that perhaps she was too polite – too well brought up to enquire about my background, or how I had acquired such a prize as Solomon's Tower. Such curiosity would no doubt have been dismissed as inappropriate and quite vulgar in her stratum of society so I decided to put her mind at rest.

'I was brought up in Sheridan Place in Newington. The Tower belongs to my stepbrother who now lives in London.'

She nodded eagerly. 'What a piece of good fortune to have such a piece of ancient architecture in one's family.'

She held out her hand to Thane who, always polite, came forward. She patted his head. 'I love *all* dogs, but he is the first of his breed I have seen in Edinburgh. Tell me, how did you come by such a splendid creature?'

I smiled. 'It was rather the other way round. He adopted me when I arrived here.'

'You mean he was a stray? How *extraordinary*.'

'I thought so in the beginning. I tried to find his owner but without success, especially as I was never sure whether he was real or a figment of my imagination. He remained so elusive to everyone I had a difficult task convincing anyone of his existence.'

'He is certainly real enough, but somehow...' she paused and shrugged. 'I know it sounds silly, but he doesn't look like a pet one would have these days. A pet such as Rufus. He looks quite old-fashioned, not of this time at all.'

She smiled. 'As if he'd stepped out of one of those ancient old hunting tapestries hanging in the other room. As if he, too, belongs, well, to times past. It must have been quite a shock when you encountered him.'

'It was indeed, especially as one of the legends of

Arthur's Seat here is that King Arthur and his knights are asleep deep in a hidden cave with their deerhounds at their side ready to ride out when Britain calls for their help.'

Elma liked that but as we talked I could sense there were some curious omissions. She had been intrigued by Thane, but apart from being a dog lover, she was not the most observant of women. My bicycle lying against the kitchen wall had not raised an eyebrow, much less a question, yesterday afternoon. Forgivable, perhaps, as she was in some pain. Furthermore, she had addressed me as 'miss' regardless of the wedding ring and although I knew her name she had never asked mine until the cab carrying her and my umbrella departed.

Contemplating these odd facts, as if interpreting my thoughts she glanced at my hands and said, 'Your husband is absent?'

A polite way of putting the question indeed. 'I am a widow.'

Commiserations and condolences followed this remark. I filled in the background as briefly as I could, omitting the details of how Pappa's sergeant Danny McQuinn had rescued my sister Emily and I as children in a kidnapping attempt by one of Pappa's villains. Twelve years old I had fallen in love then and there with Danny, swore to marry him, and even against his will, his better judgement and his protests that he was ten years my senior, I had followed him to America where he was working for Pinkerton's Detective Agency and the Bureau of Indian Affairs.

We married, I had ten years of all the love I could wish for, then one day he walked out never to return, never to know that I was at last carrying a live child after several miscarriages. Our baby son died of a fever in an Indian reservation and I kept my promise to Danny that, if he disappeared and failed to return after six months, I was to relinquish the pioneering life of Arizona in the 1880s as it was too dangerous for a woman on her own, with Indian raids and lawless white men, and I was to return to the safety of my home in Edinburgh.

'Your late husband was a policeman, Mrs McQuinn,' she interrupted, using my name for the first time. 'How interesting.'

'Interesting' wasn't quite how I would have described his dangerous life, but I could not refrain from a burst of pride: 'My father is also a retired policeman – Chief Inspector Faro of the Edinburgh City Police, perhaps you have heard of him.'

She looked at me blankly and shook her head. So much for my legendary parent, I thought, as she added, 'We came here – from London, quite recently. My husband is Felix Miles Rice – perhaps you have heard of him.'

I had indeed. And so had most of everyone else in Edinburgh. If Pappa was a legend in crime, her husband was a legend in philanthropy. A philanthropist with a finger in every pie of good works, no cause was too small or too large for Miles Rice to reach out and flourish his support and bank account. In addition to such admirable qualities he had also won the nation's respect by remaining a plain mister, one of the people who took pride in obstinately refusing the knighthood Her Majesty considered so richly deserved for his services to humanity.

Refreshing the teacups I said, 'Have you family in Scotland, then?'

She nodded. 'I am exceedingly fortunate in having a brother who has been working in a front-line hospital in the Transvaal. Alas, I would be quite alone in the world without him. We are twins and he is a trainee doctor.'

Then with a sudden change of subject she said, 'Have you children, Mrs McQuinn?'

That was a sore point; although it was possible, considering that I was in my mid thirties, that any children might be gone from home, living their own lives.

I shook my head. 'Alas, I had a child in Arizona, a baby son called Daniel...' I could still feel the tears rising; would this wound ever heal? 'But he took a fever and died there.'

She clasped her hands together, genuinely upset. 'How dreadful, how truly dreadful.' And no doubt aware of my distress, she touched my hand briefly. 'So sad to have had a child and to have lost it.'

Looking towards the window, she shook her head and said in almost a whisper, 'I have not even had the joy of those brief months. Not even days – or hours – of motherhood. Our marriage after four years is still childless. We have yearned and hoped, but no blessing of a son has come our way.'

She paused, biting her lip, and put down the cup. 'So sad. This was my husband's second marriage. His first wife died of scarlet fever. There were no children there either.' She looked up at me. 'You might imagine how he had hoped that he would be more fortunate – second time lucky.'

My imagination was up to her expectations although I said not one word, knowing all too well the disastrous influence of a childless union – even in the happiest of marriages – on the man who possessed everything and had almost the whole world at his fingertips but could not beget a living child. Kings had suffered this affliction; queens had lost their heads for their inability to provide an heir.

'A son, a son!' That was the cry as the whole world moved to the tune of a dynasty that must survive, could only survive with a male heir, and wars, the need for soldiers to fight for their country, increased this frantic yearning, although Scotland had solved this particular problem by a law which allowed a daughter to inherit.

As I was wondering what to say to break the silence that this somewhat intimate confession had imposed upon us, she smiled, and it was like clouds clearing from the sun.

'I had another purpose for my visit. I observed posters advertising a visit from the circus. I wonder if you would care to accompany me?'

I was delighted to accept and on her walk with Rufus later that week she called in to tell me that she had obtained tickets for the following day.

'If that is convenient,' she said anxiously. Assuring

her that it was so, she smiled. 'Excellent. They are agreeable seats and under cover too, should the weather be inclement.'

And, although I was within walking distance of the arena, she insisted that the carriage would come for me at six o'clock.

She departed soon afterwards leaving me wondering about this invitation. From Elma's class in Edinburgh society two ladies unescorted was unusual for an evening entertainment. Why? A 'thank you' for Thane's rescue and the use of the umbrella or – uncharitable thought – perhaps her husband had another engagement, and she did not wish to go alone or accompanied by a personal maid or a male relative.

I shook my head, mine not to reason why but to accept gratefully; a second visit to the circus in one year was an opportunity not to be missed.

Walking with Thane later I considered her two visits and my own omissions at those meetings. Why had I not told her that I was a lady investigator? And why, in our tour of the house, when she was obviously so enthralled by the Tower's past, had I hesitated about showing her the secret room?

I expect all ancient towers built in times of religious and political persecutions had them as places of refuge. Jack and I came upon it by accident, carrying a piece of furniture upstairs, when he stumbled against the panelling which suddenly swung open.

We stared into a dark room and Jack whispered in awed tones, 'What have we here? I must have pressed a hidden spring.'

The room was illuminated by a narrow slit of a window which gave enough light to reveal an ancient padded chair, its tapestry lost under generations of cobwebs, a small table and a palliasse on the floor, its bedding having provided nests for generations of mice. A uniform cape of the fashion worn in Jacobite times hung on a nail.

I pointed to it. 'Doesn't look as if it has been worn recently.'

'Aye, and the last owner must have left in a hurry,' said Jack sweeping aside the cobwebs on the table. A map yellowed with age emerged. Holding the candle aloft we peered at it.

Blowing away the dust, Jack said, 'Looks like the drawing of a battle line-up. In fact, this is almost certainly the Battle of Prestonpans, where you will remember there was a battle in 1745. Prince Charlie and his troops were camped outside here on Arthur's Seat and in Duddingston.'

'Of course. There's still a house where he stayed.'

'And presumably a soldier, either one of his men or one of the Hanoverians, we'll never know which, took shelter in this room.'

He thought for a moment. 'A slice of the past indeed. What shall we do – open it to the public?'

I shivered. 'Leave it to history.'

Jack grinned. 'Glad you think so. Gives me the creeps.'

And so it was. I doubted if anyone had entered that room since its last occupant: that unknown soldier's hasty exit without his cloak. I was certain Sir Hedley

Marsh, who left the Tower to Vince, never knew of its existence, otherwise he would have filled it with his ever multiplying population of cats.

We went outside. Looking upwards the room's narrow window was completely invisible, just part of an ivy-covered wall. Just part of the unwritten history of the mystery of Solomon's Tower.

CHAPTER FIVE

The circus was indeed something to look forward to and this was to be even better than my last visit in the spring. Easter and Whitsun were popular, coinciding with workers' holidays. One of my recent clients had promised to take her two small children but had unhappily succumbed to a severe chill, and as their nanny was unavailable that day (she was a guest at a family wedding), she asked me, as a special favour, if I would oblige. Even without the free ticket and the fee she insisted that I accept for my time, I would have been pleased to go to the circus, and the delight of those two small children would have been ample reward.

However, with no wish to disappoint Elma, I had not mentioned that previous occasion and, considering the lady whose guest I was to be, I imagined and hoped for a slightly better seat than the scramble which had meant arriving early or being confined to the back rows, elevated but requiring a lot of neck stretching to get a good view. And that had had to go to the smallest of my client's children, perched on my knee.

As Elma's private carriage was admitted by a separate entrance beyond the main gate, where queues formed early for the best seats, I began to feel optimistic for one of those reserved nearer the ringside. These were available for Edinburgh's upper income bracket and well beyond my means or, I imagined, those of the lady whose children I had previously escorted.

I certainly did not expect to be escorted by a uniformed attendant onto the raised dais, with its velvet chairs, designated as the royal enclosure.

The brass band made conversation quite impossible, so I sat back and prepared to enjoy this evening at the circus as the prelude to what promised to be a lasting friendship.

Perhaps influenced by that Balmoral visit, there was a highly Scottish influence to Hengel's Circus, with its curious newspaper advertisement: 'Like a good Turkish carpet, it takes a lot of beating'.

Tonight there was an abundance of tartan everywhere. Miss Bonnie Jean, attired in a diminutive Scottish costume, performed some heart-stopping acrobatics on an almost invisible high wire.

'Note the absence of a safety net, see how this brave Highland lassie courts death at every performance,' announced the richly moustached ringmaster, splendid in shiny top hat, boots and scarlet coat.

There were a bewildering number of acts; the arena was never empty. One following fast upon the heels of the other, and in any interval needed for preparation, a fire-eater, juggler or a sword dancer in Highland costume would appear.

The Mac Brothers on their trapeze 'rescued' Miss
Bonnie Jean and swung happily back and forth across
the roof of the tent, while far below, to wild applause,
the well-publicised equestrienne Miss Adela entered the
ring on a magnificent white horse. She was accompanied
by a couple of tartan-bowed tiny fox terriers, barking
furiously as they jumped up beside their mistress and,
as other horses joined the ring, leaping from one to the
other in perfect unison.

This performance, known as the jockey act, was
also shared with the clowns, or rather appeared to be
annoyingly interrupted by them as they defied death
under the horses' hooves by leaping up behind Miss
Adela or falling about very clumsily in front of the
other horses. Their timing was perfect, the act well
and oft rehearsed so there was never any real danger,
despite the horrified screams of the audience as one
clown seemed to disappear under the thundering hooves
but managed to roll away in the nick of time.

For me, it brought irresistibly to mind lines from
Wordsworth's poem:

> '...*chattering monkeys dangling from their poles...*
> *With those that stretch the neck and strain the eyes*
> *And crack the voice in rivalship, the crowd*
> *Inviting, with buffoons against buffoons*
> *Grimacing, writhing, screaming...*'

I remembered well from that spring performance how
Joey had led his fellow clowns in death-defying wild
leaps from horse to horse, frequently losing his balance

to shrieks of terror from the audience, but it was all part of the act. Tonight it was different. He appeared as ever on stilts, and made a great fool of himself, falling to the ground, lying there breathless, revived by buckets of water from his fellow clowns, but I wondered as he got to his feet and looked around dazed whether that unsteadiness was also in the act.

Joey certainly seemed less agile than he had been at the spring performance. I wondered had he been ill; being thinner made him look taller. No longer seated high at the back of the tent, I was now near enough to observe him closely and I felt concern and pity for the clown with his white face, his painted melancholy tears, sad eyes and huge red mouth.

Strangely enough, perhaps my concern reached him amid all the shouts and cries and applause, for several times I felt he was looking directly at me, as if our eyes met and held for a moment.

It was rather unnerving and embarrassing too, and I was glad when the scene changed and a tremor of expectation went around the audience as the animal cages were wheeled in to the accompaniment of roars and the smell of the jungle.

To a roll of drums Fernando the Fearless, the bravest man in the whole world (as was advertised), cracked his whip fiercely to maintain order among the six leopards, which obligingly leapt up onto the painted stools. This was not without a show of protest, but they cautiously regarded the leopard skin in which Fernando was attired, a stern reminder perhaps of what might be their fate if they did not do as they were told.

At last they slunk out, quelled and snarling effectively. Another roll of drums and their place was taken by the lion, Leo, king of the jungle, who suggested he might be rather more trouble than the leopards, as he must have been ten times heavier than his tamer – almost diminutive by comparison.

Fernando approached this new subject thoughtfully, armed with more caution than he had for the snarling leopards. In addition to the whip, he brandished a kitchen chair, to which Leo responded with an angry-seeming paw.

All visible things considered, I didn't really fancy Fernando's chances if he thrust his head into the great beast's mouth, my thoughts echoed by the audience's silence imposed at the ringmaster's urgent appeal concerning this dangerous action.

Although I was certain from my excellent vantage point that the head never really went between the lion's jaws, it was accomplished with all possible speed and dexterity.

A sigh of relief and ready applause greeted his triumphant bow, and the clowns once more took over the ring. As he followed the cages out so jauntily, I thought of the future, had he failed. Many animal tamers who were supremely confident lost their nerve and their lives by a piece of momentary mistiming, mauled by a watchful lion or tiger who, detecting some faint uneasiness, the smell of fear or lack of concentration, seized the long-awaited opportunity and pounced.

If tamers did not die as a result of being attacked,

they frequently lost an arm or a leg and would never enter a wild animal's cage again. I wondered whilst looking at Joey, who seemed a shadow of his former self, what became of circus performers who were injured. Not only animal tamers who had made a wrong move and paid the ultimate price, but also those other circus performers who sustained terrible injuries by falling from the high wire, or clowns who mistimed leaping under the horses' hooves or those, like Joey, whose altered appearance suggested an accident or recent illness.

A chat with the ringmaster would have doubtlessly revealed that the lions were toothless and the leopards well fed before the acts began, but what of the humans? The future of the maimed, too ill or injured was a sobering thought behind all the grandeur, the applause, the music. As for those who survived but grew too old to perform, what of them?

During the interval the clowns came and talked to the children in the audience, distributing sweets and balloons. Joey, perhaps as King of Clowns, too grand for such tomfoolery, was staring in our direction. Perhaps he was interested in the occupants of the royal enclosure, or was it Elma in particular – or myself? Whichever one of us, the effect of this attention from a perfect stranger was disquieting.

That led me to consider what they were like with the paint and wigs removed. Did they behave like everyday men when the show ended: men with wives, children and dependents? As for their jokes, the crazy gags, the horseplay and silly tricks, were they put in a trunk with the costumes until the next performance? Were they quiet and unassuming, reading the daily papers, paying the rent and concerned for domestic matters and their children's futures?

And with that curious awareness of being watched I turned, and, just behind me, saw a face from the recent past.

Jack Macmerry. Now, by his uniform, Inspector Jack Macmerry. He raised a hand in greeting.

Perhaps, I thought, it was he who had been the focus of Joey's attention. As the performance ended, the clowns gathered together in the ring, in what looked like a meeting. They looked serious, heads together, and I wondered what they were discussing.

As we emerged from the tent there was Jack again, with a group of burly, tall men, obviously policemen. They were laughing – a night out at the circus clearly a blessed relief from solving crimes.

Leaving them, he hurried to my side and, bowing to Elma, he took my hand in a firm grip.

'Good to see you again, Rose. It has been a long time.'

The look in his eyes and his wistful voice suggested that he might lean forward and kiss me, so turning hastily I introduced my companion. He bowed over her hand and, hearing his name called, he extracted himself and rejoined his waiting colleagues.

Waiting in the string of carriages trying to make their exit, I observed the shrouded sideshows of the funfair and resolved to make a daytime exploration of what excitement was on offer.

Perhaps concerned about my silence, or curious about that greeting from a policeman, Elma regarded me anxiously and she hoped I had not minded being on display. What a question!

And then she added casually, almost apologetically, that the reason for the royal enclosure was that she and Felix had been weekend guests at Balmoral Castle.

'That was when we were living in London, in St James's, and it was rather a tedious journey coming so far north. Travelling by train makes a considerable difference, of course, but it would have been much pleasanter had we then been settled in Edinburgh.'

Equally casual, I felt I should mention that my stepbrother Vincent Beaumarcher Laurie was junior physician to the royal household and also lived in St James.

'How marvellous! Such a coincidence that we are friends and both have medical brothers.' She laughed delightedly. 'Wonder of wonder – it is indeed a very small world. And do you know I have actually met Dr Laurie? He took care, excellent care, of Felix when he fell and damaged his shoulder during the grouse shoot. A charming man and I gather he is well thought of, especially good with the royal children and grandchildren who, I am told in strict confidence, of course, can be very difficult.'

The carriage had emerged from the crowd and was heading along the road to Solomon's Tower.

'At long last! That seemed to take for ever,' Elma said. And although we both smiled, I thought with pity of the hundreds who had no such good fortune and were wearily walking home, perhaps some miles away, in what was now one of Edinburgh's steady downpours.

'Do you often see your stepbrother?' she asked.

Alas, a negative response; but the discovery of Vince was a bond indeed, and sitting in the luxury of that elegant carriage, I realised that I had never had a really close female friend. Not even in schooldays and, since my return to Edinburgh, although I had met several friendly-seeming ladies among my clients, our acquaintance was not of a lasting nature.

I soon learnt to accept that gratitude was not to be mistaken for friendship, and despite being close enough whilst I was sorting out their torrid affairs, the intimacy of knowing so much about them was unhappily a detriment rather than an advantage. Indeed, they seemed anxious afterwards to forget the whole unhappy episode, and the friendship I had often hoped was in the making was nipped in the bud.

I told myself the reason was that they were too busy with their own lives, but in my heart I knew it was a sop to my pride. Business was business. I had served my purpose and the account was now closed.

Thankfully I was not expected to do anything for Elma Rice. That was a relief. We shared the same sense of humour and she knew my dear Vince.

We were approaching Solomon's Tower.

'Who was the gentleman who spoke to you back there, Rose?' Obviously curiosity had got the better of her normal diffidence.

'A policeman and a very dashing one.' She laughed

her teasing sidelong glance asking for more information.

When I said an old friend, she laughed again. 'The way he greeted you hinted that he would like to be more than that. Am I right?'

I hardly felt this was an appropriate moment to say, yes, we were lovers once, engaged to be married, in fact. And then the humiliating part. That I had delayed too long in naming the day and Jack, wearied, while in Glasgow on police business had met a new love.

Sidestepping the question with a polite smile I thanked her for the evening.

'A great pleasure, Rose. I enjoyed it very much, very exciting.'

'Indeed. Such a variety of acts.'

She seemed reluctant to bring the evening to a close so I asked, 'Which did you like best?'

'Miss Adela and those darling little dogs.'

'The clowns?'

She frowned. 'They were quite splendid, but all that absurd behaviour is really for the children.'

And a question that had been niggling me. 'What did you think of Joey?'

'Joey? Which one was he? Was he especially funny? I didn't notice him in particular.'

In which case, I must conclude that Jack standing right behind me had been the object of Joey's intense gaze.

Elma continued, 'We must do something of the same again, a concert perhaps, or the theatre.'

She left me with a promise to meet for lunch. 'That is, if you are not too busy.'

I had not told her that I was a lady investigator.

Was I ashamed to admit it or did I think such a bizarre occupation might decide her against furthering our friendship?

Especially if she discussed it with her eminent husband: I could not imagine his approval. And how did she imagine a widow could afford Solomon's Tower? Unless, of course, she had wrongfully decided that Vince gave me financial support.

Again I noticed in these small discrepancies that Elma seemed sorely lacking in observation. Or perhaps the truth was that it was a quality of which I had a superior abundance; the result of my early education where, to while away tedious train journeys, I had been taught by Pappa to observe my fellow passengers and deduce from their clothes and luggage what had brought them on to this particular railway. Although it had seemed like a game then, I had to admit that it had contributed strongly to my desire to be a lady investigator and, indeed, had even helped in solving cases.

Alone in the Tower, that night I thought about Jack, what he was doing back in Edinburgh and what had become of the young woman who had replaced me in his life. I shook my head; he was probably on a fleeting visit seeing old friends. He would be gone tomorrow, and after a two-year silence I was unlikely to ever know the truth.

Did I really care? And the answer was, strangely, yes. Although I had never wanted to be married again I greatly treasured Jack, not only as a lover but as a friend and confidant.

Never mind, the past was past. On with the future and, any day now, I would be receiving a call to take on a new case.

And that, as fate would have it, was closer than I ever expected.

CHAPTER SIX

The next morning, I opened the door to Jack Macmerry.

I was taken aback by this visitor whom Thane rushed forward to greet. A delighted, tail-wagging welcome for an old friend.

Responding warmly to this overture, Jack looked up from patting his head and said, 'Aren't you going to ask me in, Rose?'

I blinked, apologised and stood aside. In his uniform Jack looked quite splendid, and although never handsome in the Irish way of Danny McQuinn with his black hair and blue eyes, Jack had a pleasing countenance: a strong face with the sandy colouring, the broad cheekbones and the sturdy build of the Lowland Scots.

Following me into the kitchen, he laid aside his uniform cap and, rubbing his hands together in a familiar gesture, he grinned, 'Well, aren't you even going to offer me a cup of tea, after all this time?' And amused at the discomfort I was unable to hide, he laughed. 'Don't just stand there with your mouth open, Rose, looking as if a ghost had walked in. After our brief meeting again last night, didn't you expect me to come and see you?'

'No, Jack. To be honest, I didn't.'

He regarded me slowly. 'That's scarcely flattering, is it?'

'I should have thought we were well past the stage of flattering each other,' I said sharply. 'What are you doing here in Edinburgh, anyway? Visiting friends?'

'Among other things,' was the vague reply. 'As a matter of fact, I'm here on business.'

'Business?'

'Yes, police business. I'm investigating a fraud which has Edinburgh connections.' Again he hesitated, an uneasy glance, as if wishing to say more.

'How long are you staying?'

'As long as it takes to find some answers.'

'So this is just a visit.'

He grinned. 'Try not to sound so relieved.'

'I'm sorry. I didn't mean...' As I poured him a cup of tea my thoughts were racing. 'Tell me about yourself; what has been happening since we last met?'

He sighed. 'Quite a lot, Rose. Quite a lot.' And looking around, 'But I see things are still the same with you and with Thane here,' he said, as the deerhound settled happily by his feet once more, as if two years had not passed by and Jack was home again, settled in the most comfortable armchair, his long legs stretched out before the fire.

I shuddered slightly as, patting Thane's head, he

murmured, 'At least *you* are still pleased to see me, old chap.'

Thane wagged his tail and looked pleased in that almost human way as Jack glanced across at me. 'I take it that you are still a grieving widow, that the missing husband has failed to return?' he said mockingly.

Although his belittling words made me angry, I told myself that he had every reason to feel bitter. Danny's ghost had always been between us right from our first meeting, when I still believed Danny would return from Arizona and would walk in one day. To be honest, later, I learnt to accept with almost certainty that Danny was dead. It still remained the perfect excuse for not putting our relationship on a permanent basis, a refuge to evade marrying Jack.

'And what about you? Did you marry the young lady you fancied so much, the one you left me for?' I said as lightly as I could.

'I did indeed.'

'And so you are a happily married man at last.'

He held up his hand as if not wishing to hear more. 'I had no intention when I left you of marrying anyone: I was still in love with you. You surely never doubted that, Rose. It wasn't my fault we ever parted. You drove me away.'

He paused as if giving me the opportunity to deny it. When I said nothing he shrugged.

'But circumstances overcame my plan that you would miss me. To cut a long story short, the young lady took pity on me, desolate as I was, and we formed a... er...relationship. Before I could recover my senses which told me this union was going to be a disaster, Meg announced that she was having my child.' He sighed. 'And so I did the honourable thing. We got married.'

That was a relief, I thought. At least I was in no danger of an unrequited lover's return.

'And so you are living happily ever after. I am glad to hear it.'

Jack shook his head solemnly.

'Not quite, Rose, not quite. Meg died. Scarlet fever.'

'And the child?'

'She is being cared for by her grandmother.' His face expressionless, he sounded troubled, resigned.

'I'm sorry, Jack. Indeed I am.'

He regarded me without speaking and, somewhat at a loss for words myself at these unexpected revelations, I said, 'Such a tragic situation. Especially for the wee girl.'

He nodded and said slowly, 'Indeed it is. But it could have been worse. I knew from the beginning, even in those first months together, that I had made a mistake.'

Shaking his head he regarded me solemnly. 'I knew we would never be happy – the thought of long years ahead was intolerable; through no fault of her own, poor girl, she could never take your place. A sweet lass in many ways, but – oh, I don't know, I suppose I was looking for another Rose McQuinn. A woman who stirred my senses, an impossibly strong-willed woman who drove me mad, but one who I never needed to explain everything to—'

I held up my hand. 'Stop – stop at that, Jack Macmerry. Not another word.'

He jumped to his feet and seized my hands. 'I will not – I cannot stop, Rose, I will always love you. The years we had together. You can't change that. You loved another man, a dead man, more than me. Pitiful, wasn't it, living with his ghostly presence?'

I wrenched myself free. 'Please, Jack, no more. Let's have no more of this. You always knew the score. You wanted a sweet submissive wife and I wanted my career...'

I watched his mouth curl as his lips echoed the words.

'I never wanted, could never promise to be, that kind of a wife and you always knew that. You persisted in believing that you could change me.'

He looked so hurt, I said, 'Jack, I am sorry – sorry that I hurt you – and that all this has happened—'

The doorbell rang. Jack looked at the clock and sprang to his feet. 'That's my carriage. Damn it, have to go, have an appointment with the assistant chief constable – just like old times, Rose.'

That was true. And we both laughed. There was always an important meeting interrupting the flow of our life together.

Jack shook his head wryly and then said, 'May I come again and see you? We need to talk.'

I looked doubtful for he added quickly, 'Not about us this time, I promise you. But I need advice, so let's forget about the past and be friends, Rose.'

'Yes, Jack, I'd like that.' And at that moment, I meant it.

'Tomorrow, perhaps?'

'Yes, tomorrow then.'

At the door he paused. 'Your companion at the circus – Mrs Miles Rice?' He threw back his head and with a deep laugh said, 'Well done. Well done.' A pause, a shrewd look. 'Not a client, surely?'

'Of course not!'

He grinned, a mocking bow. 'You have moved up in Edinburgh society.'

Thane stood at my side and we watched him get into the carriage.

Closing the door, I sat down at the table and tried to sort out my confused feelings. Perhaps I had been harsh, always too harsh. To be honest, it was good to see Jack again, and if we could be friends, and stay that way, which I doubted, all would be well.

As for that advice he wanted, was it personal, professional, or just an excuse for a further visit?

That evening Elma had seats at the Theatre Royal for *Mrs Warren's Profession*, a daring and witty play by Mr George Bernard Shaw, whose dislike of the capitalist society (which I encountered regularly in Edinburgh) was akin to my own. As a passionate feminist and suffragette, I was an avid reader of his *Fabian Essays* and his socialist tracts.

As I expected, we were in the best seats and directly behind us was one of my former clients. We had been friends for a short while but when our eyes met there was no flicker of recognition. Sad, but no doubt, as I was becoming well known, she had her own excellent reasons for ignoring a private detective in public.

Elma was anxious to hear my comments on the play, and when I remarked upon the theme, she laughed.

'London theatregoers accept this sort of thing without question. Mr Shaw is well known for his outrageous opinions, but I fear it may be a little strong, still a little too modern, for Edinburgh audiences.

She was very knowledgeable about the theatre and as we were approaching her carriage she was hailed by a man standing near the entrance of the theatre.

'Excuse me, Rose.'

She hurried towards him, and although it was too dark to see him clearly, I could make out a top-hatted rather flashily dressed young man who greeted her warmly; he placed an arm about her shoulders. She was obviously not pleased. She left him standing and seemed anxious to escape as soon as possible.

As she stepped smartly into the carriage, he made a move and dashed across to her window. From my side of the carriage I was unable to see his face clearly, and the noise of the horses setting off made it impossible for me to distinguish the words he was shouting.

Something about their next meeting; he sounded angry and, as she leant back in her seat, I was aware that she was very upset by this encounter.

It was none of my business, but obviously aware that politeness demanded some explanation, she summoned a smile and said, 'So embarrassing, Rose. I don't even remember his name. An actor I met in London, no one of any importance.'

But her voice rather shrill and her laugh a little false spoke a different line and left me with the certainty that, at some time, they had known each other extremely well.

Indeed, her knowledge of the theatre, and of the circus come to that (how expertly she had told me about the equestrian jockey acts and she seemed to know a great deal of what went on behind the scenes in the world of entertainment), suggested that she might well have been an actress herself at some stage of her life, before she met Felix Miles Rice.

If that was so, one could not blame her for keeping it quiet. Many actresses who married rich or titled men were very keen to keep their humbler origins secret.

CHAPTER SEVEN

Jack was as good as his word. He arrived so early next morning I wondered if he was expecting breakfast to be offered: that had been the pattern of our early days together when he would look in on his way to the central office; this was before we became seriously involved, when he frequently stayed the night.

Fortunately I was an early riser and uncharitably wondered if he expected to see me at my worst, as if I had just tumbled out of bed. Rather triumphantly, I offered him a cup of tea and a piece of bread.

He shook his head. 'I've eaten already. Thank you.' But taking a seat at the table he seemed very relaxed and, irritatingly, Thane drifted immediately to his side, the master welcomed home again.

Stroking his head, Jack looked round the kitchen and smiled. 'Just like old times, Rose. Nothing has changed, not even you,' he added with an admiring glance which I avoided.

'One of us has certainly changed,' I said sharply. 'You, Jack, remember? You got married.'

As he winced at the reminder, he leant forward and said, 'And as I said, seeing you in the royal box with Mrs Rice, you have certainly moved up the social ladder.'

'You know Mrs Rice?'

'Only by sight.' He hesitated. 'Quite a coincidence you knowing her too. Everyone knows Felix Miles Rice and his beautiful wife, even in Glasgow. Not merely ornamental but full of good works, rapidly qualifying her as one of the city's eminent lady bountifuls.'

A dismissive shrug and he continued, 'But I'm not here to talk about Edinburgh society. I've come to ask you a favour, Rose.'

'A favour?' I said cautiously.

'The officer in charge of this fraud case has been taken seriously ill, and the assistant chief constable (who I knew in his lowlier early days) wants me to take it on. My Edinburgh connection, you know.' He paused and laughed gently. 'Wheels within wheels. He would love to have me back on the force.'

Looking intently at me, he was suddenly silent. 'So I'm here to ask for your help and advice – in your professional capacity.'

His words amazed me. In the past he had always been ready to pour scorn on lady detectives and had hooted with laughter at my business card: 'Lady Investigator, Discretion Guaranteed, indeed!'

Had he forgotten that my 'profession', as he called it, was the main reason why he had abandoned me? This was a new Jack indeed.

'Will you help me, Rose?'

I hesitated. 'Depends on what is involved.'

He nodded. 'Speed is involved and this is an instance where a woman investigator might make considerably more headway than the police, and I hardly need tell you that your much vaunted discretion guaranteed can be of great service to the community in this case. I am asking your help to track down a murderer.'

He paused. 'Well, what say you? Are you willing?'

I might not be willing but I was intrigued and, yes, a little flattered too. 'Tell me more. Is this to do with the fraud case?'

He ignored that and said, 'You will have read, of course, of the two girls who committed suicide within hours of one another in the slum tenements of St Leonard's, less than a mile from where we are sitting now.'

That had my immediate attention. I said I had read about it and he continued, 'There are some baffling circumstances about this case, and in all truth, it seems more like two murders than suicides.'

'The newspapers have hinted at doubts, of course. But *that's* how they increase their sales. One does not have to take such things seriously,' I said.

He sighed. 'Precisely so. But the police have only circumstantial evidence that the girls were strangled. A neighbour coming home from the public house reported that a man cannoned into him, who had rushed down the tenement stair. Questioned further, however, he admitted that he had had a lot to drink and, as he was unsteady on his feet, "pushed aside" might have been a more correct description of the encounter with the running man. Also, he had been carried away by the drama of the two girls' deaths, and cronies in the tenement had urged him to report to the police as he might possibly be a witness to identifying a murderer and – who knew? – there might also be a reward on offer.'

'What do the police know of the girls' families, background and so forth?'

'Both respectable, employed at a laundry. And this is where the doubts about suicides come in.'

'Did either leave notes?'

'No, and that seems significant to me, if not to my colleagues. Especially as Amy was engaged to be married; the banns had been called at the local church and her fiancé's ship was due in port any day. According to the neighbours Amy was very much in love, full of excited preparations, looking forward to her future life as a married woman. There was absolutely *no* reason why she should have taken her life...'

'Perhaps this fiancé had changed his mind at the last minute. That would have been *one* good reason.'

'No. When asked if this possibility had been considered, this neighbour, who insisted that she was like a mother to Amy, said she would have been the first to know. As for the other girl, Belle, she looks after her old grandfather who lost a leg at the Crimea. He, too, was distraught. He had been out with cronies that evening and she had promised to have his supper ready for him in his flat across the road.'

He looked at me thoughtfully. 'Strong evidence, don't you think? Both the fiancé and the bereaved grandfather insist that the girls were close friends, healthy and happy.'

The absence of suicide notes seemed to confirm Jack's theory.

'What do you want me to do?'

'I would be very grateful if *you'd* look into these cases, give me your opinion. You are, as *I* remember, especially good at asking questions, ferreting out information that the police don't consider important. I know from our time together that you have solved some remarkable cases thanks to what you call, if I am correct, observation and deduction.'

He paused. 'Will you do this as a special favour for *me*? This is strictly unofficial, but I think you can speed matters up. I need to get back to Glasgow rather urgently. Problems with the wee lass's grandmother's health.'

A sigh from the heart and I thought of the wee daughter who was now motherless, and realised that Jack had always wanted children, but what an irony that he should be left in such circumstances.

'I'm in despair, Rose, the lads don't seem to have many original ideas and, in fact, something I encountered before and always deplored, they have already made up their minds regarding the killer's identity.'

'Who do they think—'

'Oh, their prime suspect *would* be someone from the circus, of course.'

I knew that to be true, and it was the reason why many innocent persons had gone to the gallows. There were instances when the police decided that a suspect was guilty and obtained a speedy conviction by fixing the evidence.

'You'll do it, Rose?'

'I'll think about it.'

He smiled. 'Good. Here you are, then.' And producing an envelope he laid it on the table. 'These notes are a copy of all the evidence so far. I needn't add – for your eyes only.'

The carriage was waiting for him on the road. At the door, he turned. 'One thing that isn't in the notes which might be of use to your investigation, both girls were briefly employed at Rice Villa.'

He grinned. 'Might be useful, might mean nothing, but seeing that you are on friendly terms with Mrs Rice, I thought it worth mentioning.'

As the carriage began to move, he leant out. 'Another thing not in the notes that might interest you. Amy once worked at your old home, 9 Sheridan Place, the scene of a recent break-in, and the man who lives there now might be involved in this fraud case I came to investigate. Small world, isn't it?'

I knew nothing of the new tenants but the excuse to visit my former home, to help Jack with his enquiries, was an almost irresistible temptation.

I went inside and spread the notes he had left on the table.

Pieces of paper; lots of words that said nothing. Two apparent suicides, coincidental, curiously identical in nature. And the shocked disbelief from the statements of their neighbours hinted at murder.

I had an instinct that this was so. Curiously enough,

the happy home life of Felix Miles Rice, Elma and the two dead girls, who had briefly been part of that enthusiastic staff devoted to a generous employer, bothered me most.

Did the two girls carry something discreditable regarding their employer which had necessitated their disposal?

'You must meet my husband,' said Elma, who was now a familiar sight to be seen heading in the direction of Solomon's Tower with Rufus at her side. I was encouraged to accompany them on a brisk walk over Arthur's Seat, fortified on our return by tea and scones, the latter provided by the Rices' excellent cook.

Thane took a dim view of these outings: the idea of scampering about the hill in an undignified manner with a small yapping dog at his heels was not for Thane. Used to having me as his sole companion, he remained invisible until our return and the departure of Elma and Rufus.

'You don't like him much, do you?' I said. His imploring look said everything. 'I'll let you into a secret, then,' I said patting his head, 'neither do I.'

And Rufus liked neither of us. I decided he was a spoilt silly lapdog but the best Elma was allowed, since she confided that her husband did not like animals at all. It was on one of our walks that Elma, who rarely mentioned her husband, became expansive on that topic.

'Felix has heard so much about you, Rose. He is so delighted that I have found such a good friend to accompany me on my walks – he was never keen on the idea of me all alone on Arthur's Seat in all kinds of weather. So he is grateful to you, especially as he is always so busy and, alas, his life has little time for frivolities such as the circus and the theatre.'

She sighed. 'We do not think along the same lines in such matters: he is very serious-minded, devoted to reading the Classics, and my education failed to include any foreign language other than French.'

As she smiled I wondered again what her education had included, since up to now I knew so little of her background. It was as if life started the day she married Felix Miles Rice. Perhaps, I thought shrewdly, it had indeed. A vastly different life, perhaps.

One day she was quite excited. 'He has asked that I invite you to a little dinner party. There now. I am sure you will like each other, of course. I hope I haven't scared you off, but let me assure you, beneath that serious exterior, he is the sweetest, noblest and most generous of men; warm-hearted and kind to those in need. You will get along famously, of that I am quite sure.'

I was delighted to accept; a date was arranged, but fate deemed it otherwise and I never was able to meet Felix Miles Rice.

CHAPTER EIGHT

As I headed towards Princes Street where I was meeting Elma at Jenners, a great noise of clapping and cheering at the intersection of North Bridge and the Royal Mile indicated a group of clowns from the circus entertaining the passers-by. And, an incongruous addition, several nuns rattling tins as they circulated among the crowd.

I remembered that the Little Sisters of the Poor from the convent at St Leonard's did a city collection around the time of the harvest festival. One of the nuns, Sister Clare, recognised me and hurried in my direction. As I put a coin in the box, she whispered urgently, 'Mrs McQuinn, it is good to see you. The good Lord has answered my prayer. I was coming to call on you – will you be so kind as to look in at the convent as soon as you can?'

I was eager to hear more, she shook her head: 'I can't talk here. Please come...' and was off again, fast disappearing among the folk watching the clowns.

However, meeting Elma that particular afternoon

momentarily pushed aside all thoughts of Sister Clare's anxious face.

Elma loved shopping and it was part of this new friendship that I was included, my opinion sought on gloves and blouses and millinery, as well as lace negligees.

'What do you think? Will Felix like this one – or will he think this too daring?'

I found all of this very odd indeed and yet another example of Elma's poor observation skills: I had not the slightest interest in the latest fashions – as long as I was decently clad and warm with clothes adaptable for bicycling, I didn't care.

We were to meet in the restaurant as usual; today I found her in animated conversation with a familiar face. My old school friend, Alice Bolton, who greeted me warmly.

'So you two know each other!' Elma exclaimed.

'We do indeed.' We exchanged glances and Alice said, 'How are you, Rose?'

As we talked as women do, catching up with past events, I thought I intercepted an uneasy warning glance from Alice when Elma asked where and when we had last met.

I smiled as Alice said hastily that we met quite often for lunch. In fact, it was during our momentous and totally unexpected meeting four years ago, when I first arrived in Edinburgh, that the sinister tale of Alice Bolton's troubled marriage provided the stepping stone for the career of Rose McQuinn, Lady Investigator, Discretion Guaranteed.

A polite argument over the bill ensued between the two women and at last Alice left us with promises to meet again soon.

Some time later, with purchases made to Elma's satisfaction, we parted company outside the shop. The rain was lashing down and the doorman shepherding us under a vast umbrella hailed a cab and helped pack Elma's multitude of boxes inside.

As she settled down, she said, 'I am so looking forward to this evening. Felix is longing to meet you. Just the three of us, quite informal, so you can get to know each other. Such an awful day. Jump in and we will take you home.'

One look at the piled-up seat beside her suggested that it would be an uncomfortable journey, with little room in a hiring cab for an extra passenger.

However, as always with Elma, an argument followed and I insisted that I did not wish to return home as I had matters to attend to in the Pleasance. Despite her protests, I suspected that Elma was secretly relieved when she considered the hatboxes and all her latest acquisitions.

'Until later, then,' she called. 'The carriage will come for you at seven o'clock.'

I retreated once more into the shelter of Jenners and remained there looking at the haberdashery counter, considering gifts I could afford: presents to send to Orkney in time for Christmas, for my sister Emily and my little nephew.

When I looked out again, the heavy shower had abated into a mere drizzle and with the umbrella, my constant companion these days, I hurried homeward across Waverley Bridge, the High Street now silent, devoid of the clowns, the crowds chased away by the sudden rainstorm.

The nuns with their collecting tins had also taken shelter and I remembered once again Sister Clare's anxious expression and her note of urgency.

My visits to the convent were rare indeed. I wasn't Catholic but I received a special invitation when they had any fund-raising occasion for their orphans. The convent had a special place in my heart as it was also the orphanage which had taken in Danny McQuinn when he was brought across from Ireland by his uncle, the sole members of their family who had survived the Famine. The nuns had been very proud of the way Danny had turned out, clever and industrious, especially when he fulfilled that early promise, joined the city police and became Chief Inspector Faro's sergeant, and much later, my husband.

Now the Little Sisters of the Poor were beneficiaries of my rarely updated wardrobe. I occasionally bought new clothes these days: although I cared not a fig for looking elegant, I realised the importance of first impressions – that a lady investigator should not only sound convincing but should look convincing too. No shabby shoes or frayed cloaks in this profession. Even my wild curls had to be trained into a semblance of good behaviour and confined within a bonnet.

The nuns were very grateful, especially as the discarded garments of a lady under five feet in height were eminently suitable for the older orphaned girls in their care.

It was the bane of my life that I could have passed for a little girl of twelve in a poor light, despite being in my mid thirties. Nevertheless, my professional abilities had given me confidence and I joined that legion of womankind who, never satisfied with what nature has seen fit to bestow on them, are forever bewailing their lot. I had it all first hand from my younger sister Emily, a prime example. Taller than me, she had yearned for my curls as I wrestled with that unruly mop, yearning for her long, black, straight hair and those extra inches, not to mention a shapely bosom.

I had my bundle ready, preparing to go across and call at the convent early next morning, realising they would be up and about from 6 a.m., when a knock at the kitchen door announced Sister Clare.

She was accompanied by a small, thin girl, at first glance little more than a child, wearing the grey uniform dress that indicated she was a novice. This was her probationary period in which she still had the opportunity to change her mind. She would not receive the black dress and veils of the nuns' habit until she had taken her final vows, closing the door to become the bride of Christ, where only a few of the nuns privileged to run the orphanage were allowed to communicate with the outside world.

I invited them in, and as they sat down at the kitchen table and declined my offer of tea I noticed, after the somewhat wan greeting, that they looked pale and scared.

'This is Marie Ann,' said Sister Clare. 'Please tell Mrs McQuinn what happened.' As she was using sign language I realised that the young girl was also deaf.

The girl spoke in a faint hoarse whisper, many of her words were lost and I had to ask her to repeat herself, much to her distress. As I listened and pieced together the story it seemed that several times, when she was working in the convent vegetable garden, she had observed a man looking very intently at her over the fence.

'One evening, as it was growing dark...' Pausing, she sighed deeply, her distress obvious, and Sister Clare said in a shocked voice, 'He vaulted the fence.'

She stopped and closed her lips firmly, leaving me to consider the enormity of such action.

Marie Ann's eyes filled with tears and, shaking her head, she darted an imploring look across to Sister Clare who sighed and continued the story.

'Marie Ann was about to run indoors, quite terrified, but this man chased her – seized her arm, murmured words that she did not hear or understand. She was terrified– he sounded so savage and awful. He then put an arm around her and—' she darted a shocked look at the young girl and whispered, 'he attempted to kiss her.'

A dreadful pause followed as Sister Clare's hands busily poured out this story for Marie Ann's approval. The girl watched, her vigorous nods confirming the details.

'She struggled free and rushed indoors. One of us caught her: she seemed about to faint with terror.' Another significant pause, another shocked whisper. 'Her dress was torn at the neck.'

A moan from Marie Ann.

'We rushed out, of course, but the garden was empty—'

'A moment, Sister,' I interrupted. 'What was this man like?'

This was translated by a flurry of hands. Sister Clare shook her head. 'It was dusk and he wore a hooded cloak. She only saw he was a tall man, with, she thought, a badly scarred face.'

A scarred face, that would have been enough to frighten her, let alone being seized violently by a strange man, I thought. I asked Marie Ann, 'He tried to kiss you?'

Sister Clare gave a little scream and averted her face; a hand against her mouth so that Marie Ann could not lip-read, she drew a deep breath. 'That might have been imagination. Marie Ann comes from a troubled home.' Lowering her head, a blush of embarrassment. 'She was...er...interfered with, by her half-brother and her stepfather. She is very afraid of all men.'

I considered this piece of information. 'Could Marie Ann not tell you what he was trying to say to her?'

Sister Clare shook her head. 'We tried that, but she was too frightened, too distressed to understand. Just wanted to get away from him.'

'As the presence of an intruder in the convent grounds is a serious matter,' I said, 'this information would have been very useful to the police.'

Sister Clare practically jumped at the word 'police', which seemed to hang in the air before us. A speedy translation for Marie Ann who looked ready to burst into tears.

They both stared at me. Had I suggested a visit from Lucifer himself they could not have looked more shocked and horrified.

A tricky situation indeed. And with no desire to make matters worse, I refrained from adding that the police were looking for a man wanted for the bank robbery.

I had no wish to elaborate on the two suicides.

'If this was a serious assault, then you should have informed them immediately.' I paused. 'As you are no doubt aware, there have been serious incidents recently.'

Watching their expressions, I asked gently, 'Why did you come to me? How did you think I could help?'

Sister Clare shook her head. 'We had to think of the distress of the other sisters, having uniformed policemen wandering about, asking them embarrassing and intimate questions.'

'Surely only Marie Ann is involved?'

'No, Mrs McQuinn, when we mentioned it, it seems that others of the novices working in the gardens have also seen a man lurking about.'

'The same man?'

'They were not absolutely certain as he had only been seen from a distance.'

I wasn't inclined to take that too seriously. In a place like the convent, where nothing more exciting than a missing shoe ever occurred, one girl's terror and hysteria plus another's imagination and even an innocent stranger seeking directions is transformed into a monster.

I looked at Marie Ann. Poor little waif, I had

sympathy with her. She was no taller than I and looked childlike with her close-cut fair curls. This was the first step of initiation, the female vanity of long beautiful hair was to be sacrificed.

Sister Clare was tight-lipped as she said, 'The police would not do at all, Mrs McQuinn. Surely you can imagine, as a woman, the sort of indelicate matters that might be discussed with our young girls. We thought that a lady like yourself would be ideal to conduct a more discreet enquiry, one of your investigations that would not distress them.'

I wondered who had told them I was a private detective. Even in convents, it seemed, news got around.

Sister Clare had now turned her back towards Marie Ann who was effectively eliminated from the conversation.

She leant forward and whispered confidentially, 'There is another matter, concerning those two girls who apparently took their own lives recently. This has not been mentioned and it is something you and the general public – as well as the police – might not be aware of.'

She sighed and shook her head. 'Amy and Belle had been brought up as Catholics, indeed they still came to Mass occasionally. And as you know, suicide is strictly forbidden by our church.'

A moment while she let that sink in. 'Brought up' might indicate that they were lapsed Catholics. I had no idea if the Edinburgh City Police would consider this significant but it did throw a new clue into the matter.

Sister Clare took my silence as acceptance. 'You will help us, Mrs McQuinn.'

I wasn't at all sure what I could do to help but promised to give it some thought. They obviously considered this a foregone conclusion and were smilingly cheerful at the door and grateful when I thrust the bundle of clothes into Sister Clare's hands.

Peeping into the bundle, she withdrew first my shabby cloak and beamed at me. Shaking it out and handing it to Marie Ann she said, 'Here you are, this is perfect for you. Perfect for winter. You are always very good to us, Mrs McQuinn. God bless you for your kindness.'

She looked me up and down. 'Marie Ann is exactly your own size, Mrs McQuinn. You are both so small and neat but the good Lord made good stuff in small bundles.'

I watched them walk down the road. A hooded man with a scarred face, two suicides imperilling their immortal souls if they were, or had been, good Catholics.

This was a new factor to discuss with Jack.

The sounds of the circus preparing for the day's performance in Queen's Park travelled across the hill. As I stood in Solomon's Tower I thought about the sound from the circus, the short distance from the convent and from where I stood, and realised, perhaps for the first time, the significance of the fact that all these crimes had happened within Newington, a small suburb on the south side of the city.

And therefore, willing or no, I was part of it too. For the first time I felt vulnerable. Who was this stranger who had threatened Marie Ann, hooded, scarred? And suddenly Arthur's Seat took on a sinister aspect while I remembered those legends old as time itself.

I looked at Thane, happy at my side. Thane, whose mysterious appearance in my life four years ago had never been properly explained. I sighed; only he knew what was happening up there far above our heads, what strange hiding places and secret caves had existed long before man appeared to put down roots and live out his days on the slope of an extinct volcano.

Before the twentieth century the marks of the medieval monks' ancient agriculture across the hillside were still clearly visible at sunrise and sunset, and their names remained with the shadows of the runrigs, despite all the progress of man.

If only Thane could speak, I thought yet again. How far back did his own strange history go? What were his origins? How had he evolved so complete, so neat and tidy to come to my door one day and set himself up as my rescuer, my protector, to whom I owed my life more than once? That could have been coincidence, but several times my logbook recorded cases where I had taken the wrong turning and become the hunted instead of the hunter.

I patted his head and he rewarded me with a pleased look. But he could still disappear, be absorbed back into these wild, lofty heights for lengthy periods, which I had learnt to accept, knowing that he would always return.

Sometimes he seemed able to exist without any food from me. This was once a cause of constant concern, until common sense told me that, although acclimatised to and accepting domestic life, he was still a hunter, a killer of small animals.

At least when the dark days arrived he was always back at the Tower by nightfall, much to my relief: having him at my side as the first storms of autumn shrilled across the hill was a comfort. Fallen leaves and debris thrown up against the windows could sound alarmingly like alien footsteps.

I pushed aside these thoughts of Thane, the mystery I would never solve. Standing there at my kitchen door, to the west, hidden by trees, the convent and its grounds; eastwards, the horizons held Edinburgh's spires, the smoking chimneys to St Leonard's and the Pleasance with their grim tenements. And in between, the Innocent Railway with its daily trains, steaming their way back and forth to Musselburgh.

Just out of sight, down the road, the Palace of Holyroodhouse, the Queen's residence, with the circus established in the area known as the Queen's Park for a short season. A short season which had heralded, by coincidence or design, an outbreak of violence and mysterious death. Was it coincidence that all these landmarks close to each other were also linked with the tinkers' encampment with its gaily coloured caravans?

It would seem even to the least suspicious mind that, if Jack's theory was right, then either circus or tinkers might well be providing refuge for a killer.

CHAPTER NINE

I decided to set off for the tenement where the girls had died. A crumbling ruin among those marked down by the city developers for demolition to be replaced by more modern apartments.

Two hundred years ago, long before the wealthy of Edinburgh had moved on to build their splendid houses in the New Town, these high tenements were already warrens built without thought of style or comfort or hope of luxury, merely to herd together as many human souls into as little breathing space as possible to keep them alive.

After all, this section of humanity was not intended for comfort or luxury. Such bonuses in life would only make working people slothful and turn their families soft, thus spoiling their efficiency as human machines, provided by the good Lord's bountiful grace to keep railways and canals in order, and to prosper their betters by providing a marked increase in their stocks and shares.

If the tall lands before me, and many well out

of sight and conveniently overlooked, were soulless monstrosities, the reason was that it had never occurred to the builders that their wretched inhabitants had souls to destroy. As the decades passed, such properties lacked even the dignity of growing seedy-looking and the passing years did nothing to mellow the miserable conditions.

Where occupants struggled to raise vast families in one room, every drop of water had to be carried up and downstairs from a water main two hundred yards away, until ten years ago. Beds to make the night hours easier were most often crude mattresses thrown down on the floor, the moderately house-proud grateful for a ragged carpet from which all pattern had long since vanished, plus a few broken-down chairs and a rickety table.

Both girls, I knew from Jack, belonged in that peripheral army of servants and factory workers taking employment, however transient, that guaranteed enough money to survive. Their bolder sisters walked the streets of Edinburgh and sold their bodies instead.

Amy Bland occupied flat 6, Belle Sanders flat 5. A dignified description of what was one room, with a bed recess, kitchen sink and shelved cupboard known as an Edinburgh press. On the landing a shared lavatory for six tenants; in the absence of a nearby drying green in that overcrowded area, each flat was provided with indoor laundry facilities: a series of wooden lathes linked to the ceiling by a pulley. Sadly, this novel innovation assisted the two girls in their suicides, if such they were.

The ground floor of number 64 was occupied by a shop with the fanciful name of pawnbroker. Although his dubious connections were keenly observed by the police as a possible fence for stolen goods, he did a considerable trade as a rag-and-bone merchant, a valuable and much frequented addition to this sad poverty-stricken community.

The neighbour who had returned drunk lived in flat 2. A widow with four tiny children resided in flat 3 – presumably the kindly neighbour who could be dismissed from the enquiries as a possible suspect but might have helpful information.

Number 4 was unoccupied, utterly derelict after a burst water main, so that, too, could be eliminated.

As I toiled up the worn stone stair, the bright day outside vanished under a miasma of poverty, children crying and a darkness that I suspected took little heed of daylight. There was a feeling of hopelessness, of inevitability which must have struck anguish into any tenant reduced to living in such poverty, and I spared a thought for the widow woman with her small children and what the future might hold for them.

I arrived at number 6 rather breathless, knocked on the door and expected to find it empty. It was opened by a young woman, carrying a large bundle, her expression harassed and impatient.

'I'm making some enquiries—' I began.

Obviously in a hurry to leave she gasped out, 'You've got here just in time. If it's this place you're wanting.' My respectable appearance had not made an impression as, looking doubtfully at the bare walls, she added, 'You'll need to see the landlord.'

And deciding that further explanation was necessary, she went on, 'I'm Amy's sister and the police told me I could take anything I liked as they didn't need anymore for evidence. I'm not going far, just down the stairs to Joe's shop. There's nothing in here for me, nothing I want.' And perhaps aware that I looked moderately prosperous, she frowned suspiciously. 'Were you a friend of hers?'

I had a sudden inspiration. 'The nuns at the convent asked me to call regarding a Requiem Mass.'

She looked at me wide-eyed and laughed. 'For Amy?'

'She was Catholic, I gather.'

'Aye, baptised and all – we both were. But it's many a long day since I set foot in that church. My man was staunch Kirk, wouldna' be doing with all that popish nonsense. I canna be much help to you. Amy and I werena' friends, too many years between us, nothing in common and I live way out Liberton way. She never wanted me to get married and didna' like my man much.' She sighed. 'He's dead now, God rest him.'

Her statement didn't encourage me to ask her whereabouts at the time her sister died. 'Can you think of any reason for...for...' I faltered deliberately.

'Why she topped herself, you mean? Florrie downstairs – her with all them noisy bairns – tells me she was getting married. Married, well now. I'd never been told about that either – never showed much interest in lads, bit of a surprise that – but she might have invited me to the wedding, as her only kin,' she added, her bitter tone hinting that this was the worst cut of all. 'This lad she was marrying has never been to see me to offer sympathy either.'

'I understand that his ship is due to arrive in Leith.'

'Is that so, now?' She sounded mildly placated so I asked, 'Would you by any chance know where I can get his address?'

She shook her head.

'Were there any letters from him when you were clearing up?'

'I dare say there were, but didna' bother to read them like, none of my business. Just put them all in the fire. All except this.' And putting her hand into the bundle, she produced a framed photograph of two girls which I presumed were herself and Amy.

'Not me,' she laughed. 'That's her with her chum Belle, they were always very close. Thought more of her than any of her own family,' she added, thrusting the photo back into the bundle. 'The frame might be worth a penny or two.'

That seemed a little heartless, and had I arrived earlier, those letters she was destroying might have contained some valuable information. Not that it would be any help in finding out the truth about Amy's death and I realised that, as an interview, this conversation was going nowhere. Except for one vital piece of evidence. That Amy, because of her religion, was unlikely to have taken her own life.

I trailed down to the next floor, the screeching inside indicating that this was where Amy's friendly neighbour lived. The door was opened by a harassed young woman, holding a babe in arms and with two small children clinging to her skirts, which they were finding handy to wipe their running noses.

'Hello.' I smiled and gave the prepared story I had given Amy's sister.

'Oh, Amy would have wanted that, very devout she was. Didn't go to Mass as much as she would have liked, but she was a good Catholic. Lots of holy pictures and the Sacred Heart on the wall...'

I presumed they were in the bundle on its way downstairs to the pawnbroker.

'Are you Catholic?' I asked,

'Me? No. But I didna' hold that against her. Good-living girl, and getting married too.' Pausing, she shook her head. 'With so much to live for, I still canna' understand why she did it, wanted to end it all. Didna' mak' any sense to me.'

'There hadn't been anything worrying her?'

She frowned, said uneasily. 'Such as?'

'Well, a quarrel with her fiancé – about their wedding arrangements. These things do happen at the last minute...' I hesitated, 'or one of them meets someone else—'

'Never that! Mind you, I think her friend Belle was trying to persuade her against this chap. There were plenty of arguments before—' Biting her lip she left the rest unsaid.

'She would have told you, then, if anything was wrong?'

For a moment she looked bewildered. Then she shook her head. 'She once said I was more like a sister than her own kin.' Her eyes filled with tears. 'I shall miss them both, that I will. Many the cups of tea and a good laugh we shared.'

Screams and altercations from behind her indicated that all was not well with the remaining bairn.

She looked panic-stricken. 'I'll have to go. But yes, miss, you tell your nuns they can have a Mass for Amy.'

My next call was on Belle's grandfather who occupied a one-roomed ground floor flat in a similarly dismal tenement across the street. He answered the door firmly enough on crutches. Obviously he was now used to the loss of his right leg.

I said I was from the convent and he invited me in, hardly waiting to close the door before saying that his granddaughter would never have topped herself.

'I have a bit put away and I wanted her to come and live with me – we could have found somewhere a bit more comfortable than this. She would have none of that. A fine lass but with a will of her own. We got along fine most of the time, right fond of me she was, always remembered my birthday, came in to see me each day just to cheer me up. But she said she could never ever live in the same place with me – that I would never understand her.'

Pausing, he shook his head. 'I gave up trying. Lasses are different to what they were when I was young.' He sighed with a despairing look around the shabby room. 'I can do without lectures on the way I live, I manage fine on my own.'

Glancing towards the sideboard, I noticed the bottle

of whisky and had already identified the strong smell of spirits. An old man's consolation.

'Belle and this chum Amy she thought so much of were good Catholics. Not like me: I lapsed long since,' he added, indicating the proud photograph on the sideboard.

Corporal Will Sanders, a young soldier with two medals in a glass frame.

'Killing Russky soldiers, who were just like ourselves, worshipping the same God and all that sort of thing, put an end to religion for me. Never set foot in a church since the day I came home. Not even when my lass, her ma, died.'

A shake of his head. 'She never knew her father, scarpered when she was a bairn, but Belle and me got on well, right enough, though sometimes we had rows – she didn't approve of me taking a drink or two.'

There seemed nothing more to say and expressing my condolences I prepared to leave.

He followed me to the door and thanked me for coming. 'I think Belle and her chum would want to have Requiem Masses said for them.'

He looked at me intently, almost pleading. 'I still don't understand it. She came and visited me just hours before...before it happened. I wish you had known her.'

I didn't have an answer to that and he took my hand and said, 'God bless you for coming to see me. You're a good lass.'

On an impulse, suddenly aware of the bitter loneliness of this old man who had lost everything, I scribbled my address on a piece of paper torn from my notebook. 'Perhaps I could look in again and see you; I often pass this way.'

He murmured gratitude, gave me a bewildered look and opened his mouth as if to say something else, then shaking his head, as if changing his mind, said, 'No, nothing important,' and closed the door abruptly.

I felt I had failed Jack badly. I had not one clue to prove that the two girls who had died within hours of each other had been murdered.

They were close friends, and had they both been suffering from tragic circumstances, they might possibly have had a suicide pact. But their faith and certainly Belle's daily calls and caring for her grandfather were against that. Were there any suicide notes that the police had failed to find? The other quite minor detail, something I didn't really want to consider, was that Amy and Belle had once been employed in the Rice household.

Much as I hated anything that might upset my new-found friend, blackmail was a silent possibility that could not be ignored. Did these two girls know something from their days at Rice Villa, regarding their past employer, which had necessitated their disposal?

CHAPTER TEN

Thankfully sighting home and breathing in the refreshing air of Arthur's Seat, almost guiltily aware of the vast empty rooms in Solomon's Tower – that great hall, and others upstairs that I seldom set foot in – I was aware of a carriage rushing up the hill.

It reached me at the gate and the Rice coachman leapt down. 'Mrs McQuinn, a message from madam.' He thrust a note into my hand:

'Dearest Rose, Come at once. Something terrible has happened.'

This had to be serious; I knew that by the anguished expression on the coachman's usually stolid countenance as he silently opened the carriage door for me.

'What has happened?' I asked. He merely shook his head and set the horses off at a cracking pace back in the direction of Rice Villa.

With not the slightest idea what Elma's summons involved, the prospect of this urgent visit to her home for the first time gave little time for admiration of the handsome surroundings.

A tear-stained maid opened the door and Elma, attired in black, rushed down the stairs to greet me.

She took my hands, wringing them painfully, almost speechless as she gasped out the terrible story.

While we were having tea with Alice and shopping together in Edinburgh, Felix had taken a heart attack and collapsed in his study, to be found by his valet bringing in his afternoon tea.

The circumstances were dreadful.

She led me into the parlour, weeping. 'Oh Rose, dear, I am so glad you are here, you are the only one I could turn to.' Still clutching my hand, she sobbed out the story. 'To think all this was happening back here while we were so happy, enjoying ourselves in Jenners. Oh, dear heaven,' she moaned, 'my stupid pride, that's to blame. If only I had been with him, Rose. I might have saved him.'

I thought that highly unlikely, it wasn't the way heart attacks happened: the grim truth was one moment alive, the next quite dead. That was the rule.

Then I learnt that this was not the case. Felix had struck his head on the stone hearth when he fell. He had lost a lot of blood but was still alive, his life hanging by a thread.

'Hodge found him. It was dreadful, dreadful.' She shuddered. 'When I arrived I almost died – the sight that met my eyes, you can't imagine, Rose. There was Hodge covered in blood, everywhere – the poor man had been trying to lift the master, trying to help him, and God knows, if he hadn't called a doctor neighbour from across the way, a few more minutes and poor Felix would have bled to death.'

All I could do was sit there mutely and listen. But she was soon too exhausted to speak, dazed and shocked beyond words. She insisted that I stay the night, a guest room always at the ready was prepared for me: a fire glowing red, a nightgown provided.

In normal circumstances I would have relished staying in that beautiful room with its windows looking towards the Pentland Hills over the treetops of a spacious garden. Everything around me spoke of luxury, of comfort and wealth, but alas, this was not the case: the tragedy that awaited downstairs was inescapable.

Elma was too upset to eat. The doctor came from seeing Felix at the hospital, said little but gave her a sleeping draught. She insisted that I saw her to bed, and as she closed her eyes, she took my hand, held it tightly and said, 'Promise you will stay, Rose. Promise, you won't desert me. You'll see me through all this, whatever happens.'

I assured her that I would do so. I didn't feel much like sleeping either, but it had been an exhausting day and at last I drifted off in my magnificent surroundings, in the warm depths of the four-poster bed, to awake to the sound of a carriage on the drive.

It was eight o'clock and I heard voices in the corridor. A tap on the door, I opened it and the maid had left my breakfast on a tray outside. She saw me and said, 'Madam will be in the breakfast room – the door on the left of the staircase.'

There was a bathroom along the corridor, unheard

of luxury in Solomon's Tower, a newfangled luxury to most Edinburgh homes, and I would have enjoyed the prospect of a lingering bath, but after some hasty ablutions, I made my way downstairs.

Elma was seated at the table. She jumped up to greet me. Pale and exhausted, her shocked expression wrung my heart.

'I have been to the hospital, that awful crowded place. I went at six o'clock this morning: I had to know how he was. Oh Rose, he is still alive, at least let us be thankful for that.' She sobbed into a piece of lace and then lifting her head whispered, 'I wanted to stay with him, but they wouldn't let me, they said he was too ill. Gravely ill, as if I didn't know that. The nurse emphasised that only his extremely thick skull saved him, any normal person would be dead. They didn't give me much hope: even if he recovers, his memory might be affected.' She shuddered. 'His poor darling eyes were wide open, but he couldn't recognise me. Oh Rose, seeing him in that terrible place – he should have been at home, we could have got the best physician Edinburgh has to offer, the best nurses to attend him. But they say he must not be moved and he must stay there.'

I didn't want to distress her but agreed that he had to have constant care in a proper hospital where doctors were on hand in an emergency.

She made fists of her hands. 'It's so unfair. They won't even let me see him alone. I'm told there must always be one of these grim policemen sitting at his bedside – isn't that awful?'

I hadn't expected that swift turn of events, as she continued, 'Not even a moment's privacy between us. When I complained, they said it was necessary. That's all. But I can't think of why, can you?'

I shook my head. An injured man, possibly dying, and his devoted wife. It wasn't until later when I was aware of the true facts that I could hazard a guess for the policeman's presence. That there was some doubt about the nature of her husband's 'heart attack'.

The real reason for the twenty-four hour surveillance was the off chance that, if Felix recovered, the police might get an answer to their question about what really happened in his study that afternoon, rather than the story cobbled together from the valet Hodge's gabbled report.

All I had learnt so far was the suggestion that Felix had felt unwell, stood up to summon his valet by the bell at the fireplace but, unsteady on his feet, he had fallen and struck his head on the stone hearth. Lying there in a pool of blood was a much worse scene for poor Elma to imagine and a constant reproach to have to live with.

She was returning to her vigil in the hospital and so I went home on foot, declining the suggestion of a hiring cab, and while much regretting the absence of my bicycle, I was glad to breathe the fresh air and have my own thoughts for company.

As I entered the kitchen to be overwhelmed by Thane's greeting – he had the freedom of the Tower to come and go as he pleased, having long ago learnt how to lift the latch on the back door with his nose – the sound of a cab outside had me rushing to the front door.

Much to my surprise a very grim-faced Jack Macmerry emerged.

'I thought you were going back to Glasgow,' I said.

'So did I,' he said shortly. 'But in view of the recent happenings at Rice Villa a decision on high means I have to stay. Short-staffed and all that sort of thing,' he grumbled. 'So my domestic concerns are of little weight when we are faced with a possible murder case.'

'Murder!' I whistled. So that was the reason for the policeman at Miles Rice's side, I thought as he continued, 'The possibility is that he might not have fallen but had been pushed, and that unless he recovers, which is considered most unlikely, and can tell us the facts about what really happened, then we may have an attempted murder on our hands.'

Leaning back in the chair, making himself at home as ever, he said, 'And what do you think, being on such friendly terms with his wife? What's your opinion, Rose?'

So that was it. Jack was being especially communicative in the hope that I had a fleeting acquaintance with the husband as well as the wife.

I told him that I had never met Miles Rice or even set foot in the house until Elma summoned me immediately after the accident.

He looked at me appraisingly. 'She must think very highly of you, considering you met quite recently?'

That was a question I ignored as I told him of her distraught state.

He frowned. 'Pity that you had never met him. It is

always useful to find out what goes on behind the scenes.'

'If you mean by that, were they happy...? I can vouch for Elma: she absolutely adored her husband.'

He looked thoughtful. 'So it appears, but let's not forget none of us know what goes on between apparently happy couples once the bedroom door is closed. All our friends,' he gave me a dark look as he emphasised the words, 'would have vouched for the pair of us, imminently expecting that wedding invitation. And look what happened.' A bitter smile as he shook his head wryly. 'We all have had unpleasant surprises in that direction.'

I regarded him sternly. 'If you are hinting that Elma secretly loathed her husband and wanted him dead, I can put your mind at ease. Elma was with me in Jenners when it happened. As one of my friends and half a dozen waitresses as well as the manageress of the lady's millinery department can testify.'

Jack nodded solemnly. 'Oh, I believe you, but there are means of disposing of people one loathes without physically being present, if one has enough money and influence.' A pause. 'Did you have a chance to meet the valet Hodge, by any chance?'

'No. I didn't see him while I was there. It was unlikely that the occasion demanded that I should be immediately introduced to her husband's valet,' I said heavily. 'Anyway, he was probably too upset to meet anyone after what he had been through. Are you telling me that you think he is involved, your prime suspect, in fact?'

Jack said nothing for a moment then merely sighed deeply.

'All I am saying, Rose, is that a deeper investigation concerning this accident is needed—'

'What on earth do you mean, "deeper investigation"?' I demanded angrily. 'Here is this poor woman, heartbroken, terrified of losing her husband. Are you trying to tell me she engineered his death?'

Jack held up his hand in a gesture well remembered from our past life together. 'Hold on, hold on there, Rose!'

Then he told me, reluctantly, I thought, that it had emerged recently that Miles Rice had enemies and, indeed, was possibly being blackmailed by unscrupulous business rivals.

He shook his head. 'Some of the explanations for the happenings of that afternoon do not quite add up at the scene. The study has french windows into the garden. They were open—'

'Hardly suspicious. Perhaps he was expecting a visitor.'

'I would call that highly suspicious considering the circumstances—'

'Then maybe he liked fresh air while he worked,' I said defensively.

Jack gave me a wry look. 'Fresh air, yes. But on a chill, rainy day with a strong wind?'

And I remembered that the weather had been particularly disagreeable. Violent sudden showers – we had to run from Jenners to the carriage, sheltered by the doorman's umbrella.

'You have a naturally suspicious mind, like all policemen,' I said shortly.

He grinned. 'And like all lady investigators should

have, my dear Rose. It is, as you used to tell me several times a day, an essential qualification for the job.'

He was right, of course, it was simply that this was too personal for me. I wanted desperately to protect Elma from further distress and was grateful that at least I was able to provide her with an alibi.

'I presume the household have all been questioned?'

'Only his valet was on hand to make the master's tea and attend to any needs. Miles Rice, a generous employer, had treated the staff to a visit to the circus that afternoon.'

That accounted for the informal dinner Elma had planned and my first meeting with Felix.

Jack rubbed his chin thoughtfully, adding grimly, 'Which could also have provided useful information for a prospective burglar or killer.'

I was leaping ahead. I thought again of Hodge and wished I had met him. 'What is known about Hodge anyway?'

He shook his head. 'There isn't a lot. He has been with Rice since before they came to Edinburgh. All we could get out of the interview with him was a statement that he was in a terrible state, finding his master lying there in a pool of blood, thought he was dead—'

'What of his background?' I asked sharply.

Jack shrugged. 'Nothing criminal or suspicious, if that's what you're indicating – so far, that is. Of course, we're looking into references etcetera.'

I realised that I was quite willing, most unjustly, to sacrifice the devoted valet whom I had never met. Jumping to conclusions, the first on the scene, the one who discovers the body, is always the prime suspect in a murder case.

'A burglary gone wrong, then?'

'Mm,' said Jack. 'Considering the open french door, yes.'

He paused and said slowly, 'There is another even more vague possibility but one worth careful consideration. Two suicides that may well be murder and now the Miles Rice incident.' He sighed. 'If he was attacked by an intruder, then this is the fourth violent crime in Edinburgh in less than a fortnight.'

'And you think they may be connected?'

Jack nodded. 'I feel there's a definite link somewhere with that damned circus's arrival.' He shrugged. 'We gather from the family physician that Rice had never had a day's illness in his whole life. The hospital doctors confirm that there was nothing to indicate heart disease. Excellent health, in fact, for a man in his sixties.'

He frowned. 'Consider the timing, Rose. Since the circus has come to town for a short season rather than a short visit we will have to walk warily in the future. We can't really cope with wholesale massacres in the area, or multiple unexplained deaths,' he added sarcastically.

'The advent of the circus could be a mere coincidence,' I offered, although I was never one to believe in such where violent crimes were concerned.

Jack remembered that, too, and said: 'Wouldn't you think the word "coincidence" is rather inapt to describe what has been going on?'

I thought for a moment. 'There is another possibility, one we know nothing about. That Rice had a secret enemy, someone with whom he had an assignation that afternoon, hence the open french door. There followed a murderous attack which had no connection with Edinburgh or with the circus.'

'I've thought of that too. And the circus with its constantly moving motley collection of individuals could be the perfect refuge for a killer. Too many unknowns, and I suspect that a lot of those performers might have backgrounds that wouldn't bear too close investigation.'

'Was that what you were really doing the other evening when I met you and your colleagues enjoying the greatest show on earth?' I asked casually.

He looked solemn for a moment. 'Nothing to do with these events, as it happens.' Then with a grin, 'You ask too many questions, Rose.'

'It's the way to get answers, Jack, surely you as a policeman know that, and it is always the one that was too obvious and no one thought to ask that holds the vital clue.'

Flexing his shoulders he stood up. 'And the sooner we find this vital missing clue, the sooner I get back to Glasgow and sort out my domestic problems looming there.'

It was difficult for me to imagine Jack in the role of a devoted father. I had miscarried the one child conceived during our relationship, the reason for a hastily arranged marriage fated never to happen.

I thought of the motherless wee daughter with compassion.

CHAPTER ELEVEN

In the anxious days that followed, Elma became a constant visitor. She told me somewhat guiltily that it was a blessed relief to walk Rufus on the hill. One of the maids could have performed this task as Elma spent endless hours at her husband's bedside, watching over him, searching his still countenance for some faint return of consciousness.

Each day as we walked together she repeated her story of self-reproach, going over and over the details of that fatal fall in his study – blaming herself for being absent, as she was so often out shopping in Princes Street and looking at millinery in Jenners.

'Thank heaven you were with me, Rose dear, you are the only one who truly understands.'

I found this quite remarkable. She must have many close friends in her own circle but since we met I had become her oft declared 'most trusted friend'. Having been together at a time of crisis was a further bond, and now it seemed I was the only person whose company she wished for, reliving those moments of happiness – the circus and the play, the shopping excursions – before the blow fell that was to throw her life into disarray and change it for ever.

I, who had long been a widow, knew only too well what it felt like to love and lose a husband, and listening patiently to these daily outpourings with compassion, I thought of her alone in Edinburgh, with no family to turn to.

Wait a moment. What of her twin brother Peter, training to be a doctor?

But when I mentioned him, she looked at me, her expression almost fearful.

'Peter has just returned from a hospital in South Africa, in the war zone. Indeed, he was my very first thought, but he wouldn't be able to help poor Felix,' a sob restrained as she shook her head. 'Alas, he hasn't the experience.'

I hadn't thought of him in a medical capacity, merely as the twin whose closeness would bring her comfort.

'Where is he now?'

She shook her head. 'I'm not sure. London, I think. That was his last address.' And leaning forward confidentially. 'He would have come to Edinburgh to see me again immediately had I summoned him, I know that. But there is a complication. You see, he has formed an attachment with a young lady in London. It would not be the first time, ladies find him quite irresistible.'

She paused, smiled tenderly and then added with a dour sigh, 'It is different this time – there are hints about an engagement.'

And I got a fleeting but quite distinct idea that this relationship was not to her liking. Perhaps being a twin brought a feeling of possessiveness, jealousy at being displaced in their natural bond.

'Shouldn't you let him know? He would be a comfort and even his little medical knowledge would be a consolation to you,' I said, thinking how I had always relied on my stepbrother Dr Vince Laurie in moments of crisis.

'Oh indeed, yes.' But her words lacked conviction and she looked rather worried, biting her lip. 'We are very close...' a wan smile, 'and I long to have him meet you, my new, dear friend. I am sure he will love you, Rose.'

After Elma left I thought about Peter and her strange reactions. Perhaps she had not told the exact truth and had elevated a humble role as hospital nurse to that of medical student. Equally admirable for service to the public, but no doubt a profession that did not suit her lifestyle in the Grange.

So much snobbery about professions: lawyers, doctors, ministers were the acceptable strata but the lower echelons were not considered good company by the dinner party society. A sad truth but I thought, unworthily, to say 'my brother is a doctor' sounded grander by far than 'a hospital nurse', a profession regarded, despite the efforts of Florence Nightingale, as very low on the social ladder.

And then suddenly out of the blue, talking of the medical profession, totally unexpected as always, not a bit of warning, a carriage rolled up the road and out jumped a familiar, much loved but all-too-seldom-seen figure.

Delighted, breathless with excitement, I rushed out screaming, 'Vince!'

So wonderful to see him and, as usual, he swept me off my feet as we embraced. Thane also rushed forward to greet one of his favourite humans and we all tumbled into the kitchen where, once Vince was seated by the fire and the kettle on the hob, I asked, as always, the vital question.

'How long can you stay?'

Usually it was a few hours only, an escape from Balmoral and the royal household while the royal train rested in Waverley Station, waiting for some prince or princess to open a hospital wing or a bridge in Edinburgh.

Vince laughed. 'Blame the royal train once again. Has to collect one of the grandchildren from Kensington Palace, bring him back to Her Majesty for a short holiday. A delicate flower, this one, and unfortunately he has developed a slight complication to his recovery from a chill – a troublesome cough, I believe – and won't be allowed to travel until he is proclaimed fit and well again.'

Pausing, he grinned impishly. 'So it was hardly worth sending me on the train back to Balmoral for a couple of days.'

'A couple of days.' I laughed delightedly. It was wonderful, the prospect of having him for more than a brief hour or two. Fortunately I had a good supply of vegetables from the garden and soup was always on offer, especially Vince's favourite Scotch broth.

While I prepared the meal he brought me up to date with the latest news on Olivia and the three children. All were well, the children growing rapidly and all eager to know when I was going to London to visit them at St James.

The question and the invitation was ongoing, but alas, I never managed to tear myself away from Edinburgh and possibly, or probably, Thane. I had taken him on short train journeys, a couple of cases in the Borders in recent years, but the idea of his reactions to busy distant London had no appeal and I felt was beyond any hope of success.

'And what of you?' Vince asked. 'Any exciting news? Stands Edinburgh where it did?'

So I told him about Jack. He looked solemn, for he had been very sorry when we parted. The two men had become good friends and Vince was bitterly disappointed to learn – I saw it in his eyes – that Jack had got married, although I said it so lightly, making it quite matter of fact.

Although he shook his head sadly to hear that the brief marriage had ended so tragically, however, that Jack was now a widower caused him to brighten visibly. Never a good actor, he was totally unable to conceal his hopes that Jack's return to Edinburgh was a clear indication that we were to be together again.

His question was eager. 'And how do you feel about Jack now?'

'Sad for him – the wee daughter motherless.'

'Is that all?' he demanded. It was clearly not what he had in mind.

I set down the plates. 'All for the present, I'm afraid.'

Vince's face expressed impatience and disappointment.

'I have just heard this news,' I said. 'Hardly had time for what you are so anxious to read – as you might call it – between the lines.'

Vince was silent for a moment, then said slowly, 'I imagine the fact that he got in touch with you means that he still wants you, Rose. After all, you sent him away—'

I was glad I had not given him the details of that last interview between us as I interrupted:, 'Oh, for heavens sake, I think it was fairly mutual.'

Vince shrugged. 'Maybe. But by this time you can no longer pretend that Danny is the reason you won't marry him.' He shook his head. 'Missing he might still be, but dead he most certainly is. Surely you can no longer have the slightest doubts?'

I nodded. 'Yes, I have come to terms with it.'

'You are indeed a widow, my dear,' he insisted, 'and you are sensible enough to realise that you have been so since the day you left Arizona more than four years ago. It merely became a convenient excuse to delay your marriage to Jack Macmerry,' he added sternly.

Vince knew me too well to bother to deny that and a short silence followed while he finished his soup and tackled the bread and cheese. Declining tea he took out a handsome silver flask which I guessed contained a very expensive whisky from the royal cellars.

'What other news? How are you progressing with the typewriting machine?'

I noticed him giving it a hard look as we walked through the hall, where it sat at one end of the refectory table in isolated splendour under its leather cover, rarely removed.

I said, 'Not very well. It's a slow business learning when I can write much quicker by hand.'

He grinned, and then said solemnly, 'You'll be very glad of it someday – it's been a great boon to people who do clerical work. Such progress. I thought you would take to it immediately, the way you took to riding a bicycle.'

He had handed on the machine to me on his last brief visit. Brought it all the way from London, a present from one of his wealthy ex-patients who was leaving the country. 'Quite honestly, I was grateful but couldn't see myself ever having time or opportunity to learn to use it. But I immediately thought of how useful it would be to you.'

I hadn't wanted to sound ungrateful either but couldn't see myself sitting behind it tapping out letters, which I could do much quicker and more efficiently with a pen and notebook.

However, I had decided to try it out. Large and unwieldy as I removed it into the hall, I staggered and bashed it against the stone wall. Thankfully it suffered no damage – or so I thought – until I discovered that one of the letter keys had jammed and required considerable effort to print. Yet another reason why I hadn't continued to practise, which I hardly felt like confessing to Vince considering it was a gift that he had set so much store by.

'Keep persevering,' he said, 'it's not like you to let anything defeat you.' I smiled wryly and, changing the subject, he asked, 'Anything exciting on Edinburgh's crime scene?'

As Vince's logic and reasoning were always reliable and, in some of my past cases, he prided himself on touching some factor I might have overlooked, I brought him up to date on the two girls' suicides.

He whistled. 'Same place, same method. Unless it was a suicide pact and that seems unlikely, particularly with the absence of notes – unusual given the circumstances. For one, an imminent marriage, for the other, a disabled grandfather.' He paused. 'Surely the police have murder in mind? Isn't your lady investigator's mind intrigued?'

When I told him of Jack's suggestion that I carry on an unofficial investigation, he almost applauded, and not only for the detection idea either, I was sure. His imagination was bounding ahead to the closeness this would bring and a happy partnership on quite a different level.

I switched off his enthusiastic comments and told him about my new friend Elma and her husband's unfortunate accident.

'I believe you met them at Balmoral.'

'Felix Miles Rice. Of course, I remember him very well. A great wit and a reputation as a philanthropist. Got along splendidly with HM. Bags of charm, don't you think?'

'I haven't had the pleasure. But Elma obviously

adores him. I gather this is a very happy second marriage.'

Vince gave me a wry look. 'I hate to disappoint you, but I think you gather wrong, my dear. About the adoration, I mean. From personal experience this was not the impression we got at Balmoral. She seemed to be anxious to avoid him and it was, I suspected, mutual. A good front for the natives, but behind the scenes...' He paused and shook his head.

'Rubbish!' I said shortly. 'What you witnessed might have been just a domestic tiff, everyone has them. Even you and Olivia.'

He grinned. 'Don't I just know that! All married couples have rows,' and shaking his head, 'but not this. This gave an impression that it was somehow rooted, long-standing.' He shrugged. 'The frequent dark look, the sharp word, the scornful rejoinder – the indifference.'

'What nonsense,' I said, 'all based on a few hours acquaintance. I'm sure you're wrong, and anyway, I prefer to take Elma's word.'

He nodded. 'Your choice, as always. What about Felix?'

When I gave a few brief details of the accident, I could see the medical side of him take immediate possession.

'Poor chap. I've heard of cases like this. A coma for a few days, then...' He shrugged. 'I wouldn't hold out too much hope. Poor chap,' he repeated. 'And what of Elma? I gather there were no children.'

'She has a twin brother, studying medicine. He's

been working at the front in South Africa.'

Vince's head shot up. 'She'll be glad to have him at her side, have his support through this difficult time.'

As I valued Vince's opinion, I went into further details about the accident, the discovery by his valet and so on.

'What did the doctors say about the heart attack?'

So I told him about the excellent health record.

He frowned and seemed to come to a sudden decision. 'Do you know, I'd very much like to go in and take a look at him,' he said eagerly.

'I very much doubt that you would be allowed to visit him, Vince. He is under twenty-four-hour surveillance, a policeman sitting constantly at his bedside. All adding to poor Elma's despair; naturally she wants some privacy.'

'Naturally,' Vince echoed dryly.

I gave him a hard look.

He smiled. 'Obviously the police suspect that there might be more than a serious fall, especially where there is no evidence of heart disease.'

He shrugged. 'This could be a bad business, a very bad business for everyone concerned.'

CHAPTER TWELVE

Our conversation was interrupted by a dog barking. Rufus was heralding Elma's arrival. As I opened the door, Thane slid past me, ignoring the terrier's threatening growls. Once more it was as if Rufus did not exist.

Elma was surprised to see Vince and delighted too. And Vince was at his most charming. Before his marriage, he had a succession of unrequited loves, bemoaning his lack of success with girls – blaming his boyish appearance, his mop of fair curls, both of which had long since vanished into a balding high forehead, and a rather corpulent but still imposing figure.

A happily married man, now with an elevated position as physician to the royal household, I was witnessing a new side to my stepbrother's personality. I realised that sex is not something we recognise in our siblings and this was a very different Vince, a man who was undoubtedly attractive and very successful with the ladies, and without question most appealing to his female patients.

The Balmoral visit, where he and Elma had first met, was casually mentioned. Then, as her face clouded, Vince offered sympathy for her husband's appalling accident at which she switched to her usual angry comments. Not regarding his treatment in hospital, but her own reception and the extraordinary behaviour of those in charge of Felix, to say nothing of the grim presence of a policeman at his bedside.

Vince listened, an occasional shake of his head indicating silent condemnation of such outrageous behaviour.

'I am so sorry, Mrs Rice. Is there something I can do for you? Would you like me to go in and have a look at him?'

She considered this for a moment, and then said slowly, 'Oh, would you do that, Dr Laurie?' And clasping her hands, 'Yes, indeed. I would be so grateful. Obviously, with all your influence, they could not refuse to admit a *royal* physician.'

And as Vince shrugged modestly, she added, 'I am sure they would never deny you the right to see someone you had met in Her *Majesty's* presence at Balmoral Castle.'

The talk turned to how long Vince was staying and so it was arranged that Vince would visit Felix the next day.

I was certain, and so I imagine was Elma, that she would accompany him, but as if anticipating this suggestion, he said, 'In the first instance I believe it would be more effective if I saw him in private, in my professional capacity, being acquainted with their patient and so forth.'

Elma agreed a little reluctantly and it was arranged that she should wait in the reception area and, when the moment was appropriate after Vince's consultation with the doctors, once again pay her usual melancholy visit to her husband's bedside.

She left us soon afterwards.

We watched her cross the garden and head towards the hill, with Rufus bounding ahead, barking fiercely.

Turning to Vince, I asked, 'Any second thoughts?'

He gave me a quizzical glance. 'What do you mean, "second thoughts"?'

'I gather at first meeting you were not particularly impressed, and I am wondering whether, on closer acquaintance, your opinion has now improved?'

He grinned. 'I think she plays her part as the adoring wife very well indeed.'

'You think that's an act,' I said indignantly. 'What a horrid thing to say, Vince. Quite unworthy of you.'

He made a modifying gesture, shook his head. 'Perhaps she is as sincere as she appears in her affection. After all, it is not until we lose someone close to us that we realise their true worth. And in Mrs Rice's case that worth is considerable – a vast fortune is involved.'

I felt disappointed. 'That is extremely cynical, Vince. Not much evidence of your usual kindness of heart.'

He smiled. 'And you, my dearest Rose, are once more a victim of your excess of that particular quality.'

'What do you mean by that?' I demanded.

He shook his head. 'Only that you have known Mrs

Rice a very short while. What is it – weeks, rather than months and years?'

I felt angry and misjudged, wanting very much for him to like my new friend, but Vince carefully forestalled me. Observing my expression and guessing as of old that I was going to argue, he stood up and said, 'It's a lovely day, and do you know what I would like?'

I shook my head, still annoyed with him.

'I would love to visit the funfair down the road,' he said. 'We had the circus, of course, at Balmoral, but I haven't been at a funfair for ages. Shall we?'

'A splendid idea.'

But before we left there were domestic matters to consider. I hadn't any guest accommodation in the Tower. I thought of all those empty, damp and cold, dusty rooms upstairs and decided we could get by if Vince had my bedroom and I slept downstairs. So I asked, 'Will you be staying here?'

Perhaps he recognised the anxiety in my voice, for he smiled. 'Dear Rose, much as I would love to stay with you, I am bound to stay at the Station Hotel. There is a suite always prepared and ready for emergencies so that passengers on the royal train can literally be on call. Do you mind terribly?'

I didn't. Although it was great to have Vince in Edinburgh for a day or two, it was also a relief that I was not to provide him with bed and board since I might make an accurate guess that Balmoral provided luxuries which were no part of my spartan existence.

As we strode down the road arm in arm I realised that Vince had never been able to accept the Tower as a place to live – the circumstances of its inheritance from the previous owner perhaps still aroused uneasy memories.

I resolved to enjoy every moment of Vince's visit, whatever its length, short or long, and I was not going to let the subject of Elma sully our precious time together.

I would lay that firmly aside but it was not until I was alone that I felt sad. For as well as acquiring a new personality I did not immediately recognise, my dear stepbrother had added a cynicism, which could only be the result of his new lifestyle and the circles he moved in.

There were, however, vestiges evident of the boy I was pleased to see still existed. When we entered the funfair he threw away all dignity to the four winds, relishing the merry-go-round usually the province of small children. I was persuaded to join him a second time round, and he would have had a third.

We marched through the sideshows with their enticing lurid posters – Arab belly dancers very daringly underclad – and barkers enticing male audiences.

'Do you remember Wordsworth's great poem you learnt by heart and used to recite when you were a little girl?'

'I still remember it.'

'Do you really? Those were such fun days when our dear Mrs Brook inevitably had to take you and Emily to the circus in Stepfather's absence. Some of the lines stick in my memory:

"The Wax-work, Clock-work, all the marvellous craft
Of modern Merlins, Wild Beasts, Puppet-shows,
All out-o'-the-way, far-fetched, perverted things,
All freaks of nature...
All jumbled up together, to compose
A Parliament of Monsters."'

He paused and shook his head. 'They're all the bits I still remember.'

'Bravo!' I said.

He laughed. 'Ah, and here are the freak shows. The very thing.'

'No, please!' I hoped to avoid them but Vince insisted, sternly reminding me that from a medical point of view this was a challenge.

The fat lady and the smallest man he pronounced were all done with mirrors. He was restrained from a closer examination of a calf with two heads and a pony with five legs and came away shaking his head, sure that these miracles could be achieved by a piece of clever grafting.

At the shooting range, always a good shot thanks to his recent practice during the grouse-shooting season at Balmoral, he excelled himself until the proprietor begged him to leave.

'Go away, sir, or I'll be ruined. All my trophies gone, the stall laid bare,' he pleaded despairingly.

Vince graciously returned all he had won. Glad I was of that, too, as I watched in horror an accumulation of dreadful china dogs and hideous vases – trophies that could not possibly accompany him back to St James, destined to remain with me, their splendours hidden behind the closed doors of a cupboard in Solomon's Tower.

'Fancy having your fortune told, Rose?' And there was the booth: '"Seraphina, clairvoyant to the greatest in the land." You couldn't get a better recommendation than that.'

As we walked past, the beaded curtain raised a moment and I caught a glimpse of a large lady, with a very full head of intensely black hair, her eyes outlined in kohl.

'Very exotic. Except that I would never believe a word of it. We make our own destinies, Vince.'

He shrugged. 'Some of us do. But there are others... How did William Blake put it? "Some are born to sweet delight, some are born to endless night."'

'You may be right. But for most of us, I think life is a mixture of both.'

And I thought of how the loss of Danny, the waiting time that had become my own endless night.

As we were leaving the funfair breathless and exhausted, we were hailed by a familiar voice.

Inspector Jack Macmerry, resplendent in uniform.

Vince was delighted and rushed forward to warmly greet his old friend who he had once hoped would be his brother-in-law.

Jack indicated that he was just leaving and Vince said, 'Been enjoying the sights, have you?'

Jack smiled vaguely and I realised that, far from such luxury, he was on duty, probably here in connection with his suspicions that the circus was involved in the recent rash of sudden deaths in Edinburgh.

His job done, and now having met us, Jack was in no hurry to depart. As the two men talked, some of the tinker bairns, who were indulging in a shrill and noisy game chasing each other, cannoned into me as they whirled past. I staggered, Jack yelled at them and grabbed me.

He put an arm around my waist and kept it there.

Vince looked on approvingly. I could see by his smug expression that he was hearing those elusive wedding bells once again.

It is one of my curious instincts that I can always feel eyes watching me intently or sense conversations, in which I am the topic under discussion, switch off hurriedly when I enter a room.

And there, within the radius of Jack's arm still possessively around my shoulders, I turned sharply and saw that we were being closely observed by one of the clowns leaning against the entrance of the circus. And although he turned aside quickly, by his height I was sure it was Joey.

The incident went unnoticed by the two men deep in conversation, but it left me wondering if and when this particular clown ever removed his stage make-up. It seemed odd at midday when there was no circus performance.

Indeed, for the first time, I thought there was something decidedly sinister about this man calculated to arouse guffaws of merriment and delight.

And that was possibly the moment of truth for me,

when a lot of things I had seen and heard no longer aimlessly floated at the back of my mind but loomed into steady focus.

At that instant, Joey the Clown, under whatever happened to be his real name, became my prime suspect.

A perfect disguise. I realised that a criminal could hide out most successfully under greasepaint, the equivalent of a mask worn each day. I was also aware that my suspicions should have been first aroused when I realised that this Joey was not the same King of the Clowns I had seen when the circus was last here in the spring.

I would have loved at that moment to share my discovery with Jack, but there was no hope of a mere woman interrupting an intense discussion as they caught up on two missing years and man-related topics, including golf and whisky.

Apart from Jack's arm, from which I skilfully disentangled myself, my presence or absence would not have been noticed. But as we walked down the Pleasance and up St Mary's Street to Princes Street, Vince insisted that this meeting was a call for celebration and that we should dine at his favourite Café Royal, while my thoughts were busy building up the case against Joey the Clown.

What was his real name? Had he a criminal background? Where had he come from before taking refuge and anonymity at the circus, and how many of the performers knew his real identity? Did they know he was a criminal and were they banded together, out of loyalty shielding him from the police?

To return to that first incident. The bank robbery and the murder of the clerk. Was that when my prime suspect sought refuge in the circus? I was certain, as was Jack, of a possible link with the so-called suicides of the two girls.

I remembered the neighbour who claimed a man had bumped into him that night rushing out of the tenement where the girls died and heading in the direction of the circus. A tall man. Had he killed them both by identical methods, merely through the accessibility of the ropes on the drying racks?

But there had to be a reason and that, of course, led me reluctantly to the Miles Rice household. Did the root lie there? Had the two maids who were friends found out something to their employer's discredit?

The reason was almost always blackmail, from Jack's vague hints about Felix's finances. Was Joey a further connection, another blackmailer, the mysterious intruder who had come through the french doors that night and, when Felix Miles Rice refused his terms, viciously attacked him...?

There were a lot of 'ifs' but I felt sure there was a link somewhere and that I was going to find it.

We had almost reached Princes Street when Jack stopped and said, much as he would like to accompany us, duty called. He knew of old that lunches with Vince and at least one bottle of wine could wear away an entire afternoon and he had business to attend to.

Vince was genuinely sorry, but Jack was not to be persuaded. He promised, however, to look in and see us later.

I watched him go. Should I tell him of my suspicions? Reason said yes, share your discovery. But I cast aside reason: this was something I wanted to do on my own – unmask the killer. And that was my first and very costly mistake.

CHAPTER THIRTEEN

The Café Royal was crowded and, as this had been a sudden decision, there was no time to book a table. It looked as if we would be turned away when Vince was hailed by a gentleman who seemed delighted to see him and, obviously aware of the situation, insisted that we share a table with his wife and himself.

This new acquaintance of my stepbrother's was introduced as Mr Hengel, the owner of the circus. And Mr Hengel was something of a surprise, very different in appearance from the flamboyant ringmaster. The luxurious moustache he wore then was obviously false and the shining silk top hat effectively concealed a shiny bald head. He also seemed to have shrunk somewhat, perhaps the black high boots and riding trousers added an illusion of height.

A further surprise was Mrs Hengel, also known as the clairvoyant Seraphina. In her everyday clothes she also seemed diminished, despite the luxurious fur coat: plain of countenance, rather plump and certainly middle-aged, considerably older than the exotic lady hovering dramatically over the crystal bowl with the canary who picked out paper fortunes for a small sum.

Perhaps they both preferred to be incognito and hoped not to be recognised in their real-life roles.

The conversation was carefully hedged with the circus visit to Balmoral where it seemed Vince had been on hand in his physician capacity to deal with one of Mrs Hengel's severe headaches, their mysterious cause an overindulgence in Seraphina's activities, with too many eager clients anxious to know what the future held for them.

I gathered from the drift of the conversation that this odd state of affairs vaguely hinted that her clairvoyant personality as Seraphina was capable of taking her over and causing physical distress.

Whatever my feelings, I had to take into the equation of disbelief a deerhound who seemed to understand human minds and human motives, and who had a strange telepathic contact when I was in danger. Maybe Seraphina knew the answer to that as well.

However, I had more important matters in hand. This unexpected meeting with the Hengels suggested that I should put my mind towards diverting the conversation into a topic that might further my own, now urgent, investigation into the activities of the clowns, and of Joey in particular.

A small silence between soup and the main course provided the opportunity to say how much I enjoyed the clowns, how skilled they were and so forth.

My remarks were addressed to Mrs Hengel, a source of valuable information and, as it turned out, quite

different from her Seraphina persona. She glanced
occasionally at Vince and her husband sitting opposite,
ignoring us both, engrossed in discussing the latest
developments in medical research, which, I learnt later
from Vince, was Mr Hengel's particular obsession.

Mrs Hengel, however, seemed eager to seize the
chance of a gossip with another female. 'His great
ambition was to have become a doctor, poor chap, but
alas, it was out of the question, a dream only, for his
impoverished family had neither the understanding nor
the means to afford such a luxury, so he followed them
into circus life.'

She asked where I lived and her eyes brightened.
'Oh, that lovely old Tower. It intrigues me and I've
often wondered who lived there. You are fortunate. It
must be lovely inside,' she added wistfully and I took
the hint of a hoped-for invitation.

'Oh, thank you, Mrs McQuinn. I would dearly love
to visit you.'

'Do you live at the circus?' I asked.

She laughed. 'Oh no, we do like our comfort and we
are far too old for the rigours of a caravan, although
Mr Hengel still likes to be as near the circus as possible
in case of emergencies, you know. As a matter of fact,
we are living close by, just off Dalkeith Road, in the
Mayfield area. I expect you know it.'

'I do indeed. I used to live in Sheridan Place.'

'Really? Mr Wood, the gentleman who owns a very
nice boarding house, obliges some of our lads with
accommodation. Number 9, I think it is.'

'And that is exactly where I was brought up. My

mother died when I was quite young, so my sister and I stayed with our grandmother in Orkney, in Kirkwall, and came home for the holidays to be with Pappa—'

I was about to tell her about my illustrious father when she interrupted with an excited exclamation. 'Kirkwall! Well, I never! What a coincidence.' Her eyes lit up again. 'What a small world it is indeed that we live in,' and beaming at me, 'my ma came from Orkney.'

She paused, then added in a whisper. 'It is from her I have inherited my ability to tell the future; she had it and her grandmother too.' A small shrug and she added warily, with a glance across the table at her husband, who seemed to have forgotten our existence and remained deep in conversation with Vince, 'The story was that we came from the selkies,' she murmured in tones of awe.

I smiled. 'We have that family tradition. Seems very popular in Orkney to be related to the selkie folk.'

I wasn't prepared to go into the details of my great-grandmother Sibella who I had met for the first time two years earlier. Past her hundredth birthday, with an intriguing background of mystery, her existence was a well-kept family secret, almost, one might say, a selkie in the cupboard.

Mrs Hengel said, 'May I?' And taking my hand, she turned it palm upwards. Her polite smile disappeared, her face changed and she looked worried, biting her lip.

What did she see there? But before I had a chance to question her, Mr Hengel leant across the table and asked, 'Ready to go, my love?'

Although we had hardly exchanged more than a polite greeting, he said, 'An unexpected pleasure to meet you, Mrs McQuinn.'

As he turned his attention to Vince again and an argument over who should pay the bill, Mrs Hengel stood up and smiled wryly, glanced at the two men. With almost an apology for their lack of attention to us during the meal, she said, 'Mr Hengel thinks highly of Dr Laurie.'

Now I would never know what she had seen in my hand, as she went on, 'My husband so loves reading books, mostly about strange illnesses – I can't even pronounce their names,' she laughed.

A waiter hovered. Vince was insisting that the bill was his, Hengel arguing not at all, that we were his guests.

Mrs Hengel sighed. 'I am so sorry, Mrs McQuinn, I have so enjoyed our conversation,' and in a whisper, 'you have a very interesting lifeline.'

Although I was naturally curious, I didn't want to hurt her feelings by saying that I didn't believe in such things. Maybe I had imagined that strange look, perhaps it was only concentration – or indigestion.

We were being ushered into our cloaks and I realised that I had eaten more than my normal spartan diet and drunk considerably more wine than I should to retain a clear head.

As we left, I declined to accompany the Hengels in a carriage back to Queen's Park. At my side Vince announced that he must look into the hotel to see if there were any messages and asked if I would accompany him.

The answer was to take his arm as I was in desperate need of fresh air, and there was plenty of it waiting for us as we crossed the short distance over Princes Street.

Vince, holding on to me very firmly, announced that he intended to look into the hospital and have a look at Felix Miles Rice tomorrow.

In the hotel reception, there was a message awaiting him. I guessed the contents as he read it and groaned. 'Sorry, Rose, this is going to be a short visit after all. The train will be leaving for London in a couple of hours. Dammit, I had hoped for a couple of days. No chance to see Miles Rice, either, as I promised your friend.'

To alleviate his disappointment I told him that it was unlikely he would have been allowed to 'see' the patient anyway.

'I doubt if even your royal connection would have made the slightest difference as he is being kept under strict police surveillance until he regains consciousness – if ever.'

I followed him upstairs and took a seat by the bow window. Now I realised why he was tempted to stay in such a luxurious suite with its stunning views over the topography of Edinburgh, Salisbury Crags, and Arthur's Seat. The view was dominated by the castle, the station far below, with its threads of smoke indicating trains travelling back and forth between the north of Scotland and the far south of England and, nearer at hand, the busy traffic of carriages rattling up and down over Waverley Bridge from Princes Street to the fashionable suburbs.

Meanwhile Vince packed his valise and speculated on the reasons for the police vigilance.

'Either he will reveal all or they are expecting the killer to put in an appearance and finish him off.'

I agreed but said it was a bit hard on Elma being also excluded.

Vince shrugged. 'I expect they have their reasons, not for us to reason why.'

I had decided to stay and see him off at the station, those last two hours becoming increasingly precious. It was one of those lovely rare autumn days when the weather forgets the calendar and indulges in a bout of frivolity, pretending that it is still summer, warm and calm.

With none of those ill-famed shrill east winds blowing up Waverley Steps, we strolled into Princes Street Gardens, enjoying a seat in the blissful sunshine which cleared my head of the overindulgent lunch, before returning to the hotel for a light refreshment. In my case, a much needed refreshing pot of tea while Vince indulged in a sandwich and ordered something considerably stronger to drink.

The clocks could not stop their relentless progress, all too soon the two hours were over and it was time for yet another parting, down in the lift to the station where the royal train purred beside an empty platform in readiness to leave for London.

'Olivia and the children will be glad to see you again,' I said.

He smiled sadly. 'I wish you were coming with me, Rose.'

Although I agreed, it was a bit of a lie. I had little desire to go down to England. Edinburgh was so complete: it had food and drink and all I needed. I loved my weird little tower, safe and secure with Thane to walk the hill by day and, like an ordinary domestic pet, have him lie at my fireside in the evening.

In truth I had little desire for travel these days. Perhaps it had been cleared out of my system by those years of Arizona, with Danny working for Pinkerton's Detective Agency. No real home, only hazardous, enforced stays in pioneering shack towns with their squalor and their ever-attendant dangers. Gunfights in the streets and scenes of sudden death and violence every night as the bars closed and threw out their customers, mostly drunk cowhands.

Yes, that had been more than enough, I decided, for one lifetime.

As the train steamed out, I felt suddenly bereft, with so much still to tell Vince and not the least idea when we would meet again, at the mercy of another short stay of the royal train.

His last words had been: 'That was a splendid lunch with the Hengels. An interesting couple and you ladies got along well, lots of girlish confidences, eh?' He laughed.

I refrained from mentioning that, as we were receiving our cloaks, Mrs Hengel looked around sharply as if in danger of being overheard and, observing her husband and Vince at a little distance summoning a carriage, she had taken my hand and whispered, 'May I come and see you tomorrow if that is convenient? It is very important.'

Mrs Hengel's request sounded anxious, a note of urgency I was used to receiving from a prospective client. Could it be just curiosity about Solomon's Tower or had she some domestic crisis that required the urgent services of a private detective?

If that was so, there was another mystery. How had she heard about me? Although I was becoming quite well known in Edinburgh, it seemed odd that my reputation had extended to a travelling circus.

CHAPTER FOURTEEN

I had told Vince about the coincidence of Sheridan Place as we sat in Princes Street Gardens. That number 9 was now a boarding house, patronised by the circus performers, but Vince did not seem particularly impressed.

Sadly, I guessed that for him it was all part of a past so alien to his present life in St James that he had lost all interest in what had been our home with Pappa and his debut as a family doctor.

And quite suddenly, as I walked towards the Pleasance, I stopped in my tracks. There were urgent reasons for visiting Sheridan Place and seeing what the new owner was like. The circus connection might be important, especially as I suspected that one of the clowns might be the killer of the two girls and the bank clerk.

I also remembered Jack's information: it had been the scene of a recent break-in and had some connection with a fraud he was investigating, facts that I had not passed on to Vince.

My new plan cast all thoughts of Mrs Hengel's problems aside. As I walked the once familiar streets towards Newington, it seemed strange indeed to be in the area which held so many memories of long ago. I had not set foot in Sheridan Place since the day of my arrival in Edinburgh, when I found, instead of my welcome home with Vince and family in residence greeting me with open arms, only shuttered windows and a For Sale notice in the overgrown garden.

At first glance nothing in the handsome Georgian villas had changed beyond the trees having grown higher in the past decade, and in many cases threatening to darken the outlook from the lower windows.

Considering a suitable excuse for my visit, I had my story all prepared. As Mr Wood opened the door, I had assumed my disguise, my role this time a searcher for board and lodging for a visiting friend, a young lady. A necessary precaution to cover the unlikely possibility that I might be recognised as a former resident.

Mr Wood was a well-spoken, very ordinary but respectable-looking gentleman in his fifties and did not, at first glance, suggest the fraudster Jack was interested in.

He bowed me into the hall and while he consulted his register I looked around and discovered to my delight few visible changes since Vince had left, other than new carpets. From the stair landing, a sight so well remembered and dear to my heart, the old familiar stained-glass window of Scotland's heroes that Pappa was so proud of. Wallace and Bruce, bold warriors flourishing warlike swords. How that sight had impressed my young days and I had felt an enormous pride in the personal possession of such heroes.

A sound on the stairs and I stood aside to allow four gentlemen, presumably the present boarders, to rush downstairs. They bowed, murmured apologies. I stepped back to let them pass with no time for careful scrutiny. A rapid glance took in that one was young, little more than a schoolboy, the other three older, perhaps members of one family in Edinburgh on holiday.

As the door closed on them Mr Wood looked up from his register and said, 'I do have one single room at present. How long would the young lady require it?'

I said I wasn't quite sure, which was true enough, and he continued, 'It is quite small for a lady. There may be a more congenial room on offer later...'

Presumably a second glance had confirmed my respectability as he warned, 'The facilities of the WC will have to be shared...' And taking my silence for doubts about the propriety, he added hurriedly, 'My present guests are most respectable fellows, excellent references, of course. You probably don't recognise them, miss, they are clowns from the circus. All four of them very ordinary, nice chaps, but their ordinariness conceals amazing talents as conjurers, equestrians, jugglers and acrobats.' He was obviously proud to have attracted such distinguished boarders.

I told him I had seen them. 'But there were five. Joey, their leader, is he not with them?'

That was a disappointment, I thought, as Mr Wood shook his head and said, 'I am not acquainted with the gentleman; no doubt he is residing elsewhere or staying with friends.'

With a smile and warming to his theme he continued, 'I cannot praise the circus people too highly. They are fine folk and get along very well with our residents, especially as they return to Edinburgh year after year, and many establish lasting friendships.'

Which I thought is just the difference between the suburbs: in Newington, maybe, but unlikely among the residents of the Grange.

However, if Joey was a wanted man privacy was a special need and he would have found a safe house among his own criminal fraternity. Promising Mr Wood that I would consult my friend and let him know, on my way home, I remembered again Mrs Hengel's extraordinary request. I was not kept in suspense very long for she arrived the next morning.

A tap on the kitchen door and there she was. 'I took the short cut across the hill, such a lovely morning for a walk.'

And as I invited her to take a seat, she said, 'I am afraid this early meeting may have taken you by surprise.'

'Not at all.' And in my best businesslike manner, 'Now, how can I help you?'

She shook her head and said gently, 'It is yourself, Mrs McQuinn, who is in need of *my* help.' Again that intent stare. 'I saw something in your hand – and I knew that I must tell you immediately: it is very close and, in your own interest, I knew there was no time to waste.'

She paused breathlessly and regarded me sadly. 'I can tell by your expression that you are an unbeliever but no matter, that often is the case.' Another pause, a frown, and she added, 'You have certain psychic abilities of which you are maybe unaware.'

All very flattering but I was disappointed. If a private fortune-telling session was what she had in mind, when I was expecting and hoping for a new client and an absorbing investigation, then she was in for a disappointment.

'You are a remarkable person, Mrs McQuinn. You have travelled extensively, and in doing so, suffered a great deal in your life beyond these shores across the oceans.'

A good guess, I decided cynically. She was suddenly interrupted as Thane came over and positioned himself bolt upright at my side, instead of lying prone at my feet as usual. His eyes were fixed on Mrs Hengel with an unmoving stare, in an attitude of listening intently.

Quite unaware of this attitude, which only I observed, Mrs Hengel smiled. 'That is a remarkable dog, Mrs McQuinn.'

Leaning over she patted his head. He allowed her to do so, but still sat unmoving, statue-like; the hound awaiting instructions.

Mrs Hengel sighed. 'I love animals – all of them, wild or tamed. Mr Hengel and I have no children of our own and animals are the solace that has taken their place. I love the horses in particular. When I was young and slim,' she added, 'I was the main equestrienne act.' A little self-deprecating shrug. 'Very hard to believe now that I had once such energy and daring. That was how I met my husband. I had a very bad fall and the injury left me unable to have a child.'

She paused. 'Do you have children, Mrs McQuinn?'

'I had a baby son once, but he died of a fever. I hardly had time to know him.'

I felt the tears ready to well up, as they did unfailingly, no matter how much time elapsed since that terrible day.

'The good Lord gives and takes away,' she said. 'But when he takes away he often gives us something to replace what we have lost. In my case it was the discovery that I had psychic powers, a gift to help others.' She gave a faint smile. 'As you have undoubtedly already discovered that you have some power to help others.'

I looked at her sharply. She did not know that I was a private detective unless someone had told her. There had been no mention of this fact and it had been merely my assumption that she was seeking my professional services. Now I thought of my logbook full of investigations where I had been instrumental in solving so many problems and curing the sickness brought about by fraud and betrayals in my clients' lives.

Again patting Thane she looked up and said, 'How did you acquire such a lovely animal? One rarely sees deerhounds in towns these days. They belong in great estates – and ancient tapestries.'

So I told her briefly about our encounter on the hill, how I thought he was lost but seemed in such good condition that I suspected he had come from a former circus in Queen's Park at that time.

'They denied all knowledge of him. But it seemed that he had come from somewhere on Arthur's Seat.'

She nodded. 'No doubt one of the deerhounds of King Arthur and his knights.'

I was surprised by her knowledge of that improbable legend, as she went on, 'Oh yes, I have heard strange tales about Arthur's Seat, about ghosts and magic.' Pausing, she sighed. 'I do so love our visits here: there is something of the other world about this place, about the hill out there, don't you think?'

Without awaiting my reply, she looked towards the window. 'And this tower, too, this beautiful place where you live looks as if it has been here for ever, grown out of the extinct volcano.'

'How extraordinary. Do you know a strange thing? That was exactly what I felt the first time I saw it.'

She smiled. 'They say great minds think alike, and I think our minds – although perhaps not in that category, my dear – they function and derive their being from the same source common to mystics.'

There was nothing I could say to that, except that her observation so near to my own was faintly unnerving, as was Thane's continued alert behaviour.

'The Tower needs a lot of work,' I said apologetically, dragging the conversation back to normal, domestically conscious of untidy corners, the needed urgent application of a duster and mop.

She shook her head gravely. 'That is only the surface. Don't let it trouble you. Underneath nothing changes, the spirit of the house is unperturbed; as long as it knows it has our love it will protect us.'

Thane was still watching us eagerly, gazing from one to the other as if closely following our conversation.

'And so you never discovered where he came from. A remarkable story for a remarkable dog. But hardly surprising in a place full of magic like Arthur's Seat, which has always had secrets and will never give them up. I doubt if you will ever find out more about Thane than he is prepared to let you know.'

As she talked, she smiled at Thane, clearly fascinated by him, while he continued to regard her in that curious way of his, mouth slightly open as if smiling. It was odd, watching these two, as if they understood each other perfectly.

'He is your protection, Mrs McQuinn, part of the mystery of where your destiny has led you.'

As she spoke she took my hand, turned it over and, studying it frowning, she sighed. 'When we met I knew there was something that I had to tell you – to warn you of danger ahead. I guessed that you were a widow, and alas, I can see no tall, dark, handsome stranger coming into your life to carry you off.'

I already knew that, certain now that my handsome Danny was dead, as she continued, 'There is just a shadow, a dream of which you must beware; evil forces you are unaware of, lies disguised as truth, hate disguised as love. You are being manipulated, pulled in the wrong direction. That is all I know, it isn't much, but the main thing is that you must move with extreme caution.'

She sighed again. 'I just wish I could see it all clearly to advise you in chapter and verse. All I am acutely aware of is the danger that surrounds you. Danger, false hopes and uncertainties.'

And leaning over, she made a fist of my hand, eyes closed as if praying; she held it lightly for a moment. Then smiling she rose to her feet, suddenly practical.

'Now I must leave you for there is much to prepare down the road.'

As if aware that she had given me plenty to think about, she smiled. 'You are wondering if what I have told you will happen, or if it is just a wild guess.' She shook her head. 'In your case, I felt certain I was seeing into the future. It isn't always so. Many times young girls come hoping I will see a handsome husband and a thousand a year.' She paused. 'Seems an incredible fortune to them. And they want to know how many children and what the future holds. The older ladies are more practical, mostly concerned with family matters, who will wed among their children and so forth, and finances, if riches are coming their way and if they will have a long life. I aim to be honest. Usually there isn't anything of importance I can see and I have to be vague with those promises, so as not to disappoint them and make them feel they have wasted their money.'

She took my face between her hands, looked deeply into my eyes. 'But when we met something else took over, a sense of compulsion. You must take great care, Mrs McQuinn. That's my final word. Now Ed will be wondering what has happened to me and Seraphina. Takes a little longer to prepare for the afternoon sessions these days...' she laughed lightly, 'the wig and the greasepaint.'

Smiling, she added, 'I hope we shall meet again. If

you need me, you know where I am to be found. And I shall not require a consultation fee: knowing I have warned you is all the repayment I need, more than enough. And the opportunity to see this lovely house.'

The wistful hint was irresistible. 'Let me show you the rest of it on your way out. It will only take minutes.'

As we walked through the great hall towards the stone spiral staircase, she clasped her hands in delight. 'What a superb room, those wonderful tapestries – I am so glad to see that ugly progress has not overtaken and destroyed all vestiges of those original stone walls. A quite magnificent fireplace too.'

Very conscious of the massive oak table and the worn tapestry on chairs, as well as an abundance of dust motes caught by the sunshine streaming in through the narrow windows, I said, 'So visitors react, but alas, it is too large to heat comfortably.'

Laughing, she narrowed her eyes, and ignoring the presence of the table's solitary occupant, the typewriting machine under its cover, she said, 'I believe you, but I can see days long ago, when this hall was filled with a laird's family and retainers, great fires, great tables of food.' She sniffed the air. 'Ah yes, venison roasting on that fire.'

It was my turn to laugh at such an agreeable flight of fancy as I led the way up the spiral stair and opened the door of the main bedroom.

She hesitated. 'Cats! Extraordinary, but that postered bed was once occupied by a multitude of cats.' Turning, she looked at me. 'Now, how did I get such a silly idea?'

'Not silly in the least. The owner before my stepbrother was a very eccentric old gentleman who gave refuge to homeless cats – and their numerous offspring as they proceeded to multiply exceedingly.'

She smiled. 'Then I would have liked him very much indeed.'

'I thought the odours they had left would have been gone as he died a long time ago. I remember them being very strong indeed, in my childhood days.'

She shook her head. 'I can't smell them – I just sense them,' and as I closed the door, 'such a handsome room, but you don't occupy it.'

'No. I never wanted to sleep there. Here is my room. It's much smaller, sunnier and warmer.'

'And it has a magnificent view of the hill,' she said.

She made polite comments on the other two very ordinary bedrooms but hesitated on the landing.

'There is another room.' Conscious of the hidden secret room, I pretended her remark was a question rather than a statement. I shook my head and led the way back downstairs.

At the front door we exchanged mutual thanks. I said, 'You have given me a lot to think about and I shall endeavour to heed your warning.'

Her wry smile recognised my disbelief. She took my hand. 'We shall meet again. And my name is Sara, please call me that.'

Suddenly, at that moment I felt that I could trust her, that we were friends. 'And mine is Rose.'

Leaning forward, she brushed my cheek with her lips. 'So be it, Rose.' And to Thane who had followed our tour of the house, an admonishing finger. 'You guard her well!'

Watching her walk away down the road, I realised there had never been an opportunity to bring up the subject of Joey. At my side Thane gave a small whimper, as if he would have liked to follow her.

I said, 'You liked her, didn't you?' and repeated what I said so often. 'Oh Thane, if only you could talk, tell me what it's all about.'

As I stroked his head, he turned to me with that almost human look of understanding and sympathy; the telepathic veil we shared must for ever remain unbroken.

We were about to go indoors when we were hailed by a familiar voice walking in our direction from the hill. It was Elma with Rufus.

She greeted me warmly, clutching Rufus with his usual shrill reception at Thane, who took his departure with an almost human weary sigh, as Elma followed me into the kitchen. My first question was, 'How is Felix?'

She sighed. 'Just the same. No change. He still hasn't regained consciousness and they are still refusing to let me have just a few minutes alone with my poor darling.'

I braced myself for her usual complaints and angry vituperation against doctors and police but laying her bonnet aside she said, 'I hope this isn't an inconvenient call. I see you already had a visitor this morning. I saw her leaving – just missed each other. Another minute and we would have met.'

She was obviously curious so I said, 'She's a lady from the circus.'

Her eyebrows rose at that. 'I wasn't aware that you were acquainted with such people.' She managed to make it sound disapproving, as if it was not quite good form.

'They are acquaintances of my stepbrother.'

She looked puzzled. 'Surely not patients?'

'No. From a Balmoral visit. We met them by accident at lunch yesterday.'

The mention of Balmoral had reinstated Dr Laurie for her and I said, 'I would never have recognised her as Seraphina.'

'The fortune-teller, you mean? How strange. Was she telling your fortune?'

'Not really.' I could hardly go into the details of Mrs Hengel's visit, nor did I want to.

'Tell me,' she whispered, 'is that a black wig, or all her own hair?'

'I believe it is part of her theatrical make-up.'

'Indeed. Such an odd individual.'

Elma was clearly very curious, gnawing her lip, a habit I noticed when she was anxious. To satisfy her curiosity I told her that Mrs Hengel had been very impressed by the sight of Solomon's Tower visible from the circus at Queen's Park.

'She often wondered who lived there and so on. As she had never been inside I invited her to call.'

Elma sniffed disdainfully. 'Such curiosity, Rose. So very ill-bred. Quite rude. One never blatantly engineers an invitation.'

Regarding her serious expression, I had difficulty not laughing outright or refraining from observing how ill-bred it was to display such curiosity about my visitor.

But Elma did sound cross and even a little jealous of my new acquaintance and I couldn't resist an impish remark. 'A pity you didn't meet. Had you come earlier, I am sure she would have been delighted to tell your fortune.'

Elma looked at me solemnly. 'I have had my fortune told many times and I don't believe a word of it.'

'Neither do I.' I smiled, the moment was over. 'Shall we have some tea?'

CHAPTER FIFTEEN

Gathering my facts together later, I thought, logically, the bank clerk's death in the hold-up and Miles Rice's injury might well have been accidental, outcomes of attacks which were not meant to be fatal and could be classed as manslaughter. However, the two suicides so carefully planned and identical – considering the lack of farewell notes and taking into account further evidence, including their religious beliefs – suggested murder. Then the curious assault on the novice at the convent by a lurking strange man – was this related to the other cases?

My thoughts turned again to Joey the Clown, suspicions reinforced by the fact that he was not living with the other clowns at Sheridan Place and was a relative newcomer to the circus. This indicated that he was a man of mystery with perhaps very sinister reasons for being so.

There existed two possible sources of valuable information. First, that somehow I should engineer an interview with the clowns so that I could dig deeper, and second, that I should talk to Hodge who, according to his statement, had discovered his master lying in a pool of blood.

Elma had arrived on her now almost daily walk from the Grange with Rufus. She looked pale and more anxious than ever, gasping out that she was so distressed at Felix not recovering consciousness she wasn't sleeping at night.

'I'm so afraid in the house these days, Rose. And the servants are not much consolation, so remote in their quarters up there in the attics.'

Pausing, she studied me, biting her lip as she whispered tearfully, 'I expect it has also occurred to you that I might be the next victim.'

The thought had never occurred to me and she added, 'Whoever attacked my husband may be lurking about awaiting the right opportunity.'

I wasn't sure how she had reasoned out that some enemy of Felix might wish to include her in his revenge but when I said so she brushed it aside.

'I have heard sounds downstairs during the night and – guess what – yesterday I found a window in the drawing room left unlatched,' she said dramatically.

I was in no doubt that Rice Villa had its own reasons for feelings of unease: the fate of Felix and the assumed break-in calculated to arouse terrifying prospects in the minds of vulnerable servants.

I said consolingly, 'An accident. One of the maids might have been cleaning the windows—'

'No,' she interrupted, 'that cannot be. You are quite wrong. And Hodge who is very particular since Felix's attack is meticulous about checking windows and doors most carefully before retiring to his room upstairs.'

'How is Hodge?'

She shook her head sadly. 'A very unhappy man. I am afraid if my husband dies this will be the end of him. Felix was— is his whole life. An absolutely devoted servant.'

'Have you told him of your fears – that you believe you might also be in some danger?'

'Of course, but he thinks I am merely overanxious about security. Overanxious, I ask you! Who wouldn't be in my situation?' she demanded angrily.

In an effort to placate her, I said, 'There is something you could do. Get Hodge – or your housekeeper – to sleep on the same floor as yourself, in one of the guest bedrooms, perhaps.'

Her eyes opened in a horrified expression. 'Good gracious, I couldn't possibly allow that.'

'Why not? This is an emergency.'

'Hodge would be simply horrified at such a suggestion. He is very much aware of his proper place and, for servants, that is in their own quarters. We couldn't possibly have any of them sleeping...in the guest rooms! That would never do, most embarrassing for everyone.'

I wasn't impressed by the logic of all this snobbery in the face of mortal peril. I thought for a moment.

'Then why don't you tell the police? If you are in danger, they will see to it that you have protection.'

She looked at me wide-eyed. 'I cannot possibly do that, Rose. After all, I have no evidence – it is just a feeling...' her voice dropped to a whisper, 'a horrible premonition that someone is out to kill me too.'

Leaning over she grasped my hand. 'Please...please, Rose, I can't bear to be on my own just now – please say you will come and stay just for a day or two, so that I can get a good night's sleep,' she wheedled. 'I would be so grateful. I am so afraid. You just can't imagine...please...'

And so I agreed, my motive, alas, not merely to give Elma reassurance, but also that this would provide an ideal opportunity to strike up an acquaintance with Hodge and see if there was anything more he could tell me, perhaps some detail that he had overlooked, considered too trivial to mention in his interview with the police.

I wasn't particularly hopeful, but it was worth a chance, I thought, hastily packing my valise into the bicycle carrier for an overnight stay.

Standing by, Elma eyed my activities with consternation. Perhaps afraid I would change my mind, she said in a stricken voice, 'You do travel light, Rose. Are you sure you have quite enough? And why that machine? Is it necessary? We could hire a cab.'

I shook my head. 'If you don't mind walking and won't be offended, then I promise to push the bicycle.'

She looked extremely uncomfortable at the idea, shaking her head doubtfully, unable to think of the right words to dissuade me.

I said, 'I find this a very useful and convenient means of travelling across Edinburgh.'

Defeated, she shrugged. 'You must please yourself.

You are certainly a very original young lady, very up to date. A bicycle, and I noticed that you have a typewriting machine,' she added in a tone of surprise.

'Which I rarely use, I'm afraid. It was a gift from my stepbrother and I haven't quite accomplished the necessary art – by the time I find the letters and correct all my mistakes, I could have written several letters by hand.'

Rufus began his chorus of indignation at the sight of Thane who had reappeared, watching us preparing to take our departure.

'You don't lock up before you leave?' She sounded shocked as I closed the kitchen door.

'No need. I have nothing worth stealing, Elma. And Thane guards the house – don't you?' I said patting his head. 'He learnt long ago how to let himself in and out by lifting the latch with his nose.'

She gave a sniff of disapproval but soon returned to her former pleasant role as a prospective hostess, as we walked full of chatter about clothes she wanted me to look at, and my favourite dishes which she would instruct should be prepared specially.

It all sounded alarmingly as if she was expecting a longer stay than she had proposed. However, on that first day in Rice Villa, while Elma was taking her bath, I got my opportunity to have a word with Hodge, a tall string of a man, with an enlarged Adam's apple, turned-down mouth and a singularly unhappy expression.

He was also very nervous, despite a desperate attempt to maintain his dignified role as a gentleman's valet with all the aplomb of many years' service.

I began with sympathy for his predicament and said how horrendous it must have been, adding gently that sometimes it can be a help to talk about it.

I was a little taken aback to say the least when he replied, 'Of course, madam, you are used to asking such questions in your capacity as a private detective.'

How on earth did he know that? Had Elma told him? I listened carefully and he described the events of that afternoon, the horrific discovery of his master lying injured – his eyes filled with uncontrollable tears – and how, when he found the french window open, he presumed that sir had a visitor who had entered informally.

'What reasons had you for that?' I asked.

'Sir had asked me to lay out two glasses and make sure that the whisky decanter was at hand. He stressed that it should be his best brand.'

'Did you tell the police this?'

He shook his head. 'If I had thought there was any significance to this request, I should have done so, but the doctor said the cause of sir's injury was a heart attack. As the two glasses were an everyday order at that hour from sir and madam when they were at home, it did not strike me as unusual in any way.'

I had noticed that Elma enjoyed whisky in a discreet fashion, since it was considered unladylike and a small glass of Madeira or a sweet sherry were more appropriate to her role in society.

I asked Hodge, 'When you noticed the open window, did you see anyone in the garden?'

Hodge opened his mouth and then hesitated, shook

his head. 'It was dark and rainy. I didn't think to look outside – I was too upset.'

I looked at him and he avoided my eyes and turned away quickly. 'Is that all, madam? I have nothing else to tell you.'

Throughout our interview he had looked nervously towards the door as if expecting some interruption. His hesitant manner suggested that he knew more than he was prepared to tell, although there could have been an innocent reason for this, perhaps involving one of the servants.

As he was leaving Elma entered the room and said, 'You may go, Hodge.'

'Very good, madam.' He bowed stiffly and was gone.

'I heard you talking to him,' said Elma. 'Your usual sympathetic self,' she smiled warmly. 'You are such a dear good person.'

'We were discussing what happened – that afternoon. I thought it might help him to talk about it.'

Her eyes widened. 'Surely he didn't want to go over all that again, meeting you for the first time. That is really too much,' she said crossly. 'He is just a servant after all and should have more control over his feelings. He should know his place,' she added indignantly.

'I am afraid I rather led him into it.' I hesitated before adding, 'You know, Elma, from what he said – or rather didn't say – I have a strange feeling that he was telling...well, not lies, but not the whole truth either, perhaps protecting someone.'

Elma looked astonished. 'I wonder who on earth it could be. One of the maids, I expect, thinking she would lose her job for leaving the window open. I'm afraid, if that was the case, I would have dismissed her on the spot and poor Hodge knows that. I can be very stern and unrelenting in matters of disobedience and carelessness.'

After a pleasant supper of soup, poached salmon and an apple sponge pudding, we settled to a peaceful evening playing cards, at which Elma excelled. She had amazing luck and I, alas, have never been a successful gambler. Had we been playing for money I would have been considerably out of pocket, I thought, as I retired to the splendid guest bedroom with its cosy fire.

Glad to be alone in this unexpected luxury I read a few pages of Jane Austen's *Persuasion* before snuggling down into the soft pillows and warm eiderdown.

No sound disturbed my slumber.

At breakfast the next morning a somewhat agitated Elma met me, waving a piece of paper.

'I have just received this message from my brother Peter. He is arriving from London by train and wishes me to meet him with the carriage at Waverley Station.' With a deep sigh she added, 'He will, of course, be most anxious to visit Felix immediately when he hears what has happened. They have always been very close.'

She regarded me, for a moment, smiling steadily. 'I am unaware of his plans, but no doubt he intends on staying for a few days.'

And unless I had misinterpreted the pause that accompanied her words I felt it indicated very clearly that my visit was to be cut short.

She had hardly finished speaking when we heard a man's voice in the hall. Elma clasped her hands together as the door was thrown open and a young man appeared.

'Peter!' With an exclamation of delight she flung herself into his arms. 'You are early, I wasn't expecting to see you until we met at the station.'

They kissed and Peter disengaged himself from her embrace. 'I got an earlier train,' and, as if aware of a third party for the first time, he winked in my direction. 'What a greeting, eh? My sister is always unrestrained in her affections.'

Elma sprang away from him. 'We have a guest, Peter. This is my dearest friend, Mrs Rose McQuinn.'

He came over, smiling, and bowed over my hand. 'Enchanted, my dear.'

And as I looked at him, I had the oddest feeling that we had met somewhere before. A moment later it fell into place. He bore a strong resemblance to the young man I had glimpsed greeting Elma when we were leaving the theatre.

Observing the startled expression I was unable to conceal, he frowned. 'Something wrong, Mrs McQuinn?'

'Oh, do call her Rose, Peter,' said Elma and, aware of her anxious look which plainly indicated, more than any words, desperation that I should like her brother, I smiled and said to him, 'No, of course not, I just thought we had met before somewhere.'

'Impossible,' Elma put in, 'Peter returned from South Africa recently, and as I'm sure I mentioned, he's been

living in London. This is his first visit to Edinburgh for
– oh, about two years, isn't it?' she added, looking at
him for confirmation.

Peter nodded in agreement. I glanced at him again.
The same flashy appearance, but that glimpse in the
dark outside the theatre as Elma and I got into our
carriage had been very fleeting.

'I must have been mistaken.'

Peter was watching me, smiling. 'We all of us have
doubles,' and putting an arm around Elma, 'even
twins.'

The advent of her brother was making Elma bite
her lips more frequently than usual. She regarded him
with ill-concealed anxiety. Despite his genial manner as
the conversation turned to general matters regarding
what had happened since they last met, I felt somewhat
superfluous. After a polite interval, I announced that I
would be going home.

'You were to stay for a while,' said Elma, regarding
me doubtfully. She frowned. 'Must you really go?'

But there was little enthusiasm in her voice. Now
that she had the brother to whom she was so close,
I was no longer needed for her protection. I took my
leave, valise reinstated in my bicycle bag and, as they
watched me from the front door, their arms about each
other, I felt a sense of relief. She would be safe with
him and, if this was to be a brief stay, then she wanted
only his presence. I could understand her feelings, my
own exactly: had Vince been at Solomon's Tower on
one of his rare and fleeting visits I would have resented
the presence of a stranger.

I felt quite light-hearted, exceedingly glad to be going home again, as I bicycled through the Grange and headed through Newington.

The truth, which I hated to admit even to myself, was that although I had grown fond of Elma, who had so many excellent qualities, I didn't warm to her twin at all. A fact I was sorry to realise and I even hoped that, for once, those first impressions had been wrong.

I didn't like Peter. He did not greatly resemble Elma – although this was most often the rule with different sex fraternal twins – apart from both being of roughly the same height, with fair hair and blue eyes, and I could imagine that, as infants, they looked like little picture book angels.

I was disappointed. I had expected some sort of affinity as I had with Elma. Instead, there was only the odd likeness to the man who had spoken to her outside the theatre. Perhaps that was the trouble: it persisted and, despite Elma's assurances, I could not persuade myself that I had been mistaken.

After all, Elma should know much better than I who had spoken to her that evening, and since she claimed the man was a casual acquaintance, she was completely unaware of any resemblance.

As I reached home, with Thane there waiting to welcome me, I knew that I did not care for Rice Villa either. There was also something wrong about Elma's luxurious home, something deep and disturbing that wealth could not disguise.

I wondered if it was haunted. It had a forbidding air of sinister depression, almost, I might add, of evil, yet it was only a few years old and Solomon's Tower, by comparison, was a warm, serene and welcoming place, despite the many untold acts of violence and death its walls had witnessed during the past centuries of its existence.

I decided that Rice Villa would be worthy of a visit from the psychic Sara Hengel, but a more pressing reason for talking to her again was my endeavour to gather information about my prime suspect, Joey.

That was the night Leo, King of the Jungle, escaped from the circus.

CHAPTER SIXTEEN

It was not until daylight next morning that the cage door was discovered swinging open. Leo, mercifully its sole occupant, was nowhere to be seen, which hinted that he had enjoyed almost twelve hours of freedom.

Panic ensued. What if he was already roaming the streets of Edinburgh in search of food – or prey? Should the authorities be notified?

'No,' said Fernando and Hengel together in agreement. They reasoned that it was unlikely Leo would go where there were humans, and police would bring guns, trigger-happy ready to shoot him, a valuable animal, on sight.

There was one other possibility. All eyes turned apprehensively towards the vast unpredictable slopes of the extinct volcano that was Arthur's Seat with its many secret caves and hiding places.

They groaned. Nets and poles were distributed, and one or two rifles with stern instructions to be used only in the last resort. Heads scratched in perplexity. There had never been anything like this before, and how on earth could he be tracked down and brought back alive, too valuable an asset to be shot dead?

And how to keep this out of the newspapers and especially from those folk with handsome houses and vast gardens in the wealthy new suburbs adjacent to Queen's Park, where Leo might be at large at this moment?

Angry glances were exchanged. Who was to blame? Who had allowed this catastrophe to happen? Carelessness where wild animals were concerned was inexcusable and there had to be a scapegoat. They did not have far to look: Fernando's son, with the very ordinary name of Jimmy – not at all foreign, which was hardly surprising as Fernando's real name was Percy Edwards from Halifax.

Jimmy, aged seventeen, was one of the five clowns. His father had problems with him. Jimmy was utterly fearless and fancied himself since childhood in the role of lion-tamer. Loving all animals, he nursed the totally mistaken idea that they shared this agreeable sentiment for him.

Fernando had failed completely in trying to impress upon him that, however docile the animals appeared, he ruled them with a rod of iron and, although they obeyed, such obedience was unnatural to a beast of the jungle. Every human being was a natural enemy, captivity was unnatural and every beast's brain harboured only one desire – to escape back to the wild.

Jimmy was not convinced and he would sit on his little stool for hours outside the cages, talking to the animals through the bars, trying in his childish way to establish a bond and make them realise he was their friend.

And so it was, on the night of Leo's escape, Fernando went into Princes Street to celebrate the birthday of Miss Adela the equestrienne who he greatly fancied. To his delight, the feeling appeared to be mutual. He was to spend the night at her lodgings, especially as, amid fits of unrestrained rather drunken merriment, she leant amorously against him, insisting that he was in no condition after the amount of whisky consumed to return to Queen's Park.

Fernando, with his unshakeable sense of duty to his animals, scorned the luxury of lodging in Newington. Unlike Jimmy who resided with the other three clowns in the comfort of Mr Wood's establishment in Sheridan Place, his father had a caravan on the site, his travelling home close to the cages where, a light sleeper, he slept with one eye open (the habit of many years) and the slightest disturbance, the merest rumble from the cages, had him immediately alert to possible danger.

This arrangement suited both and on this occasion had certain advantages for Fernando's social life and his wooing of Miss Adela. Jimmy agreed readily enough to occupy the caravan for one night, left with instructions to look after the cages, impressed upon most sternly, time and time again, to make sure they were securely bolted before he retired.

As there had been no performance, it being Sunday, Jimmy regarded this last-minute procedure as quite unnecessary. However, someone – most probably Sean (although this could never be proved), one of the tinkers who roamed everywhere – was heard that night shouting and roaring drunk in the circus precincts and had accepted a dare to enter Leo's cage. Had the man been sober and in his right mind, even eager to impress his latest lady-love, he would never have tackled anything so dangerous. He got as far as unbolting the door and lifting the iron bar when the apparently sleeping Leo sprang up, roared and made a desperate bid for freedom.

This immediately sobered Sean. He rushed back to his companions hovering at a discreet distance, and all of them hastily departed, led by Sean, who in his exit from the scene had failed to replace the iron bar. The door was left ajar and Leo, who had long awaited just such an opportunity, smelt freedom – and took it.

Jimmy heard nothing. He had also seized the opportunity of his father's absence, and had been enjoying a relaxed evening sharing a few jars with the other clowns, a luxury strictly forbidden by his parent.

A naturally heavy sleeper, unused to the effects of alcohol, he was quite unconscious, unaware of the tinker's altercation outside the caravan.

Early next morning, a jaunty but bleary-eyed Fernando, feeling pretty good about the night's activities and what Miss Adela had on offer, strolled back from her lodging in South Clerk Street to the circus, where the open cage door told its own terrible story.

Anger and recriminations were useless and too late. Fernando's caravan was also empty. Jimmy had woken early with a shocking hangover. Horror-stricken by the results of his night's carouse, he had already set out to recapture Leo, fearless, confident and alone, armed with pole and net, a gladiator from the Colosseum in Ancient Rome.

Precautions such as seizing the first things he saw his father use might have been quite adequate in the circus tent, but Jimmy had not stopped to ponder on how useless they would be in the vast expanse of Arthur's Seat, even presuming that he came face-to-face with an angry lion whose temper was not known to be the sweetest, especially now he was undoubtedly hungry, deprived of his usual substantial breakfast.

Leo had forgotten in his long years of captivity how to hunt down zebra and wildebeest, even if there had been such creatures on a Scottish hillside. A few sheep scattered higher up the hill suggested hard work. As for rabbits – what were they? Small furry creatures, the only game and always in a great hurry. Beneath his contempt, they could outrun him and rapidly disappear into the safety of their warrens.

This, then, was the background to what was happening outside Solomon's Tower as I opened the curtains of my bedroom window.

As often happened in the autumn, the hill was crowned by a swirling early morning mist, obliterating distant visibility. A peaceful scene, with the sun struggling to put in an appearance heralding a mild day.

I yawned, then suddenly, to my astonishment, I saw a large tawny creature. A lion, no less, prowling not twenty yards from my garden, and fast approaching him the small figure of a boy carrying a net and pole. From my vantage point, also visible running across the hill through the mist, a group of men presumably from the circus.

I could see the boy making what looked like friendly and encouraging gestures applicable to a domestic pet to the crouching lion, who failed to understand. Its lashing tail swinging in fury indicated clearly that it was having nothing to do with any return to captivity.

As for the boy – I hammered on the glass with the sickening realisation that he would be dead, mauled to death long before the men running across the hill reached him. Powerless to intervene, nevertheless I rushed downstairs and seized the poker, perhaps imagining I could provide a distraction but with little hope of avoiding the inevitable tragedy.

Thane, lying by the fire, was awakened and at my heels as I opened the kitchen door to shout a warning.

I was too late. The lion had seized the boy and was dragging him along by one arm. As I screamed in horror, Thane leapt over the garden wall.

I yelled at him to come back. It was no use. We could not save the boy. It was like some scene I had dreamt of in a nightmare.

Thane, in his great loping run, had reached the lion and his prey. I wanted to howl with terror, to close my eyes, for the lion raised its head, turned snarling and looked at the deerhound.

Too late, too late, my nerves screamed. Too late. The boy was probably already dead, lying still and lifeless on the ground. I saw bright red blood where his arm had been. The lion threw back his great mane and roared at Thane.

And now Thane, dear precious Thane, would be killed too.

I had to do something. As I ran forward with my poker, clambering over the wall, throwing caution to the wind, it seemed that time stood still as the two creatures – the lion huge, tawny, four times the weight of the slender grey deerhound – faced one another.

Thane was very still. Just yards away from them, I was stricken, incapable of movement. For a moment it was as if we had been turned to stone, then life took over, moved on again.

Leo sat back on his haunches, lifted his head, roared again and, turning away, trotted to where the breathless, shouting men had reached the scene too late to save the boy.

Leo faced his master Fernando who, fearless as ever, approached him carefully – there was nothing like this in the programme from the circus performance, nothing in the silent audience equal to this real-life terror.

The circus men who had learnt to remain calm whilst dealing with any emergency had the net ready. They crept closer and flung it over the lion who, snarling and protesting, struggled in vain. The king of beasts was transported in the undignified manner of being carried in a net hanging from a pole to be returned to his cage, his short burst of freedom at an end.

All thoughts now turned to the boy lying so still. I remembered the lion's jaws, dragging his arm, I could see blood pouring out of him as I raced over.

Thane had not moved. He remained there motionless as if on guard over the body of the dead, or fatally injured, boy.

Injured? I approached, dreading what I must see, the remains of a torn and bloody arm, the awful signs of mauling by those terrible jaws. He was face downwards, but I saw a movement of his shoulders. At least, thank God, he was still alive, although his days as a circus performer were certainly over.

He sat up, his father reached his side. He tried to struggle to his feet; at least his legs were all right. But what about that arm?

Jimmy was shaking his head, bewildered. 'I must have fainted when he launched himself at me.' And straightening his shoulders, 'But no damage.'

'No thanks to you – and you're the luckiest lad alive,' said his father, as anger and relief banished all thought of chastisement and he hugged him to his heart.

They looked across at me. 'Anything I can do for you?' I asked. Thoughts of a pot of tea came to mind, the inevitable cure for all ills.

'No, thank you, miss.' said Jimmy. 'I'm fine.'

'But...your arm?'

He rolled up his sleeve, smiled. 'Yeah, I was lucky. Your dog must have scared him off.'

I stared, moved closer. There was no sign of injury on his bare arm. I blinked in astonishment. Where was all the blood I had seen?

Fernando was stroking Thane's head. 'You're a good

dog, able to frighten the king of the jungle. You should be in the circus, we could do with animals like you. Great in one of our acts.' Pausing, he looked at me. 'Don't suppose you'd consider—?'

'No, never.' I said sharply.

'Ah well, if you ever change your mind.'

Jimmy was hugging Thane. 'You're a great dog. Scaring him off like that.'

As Jimmy and Fernando departed, walking towards the circus, their thanks still echoing in my ears, I returned to the Tower.

Thane walked at my side, impassive as ever and, although I knew I had seen the lion dragging the boy along the ground, his arm in those mighty jaws, I had the evidence of my own eyes that there was not even a scratch. No marks of a mauling, not even a drop of blood.

'Remarkable,' Fernando's parting words. 'King of the jungle and a deerhound.'

Remarkable indeed. But as I went into the kitchen still shaking from the dreadful experience, I realised that this was not the first time I had seen Thane's effect on wild animals: the wild white cattle on the Borders had reacted similarly, bowing, retreating from his presence. And as for blood, I had once seen Thane struck in the chest by a bullet and he had returned to life, with not even a scar.

Later that day, I opened the door to an unexpected visitor. Young Jimmy, grinning, no worse for his ordeal, thrust a bunch of flowers awkwardly into my hands.

'These are for you, missus,' and looking past me, over my shoulder, he said shyly, 'I just wanted to see your dog again, he was great. I'll never forget that he saved my life, scaring off Leo like that.'

'You have recovered.' I smiled at the obvious.

He squared his shoulders. 'Never better, thank you. My arm feels a bit bruised, but I really thought my end had come when Leo leapt on me. I even felt his jaws close, his awful breath.' And with a shudder, 'Don't know how Pa can bear to put his head in that mouth every night. That was my last thought as I felt him tearing off my arm.' He glanced at it, shook his head. 'Even felt it bleeding, but there was nothing, not even a mark.' He grinned wryly. 'Must have all been in my imagination.'

And I could have told him other instances of Thane's strange intervention as he added, 'Got a terrible ticking off from Pa, but I'll be performing this evening just as usual.'

This seemed a perfect opportunity for learning more about the clowns, and Joey in particular; I invited him to have a cup of tea and a piece of cherry cake, a gift from Elma.

CHAPTER SEVENTEEN

Obviously Jimmy's appetite had not been impaired by his encounter with Leo as he accepted a second very large slice of cake and I refilled the teapot.

He sat with Thane at his side and looking across at me said, 'I saw you before, missus. You were at our digs.'

'Sheridan Place? You all stay there, do you?'

'Most of us clowns. Mr Wood is a grand fellow. Makes us very welcome. Good beds and good breakfasts to set us up for the day. Not too costly either. Seems to like our company.' Pausing, he laughed. 'Mind you, he does expect a little entertainment thrown in.'

'What sort of entertainment?'

'Juggling and card tricks, that sort of thing. Harmless stuff. Nothing spectacular like we do at the show. I've tried to persuade Pa what he's missing. Likes his grub but he doesn't seem to mind discomfort at all. Prefers his old caravan where he can be near the animals, keep an eye on them.'

Pausing, he bit his lip and looked embarrassed,

obviously remembering his own shortcomings with regards to Leo.

'I seem to remember there were five of you in the act. What about Joey, *King* of the Clowns?' I asked lightly.

Jimmy frowned. 'No. He stays somewhere else. Never told us where exactly. Just around. He hasn't been with us very long, joined the team when we came to Edinburgh.'

And that was very exciting news, confirming all my theories. I felt a glow of triumph as he added, 'Took Bertie, our other Joey's place, when he took ill – poor lad had consumption, circus life was too hard for him. Boss was desperate for a replacement, then this chap turns up, says he's used to working with horses – might have been a jockey, but a bit too tall for that. Anyway, boss was very impressed when he saw him in action – so were we. Took to it as if he had been born to wild riding.'

Shaking his head, he frowned. 'Poor chap – been in an awful accident some time; that's why he wears a mask all the time.

Pausing, he grinned as if this was significant.

'Expect that's why he doesn't want to stay with us, all sharing rooms and that sort of thing, nothing much any of us can hide. Boss wasn't too keen, but Sam – that's his name – is good with animals, brilliant with horses, great rider and he's very strong and sharp on his feet. He's never admitted it, but the lads and I decided that he's been a soldier, fighting in one of those battles in South Africa, pensioned off after his accident.

We've tried to get him to talk about it, but he just nods vague-like and won't be drawn into details.

He shrugged. 'Nice enough chap, but keeps himself to himself; main thing is that he's good with the team, reliable in our act. You'd never guess in the audience, I expect it looks like random dashing and falling about all over the place, but we've rehearsed it very carefully. We all know exactly what to do and where to position ourselves with those horses. The speed we work at, the exact timing needs five of us to make it work and nobody can afford to make a mistake. All over in two or three minutes. But lose your attention, miss your cue and it could be as dangerous as going into the lion's den, and just as fatal.'

He looked solemn for a moment, remembering. 'And daily danger makes us share everything, the good things and the bad, and because Sam is so secretive, if he wasn't a soldier, then we all wonder where he came from, why he left whatever it was he did and if he has a wife and kids tucked away somewhere nearby. We don't even know how old he is, although we guess he's in his forties.'

He shook his head, 'He's a bit of a mystery.'

He was indeed, I thought, but Jimmy's information was invaluable in helping me unravel some of it.

'What's Sam's surname?'

Jimmy frowned. 'Can't remember if I've ever heard it.' He gave me a look as if this question had surprised him. 'Nobody bothers about such things – call each other by first names, only the boss gets Mr Hengel.'

'What brought you into the circus?'

'I was born into it, you might say, never knew any other life.' And he told me about his ambition to be a lion-tamer like his father and how he had spent his childhood trying to get to know wild animals and make them trust him.

After he left, I remembered his words: his curiosity and speculation about Joey's background. A mercenary soldier fitted well, the scar could be from a bayonet thrust. I was certain, more than ever, that Sam (if that was his real name) had robbed the bank, killed the clerk and broken into houses in Newington.

Had he somehow engineered some excuse for a meeting with the philanthropist Felix Miles Rice, demanded money, and when it was refused, attacked him? A plausible theory but the only thing I couldn't make fit in were those two identical suicides of the girls in St Leonard's. And if this was the same man, what was he doing lurking about the convent and making advances to Marie Ann? Whatever they were he had succeeded in terrifying her.

Writing it all down made quite a long list for one man, and throwing down the pen, I asked myself the one vital question that refused to be answered: why?

Every crime has to have its motive, and unless Joey was some sort of a maniac or a madman who killed at random, the links were too insubstantial. The two girls who had died were friends and the similarity of their deaths suggested they had known their killer, and although they had worked briefly at Rice Villa, this had no real significance. They belonged to that peripheral army of men and women, taken into hotels, maids or waiters during the summer, or to work in fields during harvest time. Had Sam as a casual labourer met the girls then?

Certainly no link had been established between the girls and the bank robbery except that they had taken place a short distance from each other in the Newington area.

Burglaries in wealthy residential areas were random and commonplace, but where did the attack on Felix Miles Rice fit in, an incident which the police were taking very seriously indeed?

And then I came to the great flaw in the argument. If ex-soldier-cum-clown had just taken refuge in the circus when it came to Edinburgh, how had he time to plan the bank robbery, rig up the girls' suicides and attack Felix, unless he already had Edinburgh connections?

Jimmy's information had seemed so promising but now I realised there was a vital piece of the puzzle missing: I had to find Joey's – or Sam's – real identity and I did not have the slightest idea where to look for it.

I had dismissed the incident with the deaf novice at the convent as the reactions of a timid girl scared of all men, and the surge of disquiet that the presence of any strange male brought to an enclosed order of nuns. But now remembering the man's scarred face that had terrified the young girl, it fitted with the injuries Jimmy said Sam had suffered in an accident.

I went over and over the details of my conversation with Jimmy. Was I mistaken and were there two killers at large, unconnected with each other? I had a lot to tell Jack, a list of theories to put to him.

Alas, it was not to be. Jack had called the night I spent at Rice Villa and left a note that he had been called to Glasgow – urgent domestic matters to sort out, which I guessed concerned his wee daughter.

I had just laid my logbook aside when Elma arrived on her daily visit. She came upstairs, apologising for disturbing me, and looked quite distraught, holding a shivering Rufus in her arms.

'I don't know what's come over him, Rose. Do you think he might be ill?' He certainly didn't seem his usual aggressive self, licking her face. Nervously she went on. 'It's all so sudden, Rose. He was perfectly all right when we left home, ate all his food, eager as always for his walk and then, when we got on to the hill, he started sniffing about, behaving so oddly, and rushed back to me. He seemed scared to death.' Pausing, she gave me an accusing look. 'I thought your Thane had attacked him but he was nowhere in sight.'

'Thane would never attack your dog, Elma,' I said firmly. 'You say he was fine until he went sniffing about.'

'That's right. Something has terrified him.'

When I laughed out loud, she looked at me reproachfully and cuddled him closer. 'I don't think it's funny, Rose. He might be seriously ill – dying, my poor wee darling.'

'Do sit down.' I cleared some books off the chair beside my desk. 'I can give you the answer. There is nothing wrong with Rufus beyond a case of fright, I assure you.'

'He's never frightened.' She hugged him closely as if to protect him. 'You're a brave wee thing, aren't you, my darling?'

Ignoring that I said, 'What terrified him was that he caught the jungle smell of a lion from the circus.'

She jumped up and shrieked. 'Oh no! Is he still out there?'

'Sit down, please, and listen.' And I told her the dramatic story of the morning's events, Thane's rescue and Jimmy's visit and our conversation about the clowns living in Sheridan Place, my old home.

'All of them?'

'No, just four of them.' And because in Jack's absence I had to confide my suspicions, I told her everything about Joey, and how Jimmy had described him as a man of mystery.

At the end, she said, 'Are you thinking the same as I am, Rose?' I shrugged and she whispered, 'Do you think he could be the killer the police are looking for?'

'Maybe.'

And so we went downstairs to the warm kitchen and over a pot of tea we put the pieces together. Sweeping aside my own uncertainties, where I had only speculated Elma persuaded me that I had come up with the killer's identity.

'We are good together, Rose. I think I'd make rather a good detective, don't you?' she said triumphantly.

I merely smiled and she frowned. 'But how are we to prove it? We'll have to think of something.'

'And that will need to be soon. The circus is leaving at the end of the week.'

'What about your policeman friend?'

'Away in Glasgow.'

And I remembered Jack's note: 'If you have any vital information to report, talk to Inspector Gray.'

It was very frustrating. I had so much to tell Jack, who at least took me seriously. Although I had met the inspector several times I got the distinct feeling that he was not impressed by the presence of a lady detective on his patch. Polite and a little patronising, my activities were regarded by Edinburgh City Police with contempt, something of a joke.

He was hardly the person to whom I would wish to unload my theories with nothing to support them – a list of coincidences and conjectures which would hardly even qualify as circumstantial evidence.

Now with Jack offstage I must sit back and patiently await newspaper reports of any progress the police made and chose to make public. I expected progress to be slow and, as Jack had observed on more than one occasion during our relationship, patience was not one of my virtues.

But curiosity certainly was. I had to know the outcome so I was determined to continue on my own, lead where it might, in the hope that I would have progress to report to Jack on his return.

At least I had one confidante, my friend Elma. With her boundless enthusiasm as my new advisor, she would discourage any flagging spirits on my part. If that did nothing else, her adopted role would provide a welcome change from listening to her daily anguish about Felix and the hospital's heartless treatment of an anxious wife before Peter had arrived to accompany her each day.

I gathered they had made friends with the police guard, who was probably glad of their company for an hour or two.

CHAPTER EIGHTEEN

There was more dramatic news on the way. The coma slowly draining away the life of Felix Miles Rice continued and was to claim an innocent victim.

On the night after Elma's last visit when she had decided to help me with my investigation, Felix's valet Hodge took his own life by walking into Duddingston Loch. 'Of unsound mind, distressed by the accident and his master's grave condition,' was the verdict which everyone at Rice Villa, including Elma, accepted.

Everyone but me, that was. If Felix had died there might have been a reason for Hodge blaming himself, but I was a strong believer in the old saying that where there was even a flicker of life there was still hope, and although his life hung on a thread, there were plenty of indications that Felix Miles Rice was a fighter.

Our brief interview had convinced me that Hodge knew more about the events leading to Felix's attack than he was prepared to admit or had included in his police statement.

He was protecting someone. And then, because it

was the way my mind worked, as I went over every detail very carefully I remembered something that might well have been vital evidence.

Normally a sound sleeper, I had woken in the early hours of the fateful morning of his suicide. Something had disturbed Thane.

He had growled and I'd heard the rumble of a carriage on the road outside the Tower.

Traffic on the village road to Duddingston, past the loch and the church, was a rare occurrence at three in the morning. The grandfather clock on the landing had obligingly struck the hour and, with moonlight streaming through the window, I'd lain awake for some time.

So when I later heard the account of Hodge's suicide, my mind returned to that carriage. Was it likely he had left Rice Villa and taken a hiring cab to his grim destination? I didn't think so; my probing detective mind headed towards an altogether more sinister interpretation. Convinced that Hodge knew a great deal more than he was prepared to admit about the events leading up to his master's attack, the irresistible assumption was that he had been lured from Rice Villa and murdered, then transported as a dead passenger in a closed carriage to the loch.

Only his murderer knew the answer, but it was highly unlikely to have been the Miles Rice carriage.

Initially I had been shocked by Elma's news when she had first arrived with Rufus to tell me of Hodge's suicide, but once I had had a chance to consider the implications of the valet's death, my theory that Hodge had been murdered intensified. After thinking it all through carefully, I told Elma of my suspicions.

She laughed. 'Rose, you can't be serious. Who on earth would want to murder poor old Hodge?'

'Someone who reckoned that he knew too much about Felix's attacker.'

Her eyes widened at that. 'But surely, Rose,' she protested, 'Hodge found him – you can't be suggesting...' She paused as though overcome by a dreadful thought too difficult to put into words. 'I can't imagine him quarrelling with poor old Hodge, but if they did have a fight over something or other... Felix could lose his temper. He doesn't suffer fools gladly – and if Hodge knocked him down,' she added slowly, no doubt picturing the scene, 'then perhaps he was afraid that when Felix recovered he would lose his job. Guilt could have made him take his own life: he was so conscientious, he would have felt his life was completely ruined. All those years with one master, and then dismissed without the remotest possibility of a reference.'

I did not mention that guilt was more likely to have made him pack his bags and depart from Rice Villa than end his life by walking into a loch on a cold night. She went on, 'Should my poor Felix not recover, then Hodge naturally feared that he would be unable to live with the terrible consequences, that he had taken his master's life.'

Such reasoning seemed too way out for me to even remark upon and I sat down at the table. 'There is one vital fact missing from your argument. When I talked alone to Hodge in your house, I was certain by his manner that he was protecting someone.'

She frowned, moving that thought around in her mind for a moment. Then shook her head and said calmly, 'Why would he want to protect anyone who had hurt his master?'

'I've no idea, Elma, but in a way I feel responsible for what happened to him.'

'Why on earth should you blame yourself? That's a mad thing to imagine.'

I shook my head. 'I think he guessed that I knew he wasn't telling the whole truth.'

She shrugged. 'Well, we'll never know now, will we? Whatever he knew or didn't know has gone to the grave with him.' She sighed, 'My poor Felix, he will be distraught when he recovers and hears about this.'

I looked at her and thought she hadn't considered that Felix was also just as likely to carry the answer the police wanted to the grave.

'Peter is very upset, he thought highly of Hodge.' She smiled. 'I think he was a little envious of a gentleman having a valet, you know. Had half a mind to ask Hodge to 'do' for him.'

Her face darkened. 'Poor Peter, he had no idea the doctors wouldn't even let him – a member of the family and with his medical training – over the threshold. However, the nurses are so nice and sympathetic and I persuaded them to let us both sit at the bedside.'

She sighed deeply. 'Sometimes we sit for hours, Rose, but we don't mind, it is such comfort to be together and everyone knows us. Even the police guard, such a nice friendly chap despite his authority.'

It was around this time that Peter began accompanying Elma on her day walks over the hill. I had a strong suspicion by the drift of our conversation about the mysterious and sinister deaths that she had confided in him.

While Peter was critically examining the ancient tapestries in the great hall with the eye of someone, she hinted, who knew a great deal about the value of antiques, we were alone in the kitchen and she whispered almost by way of apology, 'Peter and I are very close, always have been. There isn't anything we can't tell one another.'

I wasn't too pleased about that; I wished I had thought to ask her to keep to herself my suspicions about Hodge's death. What she told me clearly meant that being a twin meant having no secrets, and confidences were shared as a matter of course.

Now Peter seemed as keen to display detective abilities as his twin, although his theories were of little use and too fantastic to be remotely worth even a momentary consideration.

Meanwhile the circus was preparing for its farewell performance. In a few days they would be gone, carrying away my prime suspect, at large to kill again.

The problem was that even with two very amateur detectives I failed to get a satisfactory motive, apart from a bank robbery that had gone wrong, and two suicides that were still an enigma and might not even be connected.

Felix was the greatest mystery of all. Although we agreed that he had been expecting a visitor that afternoon – a visitor whose identity I was certain Hodge had known and failed to reveal – it seemed highly unlikely that the visitor was Joey, especially as both Elma and Peter assured me that Felix never went to the circus and dismissed such entertainment as very low-class indeed.

Sometimes I found myself both baffled and irritated by their well-intentioned enthusiasm.

If only Jack would return. Of course, I had the option of consulting Inspector Gray with my theories, none of which anyone, least of all a detective inspector, would credit as hard evidence.

Then, perhaps as fate would have it, we had an unexpected meeting in Jenners restaurant where I was awaiting the twins' arrival. As always they were late and Inspector Gray had to pass close to the table where I was sitting to pay his bill.

A greeting, chilly but civil enough, as he bowed over my hand. He had never approved of me, of course, and I knew, via Jack, that he considered the idea of lady investigators quite ludicrous. Added to this he had, in the earlier days of my association with Jack, decided that a female sleuth was a bad influence on one of his team, a positive deterrent on Sergeant Macmerry's hopes of promotion.

Polite but uncomfortable at this unexpected encounter,

he asked after my father. What news? And as always I had only a lame reply – that he was well and travelling in Europe. I did not mention his companion, the writer Imogen Crowe, although I was certain that Gray knew of their relationship.

An opportunity not to be missed, I asked him how his investigations were proceeding.

This took him by surprise, his eyebrows shot up, a look of consternation as he asked, to what was I referring?

'The poor bank clerk, of course, and those two mysterious suicides.'

He regarded me silently, his face expressionless, and then with almost a twitch of amusement, he shrugged my remarks aside.

'My dear young woman, allow me to assure you that we have everything in hand. There is absolutely nothing regarding these two incidents of which you have no doubt read sensational accounts in the newspapers that need concern you in your role as a private detective.'

I bristled at his tone; he could not hide the sneer as he added, 'If, however, though unlikely, we felt at any time in need of your services, then we would not hesitate to get in touch immediately.'

His patronising tone infuriated me and, as I espied Elma and Peter approaching, I rose from the table and determined to have the final word. I said stiffly, 'Then may I suggest you give some attention to the circus.'

'The circus?'

'Yes indeed, the circus at Queen's Park, before they move on and you are too late to catch your killer.'

At that, with as much dignity as I could muster, I left him and walked quickly across the restaurant to lead Elma and Peter to another table.

CHAPTER NINETEEN

An invitation arrived to the farewell performance at the circus. I decided this was probably inspired by Thane's rescue of Jimmy from the lion and decided to accept.

The ringside seats were only slightly less expensive and elevated than those on my visit with Elma and I regarded this as an unexpected opportunity not to be missed, especially with the possibility of engineering a meeting with Joey the Clown.

I wondered if Elma and Peter would be going. When I mentioned it, Elma yawned, 'Oh no, not again, once is quite enough for me, and quite frankly, it isn't Peter's style at all – far too unsophisticated. Concerts and plays are his thing, he loves the theatre...'

As she spoke, my first possible fleeting glimpse of Peter flashed into my mind, greeting her in the darkness. I had to be wrong, of course, for she had denied it vehemently. And as Peter was in London at that time, I had to take her word that I was mistaken and it was some acquaintance who bore a resemblance to her twin. But the memory refused to be banished.

She was saying, 'Peter and I would much rather climb to the top of Arthur's Seat and watch the sunset than sit watching a lot of dreary circus acts. Much more worthwhile.'

Peter was now a constant visitor and accompanied Elma most days on her walks with Rufus before their hospital vigil. She told me that one day, caught in a heavy shower, they had raced over to the Tower. Although I was absent they found the kitchen door open and had taken shelter until the rain ceased.

Anxiously, she hoped that I didn't mind. I assured her that they should feel free to do so any time. 'Just make yourselves at home.'

She looked pleased and relieved when I added that Thane, knowing they were my friends, would tolerate their presence, although the same could not be said for Rufus if he accompanied them, in which case they must excuse Thane. He had never learnt to accept the little terrier's shrill barks and growls and would make a dignified exit.

The circus was blessed by Edinburgh's very best weather for its last performance: a mild cloudless evening with a glowing sky.

As I walked the short distance down the road to where artificial lights gleamed a welcome, crowds were already headed towards the arena. For those who could afford such luxuries, carriages rolled in from the city, whilst poorer families with young children arrived on foot, those from more distant parts of the city in horse-drawn omnibuses or trains.

Over all there was a feeling of excitement, of anticipation, the brass band playing sentimental ballads, the smell of sawdust and the faint jungle-like whiff of the still-invisible animals. Arriving early had the advantage of front seats in the blocks of wooden benches stretching up to the back of the tent.

My reason for arriving early was the hope that I could have a word with Sara Hengel but I was out of luck. The beaded curtain of the tiny ornamental caravan used for her consultations was closed and faint voices within indicated that she had a client.

From my reserved seat, I enjoyed the interval by people-watching.

At last the scene was set: the overture played, the ringmaster welcomed us, the entrance of the jugglers, the trapeze artists and wire-walkers was led by Miss Adela on her magnificent white horse. All were as I remembered from my first visit, as I eagerly awaited the entrance of the clowns.

I was in for another disappointment. Tonight there were only four. Jimmy I recognised, and his three colleagues from Sheridan Place, but I waited in vain for the King of Clowns.

The tallest and most impressive, Joey, was missing and what followed was a shortened and somewhat diluted version of the clowns' 'thrilling death-defying' ride with Miss Adela and her horses.

I suspected that this was only obvious to anyone like myself who had seen their original performance. To newcomers witnessing their daring exploits, getting in each others' way, leaping up beside Miss Adela, shouting and screaming at one another, apparently in constant danger of being trampled under the hooves of the fast-moving horses, their equestrienne act was still breathtaking and the applause that followed showed that the audience, at least, were not disappointed.

Joey's absence, however, worried me so much I could hardly concentrate on the rest of the acts. Even Fernando and his animals: Leo going through his paces, with the climax of the ringmaster's command warning the audience to absolute silence as Fernando thrust his head between Leo's jaws.

A moment later it was over; Fernando, unscathed, bowed, all smiles and Leo actually yawned, to everyone's amusement. I applauded too, the fierce lion obviously bearing little resentment for his discovery, perhaps realising that escape was pointless, particularly considering the advantage of having all meals delivered to his cage without the necessity of hunting down his prey.

Leo's escape had been a boon to the popular press. Newsboys at city corners shouted, 'Lion escapes from local circus.' Sensational newspaper headlines also bestowed unexpected benefits of publicity on Hengel's circus, undoubtedly accounting for the sell-out of the farewell performance. Although the press had embellished the ferocity of the lion and the bravery of the circus men who had recaptured him, they had omitted any mention of Jimmy's peril or Thane's rescue.

Now the audience refused to let the performers go. Wild applause. They rose, stamped their feet, demanded encores. At last the ringmaster came forward, and promising a return in the spring, thanked the audience and his performers, each coming forward and giving a bow of appreciation.

It was indeed over, and while everyone stood to attention as 'God Save the Queen' was played, any hope of an early exit was impossible. I was hemmed in on all sides by an audience reluctant, even now, to let the performers leave as the clowns, running among the rows of seats, distributed balloons and sweets among the children.

At last I was free and made my way swiftly across to Seraphina's caravan. Perhaps she might know the reason why Joey hadn't appeared on this, the most important of nights.

She wasn't there. The caravan was closed, locked. I looked round in despair, in search of someone who might have information about the clowns. At last I returned to the tent in the hope of seeing Jimmy. Any excuse – to thank him for the ticket, say how much I had enjoyed the performance.

Luck was with me. Clowns, performers and non-participants were already engaged in busily dismantling the trapeze and other effects for the first stages of their departure.

Nonplussed by the untimely presence of a stranger, heads were raised from hammering and lifting. Then I heard a voice.

'Missus – it's you. Thought I saw you right in the front. Did you enjoy the show?'

It was Jimmy. I gave a sigh of relief, turned gratefully, said it was so kind of him to get me a ticket for such a great occasion.

A boyish blush. 'We all enjoyed ourselves no end.' He grinned and said impishly, 'Leo was in good shape, didn't you think? And I wouldn't have been here tonight if it hadn't been for that dog of yours – I've been telling everyone about him. He ought to be with the circus, that's what.'

I made appropriate noises and then said, 'I noticed you were one short – your leader Joey – what happened to him?'

Jimmy frowned, put down the hammer. 'Don't know...exactly, that is. Heard that he had an accident, twisted his ankle. Came limping along to collect his money before we move on. Boss wasn't at all pleased, you can bet, but there was no way he could leap about on horses – all that timing on cue, dangerous work like it is – and we had to rehearse again at short notice.'

'What a pity,' I said. 'Sad for him to miss the last night and all the praise every one of you deserved.'

He grinned. 'Aye, that's the way of it, missus. That's circus life for you. Never know from day to day what might happen. Just have to keep hoping the next accident won't have your name on it.'

I smiled sympathetically. 'I expect he will be going back to Glasgow with you, though.'

Jimmy shrugged. 'Haven't heard, missus. Nothing definite.' He was obviously finding my tendency to chatter rather curious at such a time when all hands were urgently needed. He gave a polite grin, which could only be taken as dismissal, and he looked towards his colleagues, all frantically busy and darting impatient glances in his direction.

'Have to get on with it, missus, plenty to do. Maybe we'll see you when we come back next spring.'

I could hardly detain him with further questions about Joey, so thanking him again and wishing him well, I walked away and at the entrance to the tent spotted the one person who could perhaps help.

Mr Hengel had just arrived on the scene. Changed out of costume and *sans* top hat (revealing his bald head) and luxuriant moustache he was barely recognisable as the imposing ringmaster of half an hour ago, now in earnest conversation with the men labouring over the dismantling process.

Feeling self-conscious and even a bit brazen I walked towards them and said, 'Mr Hengel.'

Turning, he looked surprised to see me and I quickly went into my routine of delight at the show, the well-deserved applause, etc. etc.

He looked a mite confused and not a little impatient at such adulation from a member of the audience. Fortunately, as I spoke, he recognised me again as Dr Laurie's stepsister. Protocol demanded that he bowed and escorted me back towards the tent's exit, where I thanked him for my free ticket and said how marvellous the clowns were.

That got his attention. 'Indeed, and we are all grateful for that remarkable dog of yours. Young Jimmy would have been a goner. What an astonishing story.'

I took a deep breath. 'I noticed that the clowns' leader was missing. Jimmy said he's twisted his ankle, poor man. Tonight of all nights...'

One of the workers was making a determined approach.

Mr Hengel eyed him and said, 'Good to see you again, Mrs McQuinn. My regards to Dr Laurie.'

'And mine to Mrs Hengel.'

He smiled. 'If you'd like to see her, I think she'll be in the dressing-room at this moment – at the back over there...' he indicated.

'She's helping pack up the costumes.'

It was now almost dark outside but the circus lights guided me to the caravan. I climbed the steps and there was Sara and some of the women carefully negotiating costumes towards giant hampers.

She looked up, smiled and straightened her back. 'You enjoyed the show?'

'I did – now, do let me give you a hand.'

'Are you sure?' she said gratefully.

As we carefully folded away all the spangles of the trapeze artists' sequin-encrusted costumes, the masks and wigs of the clowns, I brought the conversation round to the missing Joey.

'Too bad, he was such a showman.'

She sighed. 'Poor fellow. An accident – not much but enough to put him out of the act.'

Murmuring sympathy I asked if he would be going on to Glasgow.

'Don't think so. Fancy that's the last we'll see of him. He hasn't renewed his contract with Ed. As often happens, the way of things in the circus: performers have other plans, get better offers.'

'So will he be staying in Edinburgh?'

She shrugged. 'No idea about that. Bit of a mystery, Mr Sam Wild, that's what he calls himself. Not the usual kind for circus life, mind you. He's an educated man, so whatever his reason for being briefly with us, something better will no doubt turn up.'

So Joey now had a name. That brought a moment of triumph – that this enquiry was leading in the right direction. 'Where does he live in Edinburgh?'

She looked up sharply, obviously surprised by the question, and I guessed she had sensed my strange interest, so I said hastily, 'I mean, has he relatives, a wife?'

She shook her head. 'No idea. No wife as far as we know and he told Ed he bides in some lodging near the park. Well, that's that. Thanks for your help.'

And as we closed the final hamper she said, 'It was good meeting you. I hope I didn't scare you that day.' And looking at me solemnly, she added, 'You are surrounded by danger: it hangs like an unseen menace around you.'

She took my hand, held it firmly, and said earnestly, 'You are beset by things which are not what they seem, dear, false paths and decisions which you must avoid. That is all I can tell you. I wish I could see definite things, but your future is confused. Remember, my dear, take great care how you go and trust no one.'

Next day it was as if the circus had never been in Queen's Park at all, except for the bruised grass, the mud and wheel marks of the cages and caravans, the acrid smell of burning rubbish, ashes of fires lit to destroy the debris of their stay.

They were gone. But not all of them. One of the

most dangerous who now had a name, Sam Wild, remained in Edinburgh on the lookout for his next victim.

I was resolved to track him down unaided and alone – somehow – with Jack away, and Inspector Gray out of the question.

I would not have been so sanguine had I known that hunter was now hunted – that the trap was set and about to close.

With myself marked down as the next victim.

CHAPTER TWENTY

Dave the postman rarely delivered letters of any importance to Solomon's Tower. At best a birthday card from Vince or Emily and a picture postcard from Pappa and Imogen, dutifully sent from some exotic city I could never hope to visit.

Other communications were business requests from prospective clients, or letters concerning a current investigation. Not many of those lately. I didn't know whether to be anxious at this lull in my professional activities, or relieved when I had matters of such importance to occupy my investigative powers, but I eagerly awaited a letter from Jack that might inform me of when he was returning to Edinburgh or sending his Glasgow address. I felt diffident about writing 'care of the Glasgow City Police'.

On this particular day I had been replenishing my larder from the grocer at St Leonard's. A few doors away was the tenement where Belle's grandfather, Will Sanders, lived. I thought of the lonely old man and decided to put him on my visiting list.

Armed with provisions, I waited and heard him stumping towards the door. With profuse thanks he asked me in but, taking the seat opposite, he seemed preoccupied, a little put out by this unexpected caller.

Then, taking a deep breath, he pointed to the newspaper lying on the table. 'I might as well come to the point, Mrs McQuinn, I'm right upset by all this – they're hinting that my granddaughter and her friend Amy were murdered.'

These were my own feelings, although I was surprised when he added, 'Sounds as if they're hoping to make an arrest soon.'

That was news indeed, and I wasn't sure how to respond as, shaking his head, the old man said in a voice of desperation, 'It wasn't like that at all – but you know what the police are like when they get an idea and fix their claws into anyone.'

He shook his head and added slowly, 'I could tell them the truth if I wanted to – I know exactly how it was and I don't want some innocent fellow to be taken and hung for something he didn't do.'

I took a deep breath and asked, 'Would it help if you were to talk to someone?'

He looked at me intently, as if considering for a moment, then shook his head and said almost apologetically, 'I am not sure that you would understand, lass. I don't really know myself.'

Then jabbing his finger at the newspaper again, 'All I can say is that they've got it all wrong. I could tell them if I wanted to.' And then, as if he had said too much already, he closed his lips firmly, sighed and with an abrupt change of subject began talking about the new casualties list from South Africa.

I thought about his words as I went home. Very commendable and public-spirited, but the doubt remained. Did the police have new evidence that I knew nothing about?

At the Tower, to my surprise Elma opened the door, Rufus in her arms, Thane absent as usual.

'What a relief! I wondered where you were, hoped you weren't away for the day or something.' I followed her in. 'You don't mind me making myself at home, do you?'

I smiled. 'Of course not, you are always welcome, you know that,' I assured her, as I picked up the letters on the kitchen table.

One was from my sister Emily in Orkney. The other with an Edinburgh postmark with my address printed...

'Anything exciting?' Elma asked.

'I'll read them later.'

'Oh, do read them. The kettle's boiling – I took the liberty – I'll just make the tea, shall I?'

'Yes, if you please.' I scanned Emily's letter first. Short and sweet: trials with weather and delight at my wee nephew's progress. Laying it aside, I tore open the other envelope and drew out a sheet of paper. It contained seven words in capital letters:

'BE WARNED, YOU BUSYBODY, YOUR TURN NEXT.'

'NEXT' was underlined. That was all. No signature. Nothing. I turned it over, looked at it closely, feeling suddenly chilled.

Elma came over with the tea. 'Something wrong?'

I handed her the note. She read it and giggled.

'What on earth does it mean – busybody? Is it a joke of some kind?'

I took it from her. 'I don't think so...'

She put a hand to her mouth. 'Oh, Rose. You don't think...?' A look of horror.

'A note from the killer.' I tried to sound calm.

She gulped. 'Surely not, Rose. You're imagining things.'

'Think about it, Elma. What if he killed those two girls and the bank clerk?' I paused and added slowly, 'And what if he was the man who attacked Felix?'

At that she gave a slight scream. 'Felix? What on earth gives you that extraordinary idea – that it was the same man?'

So I told her about Joey the Clown having disappeared from the circus. That as far as anyone knew he was now at large, in Edinburgh, address unknown.

'But how can you connect him with Felix?' she demanded sharply. She looked frightened now.

'I don't know. It's just a theory.' I shook my head. 'I can't shake off the feeling that all these events are connected. They have some common factor I haven't yet discovered, the missing piece of the puzzle.' I waved the note at her. 'But one thing is certain. Do you realise what this means?'

She shook her head. And I continued, 'It means, Elma, that I am on the right track and Mr Sam Wild—'

'Sam Wild?' she interrupted.

'Yes, that's his name – or the name he's using. And Mr Sam Wild is scared because he knows that I'm on to him.'

Elma sat down at the table. 'Rose, why don't you come and stay with me for a while? Just until all this is sorted out, I mean.' She whispered, staring over her shoulder as if the letter writer might be about to enter the kitchen and murder us both.

'No,' I said firmly. 'I am staying right here.'

'Aren't you afraid – alone in this isolated place?' She looked horrified.

'Of course not,' I said. But that wasn't true. 'Thane will take care of me.'

She looked doubtful. 'You have more faith than me, Rose. He's only a dog, after all. How can he know what's going on in a killer's mind?'

I smiled. I had never told Elma my reasons for putting my trust in Thane. It all sounded so incredible, and although she and Peter were now aware of my alter ego as a private detective, they never referred to it. I guessed that, privately, they didn't take it any more seriously than Inspector Gray.

We were interrupted when Peter appeared at the door. He was full of enthusiasm for the local train, the Innocent Railway, which ran from St Leonard's to Musselburgh where he had been meeting a friend from his army hospital days in South Africa. An officer who had been invalided and sent home recently.

Leaving the train Peter had decided to come by and collect Elma. A convenient arrangement as she wanted to get back to their daily sojourn at Felix's bedside.

'Will it never end?' she sighed sadly. Before they left she insisted that Peter be shown the mysterious note.

His only comment, that it was someone's idea of a joke and that I should ignore it.

Twins close as they were apparently did not share the same view in this instance. How I should deal with it provoked an argument between them, although Peter had taken my theories about Joey the Clown seriously.

And that was where Elma, who had gained a point, said, 'Seeing that he has now left the circus and is in Edinburgh, on the loose, I think Rose should take this threat seriously.'

Peter looked at me and shrugged. 'You could, of course, make it official. Take it to your Inspector...Gray, wasn't it?'

I couldn't see the inspector getting excited over the note; he would never take it as a serious threat and would merely regard it as a joke of some kind.

Finally I eased them out, assuring them that they were not to worry, repeating that Thane would protect me. They both regarded this information smiling but dubious, as if Thane would be as useless as Rufus in the face of real peril. Understandable, as I hadn't told Elma the details of what I had actually witnessed of Thane's dramatic rescue of Jimmy, since neither he nor I had anything to show in evidence of his apparent mauling by the lion.

Before I went to bed that night, making sure that both front and back doors were securely locked and bolted, I decided to test Thane as a bloodhound and gave him the note to sniff. He did as requested and gave me a bewildered look.

'Pity you can't read,' I said and looked at it again. Something about those printed words disturbed me, even more than the text. Something I knew...

Despite my safety precautions I slept lightly and a sound far off had me immediately wide awake.

Thane had leapt from the rug at my bedside and rushed downstairs. Dawn was just breaking and I realised that probably he needed to be outside and I had locked the door, a perfect nuisance as he could normally lift the latch with his nose.

I stood shivering barefoot waiting for him to return, watching the moon fade above the hill. Thane wasn't long, whatever he was about, but instead of coming in, he stood at the door and looked at me quizzically.

I knew that look. There was something he wanted to show me.

It was very cold and still quite dark and I was very tired. I peered out and said firmly, 'No, Thane. Come inside. I am not coming out.' And I pointed to my bare feet, turning rapidly mauve in the chilly air. 'It can wait until breakfast time. I'm going back to bed.'

I rebolted the door and he followed me upstairs where I burrowed into my still-warm bed. It took some time to get back to sleep. Restless, I dozed after bad dreams which I could not remember.

I wasn't best pleased to be awakened by an early morning visitor.

CHAPTER TWENTY-ONE

Jack had returned. I hadn't time to get dressed. He tapped on the window as I drew on my robe and rushed downstairs to open the door.

I was delighted to see him; he kissed my cheek briefly and would have extended that to something a little longer had I not backed away very firmly.

Seating him at the table as I prepared breakfast, I could hardly wait to tell him my news as I listened somewhat impatiently to the saga of what had been happening in Glasgow.

Jack's late wife Meg had a married sister who was childless. She and her husband had decided that fortune had smiled on them and they would adopt 'wee Meg' who had already found a place in Pam's heart.

'It will all be done legally, of course. I'll keep in touch and visit the wee bairn quite regularly.'

But this was a different Jack and he couldn't conceal the relief in his voice, the problem of fatherhood and a motherless daughter solved.

Which, he pointed out, now gave him more time to

devote to matters in Edinburgh. Namely, solving crimes and also – his affectionate glances in my direction said plainly – resolving the ongoing problem of our relationship.

At last, having consumed bacon and eggs, he buttered another slice of bread, took a second cup of tea, sat back and said, 'And what has been happening here? Any news?'

'Quite a lot.' At last, patience rewarded, I got out my logbook and in a very businesslike manner went over all the details of events since last we met, including my meeting with the inspector.

When I told him that Gray wasn't even interested in my theories, Jack shook his head.

'He's a busy man, Rose, and he doesn't think there is a case. He and his colleagues are quite content to accept the two suicides, strange as they seemed—'

'You haven't heard the latest, then?' I interrupted. 'The newspaper report?'

And I told him of my visit to Belle's grandfather and his concern that an innocent man could be charged.

'Sounds as if he has some evidence,' said Jack. 'That could be the only reason he was so certain.'

'A suicide note he has found, you mean?'

'Or has concealed for his own reasons. I think it's worth a visit. We're still on the lookout for the bank robber; a miserable enough amount – just a few pounds – was stolen, hardly worth killing anyone. I suspect one man's desperate need for money. The clerk was killed accidentally.'

He shook his head. 'A small local bank too. It

certainly had no indications that this was an organised
bank raid, carefully planned. And if that had been the
case, there would have been more than one man, and a
gang would certainly have attempted others. No sign of
that and every day the trail grows colder.'

He shrugged. 'Any day now I expect it will
be officially written off as "by person or persons
unknown" and that includes the verdict on the poor
fellow's death.'

Jack had heard about Hodge so I told him my
theory regarding the carriage during the night going
towards Duddingston Loch and the sinister possibility
that Felix's valet was already a dead passenger inside,
to be conveniently dumped into the dark waters.

'A pity you hadn't been wide awake and able to give
a description of the carriage.'

I looked at him sharply. He wasn't taking this
seriously either as he said, 'What reasons have you for
believing that he was murdered?'

I told him about our interview, how I was sure he
was shielding someone, and he merely shook his head
sadly.

'Rose, you and your feelings! You never learn, do
you?'

'What do you mean by that?'

'Circumstantial evidence. Feeling that something is
amiss is just not enough, you surely know that from all
your experience as a private detective. As for the idea
of that carriage – you are letting your imagination run
away with you again.'

Before I could protest, he said hastily, 'And to more

practical matters. Does your friend Mrs Rice report any improvement in Felix's condition?'

'Only the doctor's reports. Peter and she go in every day and there's this ridiculous policeman spending hours of wasted time – at the public's expense, no doubt – sitting at his bedside.'

Jack frowned. 'That ridiculous policeman at present happens to be Constable Hoskins, one of my best lads, and I can ill afford to be without him.' He shook his head. 'Anyway, I doubt whether they'll be able to keep Miles Rice alive in a coma much longer. Too difficult. I don't think he'll ever speak again and no doubt there will be a decision to remove the police guard. Can't come soon enough for me.'

As Jack changed the subject I was thinking of poor Elma, wondering if they would keep Felix in hospital until the end or let her, as I knew she would wish, have him brought home again with a private nurse, which she assured me they could well afford, to take care of him during his final days. I could sympathise, it was all very distressing for her.

'Anything of more importance?' Jack asked.

'Yes, indeed there is,' I said, proud of having saved the most important piece of information to the last. 'Have you heard of Sam Wild?'

He looked sharply at me, leant forward. 'Sam Wild. What do you know of Sam Wild?'

'Only that I have good reason to believe he is also known as Joey the Clown at Hengel's circus.'

Jack sat back in his chair. Frowning, he looked very thoughtful indeed, if not actually worried, although when I asked him if he knew the man, he shook his head.

He didn't convince me so I told him young Jimmy's version: that Joey was a man of mystery who didn't live with the other circus clowns.

Jack listened, nodding as if in agreement from time to time but he wasn't as excited or even, it seemed, any longer as interested in this piece of information which I considered vital to the killer's identity.

'He must be still somewhere in Edinburgh, lodging near the circus. Think of the opportunity, the coincidence—'

Jack frowned. 'Coincidence?'

'Don't you see – surely? All the deaths took place in the central area of Newington. It shouldn't be too hard to trace a tall man with a badly scarred face – without the clown's greasepaint, the wig and so forth, which he can hardly be wearing now.'

As we spoke Thane was dashing to the door and then back to me. 'Oh, I'd almost forgotten. Thane was disturbed in the early hours this morning. I think he found something outside he wanted me to see, but I wasn't tempted to go out in the dark.'

'Let's have a look, then.'

We followed him and he ran to the kitchen window, stood up with his paws on the sill.

I couldn't see anything at first, then Jack pointed.

'Nothing there. Just a smear of paint.'

What on earth could that mean? Had someone tried to break in and Thane had tried to warn me? When we went inside I showed him the note.

He took that seriously enough. 'You should be careful, Rose.'

'I'm not in any danger – after all, I have Thane.'

'From what you've just told me – and that mysterious white paint – you could be in considerable danger.

I didn't see the connection at first and he repeated, 'White paint, Rose. Think about it. We've been talking about clowns and that is probably greasepaint. You know, the kind they use,' he added heavily.

And all of a sudden a lot of things came together and I was suddenly scared as he looked at me and said slowly, 'Rose, I think I should move in with you – just for a while.'

I laughed, although I suspected it was just the kind of opportunity Jack was looking for. 'I don't need a guard detective – I have a guard dog.'

He ignored that. 'I was about to ask you, anyway, if I could be considered as a lodger – without any commitment, if that's what you're looking so nervous about,' he added hastily. 'I'm not trying to further my case, although you might as well know that I still love you – that has never changed – but I give you my solemn word that living under the same roof I would not take any advantages—'

Again I laughed rather cynically at that and he said severely, 'I'm living in police lodgings at the moment but have my name down for a flat in Lutton Place. I need somewhere central, just a couple of weeks – maybe less – until it's ready for occupation. Go on, Rose,' he wheedled, 'it'll be fine and I promise to behave like a proper lodger. Pay you rent and I'll sleep downstairs, bring a bed down to the great hall.'

At my doubtful expression he went on, 'A necessary precaution, if sleeping on the same floor worries you that I might sleepwalk and imagine it's the old days again,' he added impishly, hoping to sound sarcastic, but unable to conceal the bitterness such memories brought.

'I'll have to think about it, Jack.'

'Well, don't take long about it.' He jabbed a finger towards the note on the table. 'The writer just might mean business and you may not have a lot of time to make up your mind.'

'Thanks for the cheery prospect,' I said.

'Maybe the attempted break-in doesn't worry you – but it certainly has given me food for thought and I'd like to be near at hand until we have sorted out the whereabouts of this Sam Wild. Innocent or guilty, until we know the truth you might well be in danger.'

I wasn't fooled by his solemn tone. Aware that Jack could always make the most of any advantage.

I refused to take it seriously...then. But Jack was right; I still had a lot to learn, as I found out sooner than I thought.

CHAPTER TWENTY-TWO

Jack moved in and suddenly my life changed. I did not think having him stay in the Tower would make all that much difference but it did. He had the ability to make himself at home and he proceeded to do so with a vengeance.

Although he would have denied it – perhaps it was because I was no longer used to having a man about the house – he seemed to be a very large presence and I was for ever tripping over him.

He came on a Saturday and by Tuesday I felt as if the time lapse of two years had never happened except that we slept apart. As proposed, he had moved the bed from the spare bedroom into the great hall. There it stood in a corner in solitary splendour, with only the table and that monstrous typewriting machine snug and unused under its black leather cover to keep him company.

The weekend was pleasant, I must admit. Glorious warm sunshine, almost unseasonable, with the trees doing a dress rehearsal of adorning their leaves in that splendid array of autumn colours.

We walked with Thane on the hill and Jack hired a carriage and drove us to East Lothian where we had a picnic at Yellowcraigs while Thane, apparently enjoying the role of a domestic pet, darted in and out of the water, much to the delight of Constable Hoskins and his wife who were on a similar expedition with their three young children.

Jack was always good company and he was at his shining best, full of amusing anecdotes, throwing dignity to the winds and playing rounders with his constable and the children, light-hearted and happy to shed the solemn life of a senior detective.

Just occasionally I caught a wistful look as, laughing, he held the smallest and most beguiling two-year-old above his head. I felt a pang for Jack then, a glimpse of the father he might have been, and wished the wee lass in Glasgow had been a wee lad.

Overhearing his conversation with the constable while Mrs Hoskins and I discussed womanly topics and we all demolished the pile of picnic sandwiches, I learnt a lot of Jack's two missing years, the places he had visited. He had even visited America – New York, in fact, which was a great surprise.

When I asked him about it later, he said, 'Of course, I couldn't afford it, this was a special assignment.'

But he refused to be drawn on the details and I didn't pursue the subject. The voyage, however, with its dramatic moments of a storm whilst crossing the Atlantic was something else we had in common.

He was suddenly a friend, long lost and returned to me. He made no gestures in the direction of the returned lover, in fact he was most scrupulous about that, taking my arm to help me over the rocky shore or into a carriage, but that was all. He kept his word and never referred to our earlier relationship. He never attempted to kiss me goodnight or make any gesture, or spoke any word that I might interpret as a romantic overture.

We sat by firelight in the evenings, which were drawing in, reading and often discussing books which we had both enjoyed and, apart from Thane's new obsession for staring out of the kitchen window for hours on end, it was just like old times, with a good supper and a bottle of wine, mostly consumed by Jack, whose head for alcohol was better than mine.

The crimes and the connection with the circus, so much part of our recent lives, were laid firmly aside. Jack refused to discuss what he called 'business'.

'Let's enjoy today, Rose. It's all we have really.'

His voice was so sad that I looked at him intently. He was staring uneasily in the direction of Thane who, once content to lie at Jack's feet, had now abandoned him to stand guard at the kitchen window, occasionally wagging his tail at the darkness or the starry sky.

'I don't know what he finds so fascinating out there. What on earth does he see? It's black dark,' said Jack.

He was quite hurt and I didn't feel it was the moment to remind him that animals, unlike humans, had the gift of night sight.

Watching Thane, Jack gave me a bewildered glance and said thoughtfully, 'Don't you think it's about time you put up some curtains, Rose?'

Curtains had never occurred to me. All the other windows in the Tower were shuttered, and as I hadn't any prying neighbours, I had no feeling that my privacy was endangered, and besides, I rather enjoyed looking out at the starry sky above Arthur's Seat.

'Does it worry you?' I asked.

He shook his head. 'No, but it obviously worries Thane.'

And for the first time I felt a twinge of alarm, the unseen presence of violence and death. Was Jack making light of something that was in fact a warning? I was safe enough with him here, but would I ever again look out into the darkness beyond the Tower that had seemed so protective, once I was in the house alone, my footsteps echoing as I remembered that warning note?

'I'll think about it.'

And Jack grinned. That was my usual compromise.

No more was said, we wished each other goodnight and Jack bolted the door. He insisted on doing so despite any inconvenience to Thane sleeping on his rug at my bedside.

Insisting that it was just an extra precaution he said, 'If Thane needs to go out, I'll hear him.'

I thought that was doubtful. Jack would hear nothing from the great hall, and as I knew of old, his snores indicated that he slept very soundly indeed.

When he left after breakfast on Monday morning, I decided I must tell Elma about my new lodger when she arrived over the hill with Rufus for her morning walk, without Peter for once.

She crowed mischievously and wagged a finger at

me. 'You are a sly one, Rose. Pretending when we met him at the circus that first evening that he was just a friend.'

'And so he is,' I said shortly. 'He just needs somewhere to stay.'

'I'll bet,' was her dry comment.

We went into Princes Street to look for suitable curtain material and she seemed less enthusiastic about shopping than usual, presumably because the subject of our quest, making curtains, was of little interest and belonged in the domestic province of the Rice Villa housekeeper: a treasure, I was told, who absolutely adored Rufus.

It was later as we were having tea together that another strange idea for her offhand behaviour occurred to me. I casually mentioned Peter and asked where he was.

In reply she almost snapped my head off. 'Peter? I don't know. Why ask about Peter now?'

And at that moment I thought I had made an important discovery.

In the short time we had known each other, much to my surprise, I was, in Elma's own words, her 'greatest friend'. I liked her sweet nature and generosity, and was prepared to forgive her snobbery, writing it off as a minor flaw, the result of our completely different upbringings: her family background, rarely mentioned, an estate in Surrey.

However, try as I might, I had never felt drawn to Peter, although the twins were so close. Now it occurred to me in a lightning flash of intuition why she was so upset about the possibility that Jack was moving back into my life: the reason was Peter.

I thought of all the occasions when she was desperately anxious that I should like him, insisting that we were to be great friends, always drawing the three of us together, while I was sure he did not enjoy those morning walks across the hill from Rice Villa.

They were just to please Elma. As I endeavoured to arouse her enthusiasm on that shopping expedition, it suddenly dawned upon me that Elma was less interested in curtain-making than matchmaking.

Inspired by the heroines of the Jane Austen novels we both loved, Elma had decided that I should marry her twin, Peter.

I also remembered that, without even a meeting, she stubbornly refused to accept the young woman Peter had been courting while in London. I could hardly with decency query Peter about her – we were not on such terms of intimacy – and as she was never mentioned I presumed that she had been discarded, whether or not at Elma's insistence, when he came to Edinburgh, in the hope that he would marry her new best friend.

What a preposterous idea! I longed to have it out with her, tell her that life doesn't work like that. To say tactfully, without causing offence or hurt, that I did not want, or would ever even consider, marrying her twin.

If I needed confirmation of her displeasure it was when neither she nor Peter appeared during the next few days.

I thought little about it, busy with a tape measure

and scissors, and longing for a sewing machine; I had not been this domestic since my pioneering days with Danny when we were always trying to put a temporary home together just a step or two ahead of the next Apache raid.

I had stood back to admire the result of my new kitchen curtains when my life as a private detective suddenly gathered pace. A letter from a prospective client urgently requesting a meeting to undertake an investigation.

Paid work at last, another item for the logbook, another much needed addition to my income and off I went on my bicycle the short distance to South Newington.

Mrs Craig lived in one of the large houses almost next door to the convent of the Little Sisters of the Poor. An elegant lady, most welcoming, and I received a most civilised reception as I was led into the handsome drawing room, with afternoon tea brought by a uniformed maid. As we nibbled dainty sandwiches, she leant closer and whispered the details of her domestic problem.

A valuable ruby ring had gone missing and she suspected her personal maid, inherited by her three months ago, a long-serving much loved member of her recently deceased mother's household.

Had she thought of informing the police? I asked. Mrs Craig shook her head vehemently. 'There are reasons why I wish this to remain a private investigation. First out of respect for my mother, who was devoted to Winton.'

She shook her head sadly. 'The stolen ring is very old. It is also, I think, rather ugly and old-fashioned. But it is a family heirloom, two hundred years old and my husband will take its loss very badly indeed. Mr Craig, I am afraid, will not hesitate to notify the police.'

The shudder which accompanied this said louder than any words that the domestic strife envisaged would be intolerable and was to be avoided at all costs. So making a note of the details, a description of the ring, I agreed to take it on.

My first visit, as always in cases of stolen jewellery, would be to the local pawnshops.

Wheeling my bicycle past the convent, I had just reached the road when I was hailed by Sister Clare. She was alone and heading in my direction.

'I thought I recognised you, Mrs McQuinn. I am so glad to see you.' Tactfully she did not enquire about my business with one of the convent's neighbours. 'I don't wish to trouble you when you are so busy and,' pausing she shook her head, 'the incident is of little significance really.'

She looked at me, her anxious expression clearly asked that I be told, so I walked down the drive with her.

'Every Sunday after mid-morning Mass we provide a soup kitchen for the lonely and needy in the district. Despite the opulence we see around us in this area, just down the road there are still many poor people, ex-soldiers among them and disabled veterans unable to obtain employment.'

I thought of Will Sanders as she added, 'Poor starving folk, God help them.' We had almost reached the convent steps. I waited patiently for her to get to the point.

'This Sunday, Marie Ann – you remember her, our young novice we gave your cloak to; so kind of you! – well, she was on duty and came back in a bit of a state, poor girl. Terrified she was – I finally got it out of her, she had recognised among the men coming forward for their bowl of soup, the man with the scarred face...'

She paused dramatically. 'The very same who accosted her in the garden that day. Of course, he was well wrapped up, scarf and so forth, and she could have been wrong, but I had no idea what should be done about it. Hardly a matter for the police, or for you, Mrs McQuinn, to deal with.'

I was in silent agreement. Alarming, maybe, but again not a shred of real evidence.

'I thought, when I saw you, that I should mention it. I'll tell her I talked to you.'

And as she stood there looking at me, she smiled, head on one side, and said a strange thing. 'Marie Ann is so like you – I mean what you must have looked like as a young girl, both so small and neat, same height, that lovely curly hair.'

Just an ordinary polite remark. It wasn't until much later that the significance struck me.

CHAPTER TWENTY-THREE

That evening I told Jack about the soup kitchen incident at the convent and the possible link with Joey, or Sam Wild as we now knew him.

Jack shrugged it aside. 'You're so dramatic about everything, Rose. You should watch it, not good for your profession, you know, all this intuition, when hard facts are what is needed.'

'You haven't got far with your hard facts up to now,' I reminded him, feeling angry and misjudged.

'Let's look at it, then. A young novice at a convent full of nuns who probably imagine that every man who looks in their direction has rape in mind.'

'That's not fair,' I protested. 'This girl had been repeatedly raped by the men in her family; that was why she took to the convent – to escape.'

'To escape all men,' said Jack dryly. 'That's exactly what I'm saying. We are not all monsters, beasts—'

'The scarred face,' I interrupted.

'I was coming to that. Think of how and why. I don't imagine that among a lot of war veterans in

Edinburgh, Sam Wild – if it was he – is the only one
left with a scarred face. There must be dozens of men
wandering around who were invalided out of their
regiments.'

We had finished supper and settled by the fire. Just
like 'the old days', as Jack was pleased to call them.

There was one difference. Jack grumpily returned to
the subject of Thane's odd behaviour. The curtains had
made little difference. Thane had soon discovered that
he could get behind them and continue his vigilance
undisturbed.

Thane's daytime behaviour had also undergone a
change. He spent much more time apart from me, out
on the hill, although he returned before dark.

Jack wasn't pleased. He regarded Thane very much
as our dog in the same way as Rufus was regarded
by Elma or as any owner regarded their domestic
pet.

But this was not, and had never been, the case with
Thane. Now, as always, the old fears returned to haunt
me: that Thane didn't belong to me – or to anyone
else for that matter – and I must face the fact that he
would not stay for ever.

One day he would return to the wild, and my
new fear was that this change in Thane dated from
Jack's return. Did it indicate that, with a man about
the house, I was safe and no longer needed his
protection?

Relieved at the prospects of a new case, I set off down
the road to the Pleasance; my first port of call would

be the pawnshop adjacent to the tenement where the two girls were found.

It did not look promising, more rag-and-bone shop than one a servant would approach to dispose of a valuable stolen jewel.

The rather scruffy owner, bleary-eyed, unshaven, looked at me doubtfully when I asked to see rings. Somewhat reluctantly he produced a tray of sad-looking specimens, obviously wedding and signet rings handed in for a few coins.

When I said that it was a ruby ring I had in mind, he laughed, and looking at me as if I had gone mad, he pushed the rings away and said if that was the sort of thing his class of customers brought in then he'd soon be moving into premises in George Street.

As the old soldier, Will Sanders, lived just across the road I had brought a few provisions in my saddlebag. Parking the bicycle, I knocked at the door, usually open. There was no reply but a curtain next door twitched and a woman's face looked out at me. Raising the sill she said, 'Haven't you heard, lass? The old chap has been taken to the infirmary. Had a bad turn, fell down in the street, tripped and broke his wrist. Poor old soul, can't manage now. And no one to look after him anymore.'

I decided to visit him, especially as the infirmary he had been taken to was an extension of the hospital where Felix Miles Rice languished in a private ward. A boon for the lucky few, but that was still an aggravation for Elma. She insisted that he should be transferred to an expensive private hospital, but since the police were involved in watching over him, she had been forbidden this privilege.

I was not the only visitor that day. As I was walking towards the entrance I was almost bowled over by a familiar figure. Elma's twin Peter. He would have rushed past me, but I seized his arm.

'Hello. You're in a mighty hurry,' I said.

He shook off my hand. 'Something awful – awful.' And white-faced, without even his usual polite bow, he dashed across the road. I wondered what had happened; presumably, he had been making an abortive attempt to see Felix and had been turned away.

I continued into the reception area and was directed to the male ward where Will was awake; his right wrist in splints heavily bandaged, he was protesting to the nurse, wanting to know how long he was being kept in this place. She gave me a sympathetic look and said it was just for a day or two to see how he got on.

He brightened up when I handed the provisions over to him. He hated hospitals, remembering bitterly his last sojourn when he lost his leg at the Crimea. I managed to slide away from those reminiscences by persuading him to tell me something of his early days in the Highlands before he had gone into the army.

As I was leaving he said, 'You're a good lass, Mrs McQuinn, and there's something here I would like you to have for safe keeping.' From under his pillow he withdrew a wallet and took out a folded sealed envelope. 'I wouldn't want this to fall into the wrong hands. Belle would never want this to be made public. But someone should know the truth and I feel as if I can trust you.'

He paused and said dolefully, 'Give me your promise that you won't open it unless I don't come out of here alive.' And glancing at the line of beds, the sleeping or groaning occupants, 'There's some gay queer ones in here, they'd rob the sugar out of your tea if they could. And even some of the nurses, I don't like the look of them, always after me, wanting to plump up my pillows – my wallet might not be safe from thieving hands. Not much they can pinch, but this – it's precious.'

I promised to look after the letter. Did it contain money, or was it the missing suicide note from his granddaughter or Amy?

The rain had begun. The search for Mrs Craig's ring at the city pawnbrokers must wait. I preferred not to get soaking wet on what promised to be a long and tedious task bicycling between city and suburban streets, locations with which I had become very well acquainted through my years as a lady investigator, for this was not by any means my first foray into the stolen-jewellery market.

When I reached home I found Jack already installed. He had left the central office early that afternoon and I heard him moving about upstairs. I thought for a moment, then decided to keep Will's letter a secret.

Jack came down to greet me. 'Just looking for

something to keep my clothes in.' I followed him into the great hall where he had discovered a new toy, deciding to acquaint himself with that lost cause, the typewriting machine.

Always fascinated by new gadgets, he was teaching himself and plodding slowly, finger by finger, as he searched for the right letters, assuring me that such ability would be extremely useful in my profession, for writing letters, sending bills and so forth.

Jack had bought paper and in no time at all the table was littered with his practice at mastering the keyboard which, judging by the numerous discarded attempts, was giving him a very hard time.

His garments, also discarded, were scattered around and the normally pristine and unused great hall with its stone walls, high windows and ancient tapestries now looked wincingly untidy.

Giving his request some thought, I decided that as Jack had moved in with only a valise for a day or two, this signified that he intended longer, indeed even a permanent residence. Wondering how I could tactfully raise that subject, I found him a discarded and not too large cabin trunk in one of the attics.

In my bedroom I realised Jack had been searching there for something suitable and the first thing I noticed was that some of the objects on my dressing table had been displaced. I have a sharp eye for such things and the studio photograph of Danny and me, taken in happier days in Arizona, had been moved from its central position.

When Jack and I were lovers, this one and only

memento of Danny, irreplaceable and greatly treasured, had been tactfully relegated to a drawer, and in our new relationship as landlady and lodger, I had never considered removing it once more.

Jack obviously had. Another indication that he considered he was here for good. Danny was his dead rival, part of my past that must be banished for ever.

CHAPTER TWENTY-FOUR

My new assignment was destined to be the shortest on record. A letter from Mrs Craig asked me to call as soon as possible.

Over the usual hospitable afternoon tea, I heard an extraordinary tale. After our meeting, she had been visited by an old friend of her mother who was passing through Edinburgh.

'She was surprised to see Winton, the maid in question, and once we were alone she did not beat about the bush. She asked me if I ever lost any item of jewellery. When I told her about the ring, she said, oh yes, my mother also lost pieces of jewellery on an almost regular basis. However, if she informed Winton of the missing piece and asked her to keep a look out for it, in every instance the chances were that it would be replaced.

'With nothing to lose I took her advice. I described the missing ring, this family heirloom, how I suspected it might have fallen off the dressing table and rolled away somewhere out of sight. I added how upset Mr Craig was.'

Mrs Craig stopped and laughed. 'You will never

credit this but the very next morning there was the ring. Not on the dressing table but back in its velvet case in the jewel box. And not a word of explanation.'

Pausing, she smiled wryly.

'All of which, of course, proclaimed her guilt.'

'She will have to go, of course,' I said.

Mrs Craig shook her head. 'No. I think we understand each other and perhaps it is some kind of a game with her. She is a good servant, and for my dear mother's sake I want to keep her. I hope she got the message. If it happens again, however, I doubt whether I will have the same patience.'

Mrs Craig thanked me profusely for all my trouble and handed over my fee, which I was almost, but not quite, ashamed to take for one visit to a pawnshop.

The Indian summer continued. Thane and I enjoyed two delightful days outdoors without any appearance from Elma or Peter and, I must confess, I was rather relieved. The daily repetition of Elma's tale of woe regarding Felix and the hospital authorities was rather wearisome and I did not get any fonder of her shrill little dog, nor he of me.

I felt almost carefree. In time, the crimes that now intrigued me would be laid aside, resolved one way or the other, cases closed, old news, and that would include the elusive Sam Wild. I had boundless optimism that another domestic investigation would soon arrive to tax my detection abilities and decided to make the most of this peaceful interlude.

And, as so often happens when we feel overconfident,

this was merely the lull in the approaching storm.

A storm from which my life would never again emerge to greet with the same tranquillity those cloudless blue skies.

It began for me the following morning. The Rice carriage rolled up and a distraught Elma leapt out and rushed to meet me.

Barely able to speak, in floods of tears, she gasped out, 'Oh, Rose, it has happened....'

'Felix?'

'Yes. He has died – at last. It's so awful.' She shuddered. 'So much worse than I expected.'

I was sympathetic: although it was inevitable, perhaps she had faith, knowing his indomitable strength, that he would recover from the coma.

'I had to come and tell you, dear Rose. I am on my way into town to meet Peter. So much for us to do.' She shivered. 'Funeral arrangements, mourning clothes – a thousand things to take care of.'

I presumed she had just heard the sad news and this time she did not ask me to return with her, nor was my valued opinion sought regarding what she should wear for this solemn occasion. For which I was truly thankful that she had Peter at her side to see her through the sad days ahead.

She held my hand tightly as I saw her to the waiting carriage.

Kissing my cheek, as I murmured the required condolences, she said, 'Peter is very upset, as you can imagine.'

'I met him at the hospital on Friday.'

'Friday?' She gave me a stricken glance. 'The day...
oh!' A frantic nod. 'Yes, he looked in – I had lost an
earring, a diamond!'

Closing the carriage door, she leant out of the
window.

'What on earth were you doing at the hospital,
Rose? Nothing serious, I hope.'

'I was on my way to the infirmary to see an old
gentleman I know who lives in the Pleasance. We didn't
speak. Peter was in a great hurry,' I added.

'Oh!' she said non-committally and tapped the
window for Benson to start back to Princes Street. 'I
wish I could stay. But there is so much to do. You will
excuse me rushing off, dear, and please, please come to
the funeral. I need you to support me,' she said with a
wan smile.

I heard the story of Felix's last hours from Jack that
evening. He had died that same afternoon I was visiting
Will Sanders. If Peter had just heard, then it accounted
for his highly emotional state as he rushed out.

'I wish he had told me,' I said to Jack who shook
his head.

'What could you have done, Rose?' Biting his lip he
regarded me thoughtfully in that irritating way; I knew
it well, it indicated there was something else he had on
his mind and didn't know whether I should be told or
not.

'Well?' I said.

He shrugged. 'It isn't as simple as that, Rose. There
is a suspicion that Felix didn't die as the result of

his coma. For the last couple of days, amazingly, he had been responding, showing faint signs that he was regaining consciousness. A remarkably strong man, Felix Miles Rice, and the doctors were all amazed.

'Which makes it all the more infuriating that someone murdered him. Despite all our precautions. I'm afraid our police guard, young Hoskins you met, remember, had left the ward for a few moments. Good chap, one hundred per cent reliable, but he had a violent stomach upset. His missus and the children have had it too. Something they'd eaten. Urgently needed the WC, couldn't wait to search for the ward nurse who was absent doing her rounds.

'Hoskins was sure it would be all right, quiet time in the wards, patients sleeping, no one around until the visiting hour. He was away for five minutes...five minutes!'

Jack gave an exasperated sigh. 'That was longer than he intended, but when he returned Felix had stopped breathing. One of the pillows and the bedclothes were scattered on the floor, it looked like a bit of a struggle, and by the colour of Felix's face, he suspected that he had been smothered.'

'Then, who killed him?' I asked.

'The answer is obvious. Whoever attacked him in the study had been lurking about. The person Hodge saw, for which he paid with his life, also killed Felix.'

There was plenty to mull over and in the Tower Thane wasn't the only one behaving oddly. Jack was more than ever preoccupied and, what was more unnerving, sometimes I caught him off guard, staring at me in a brooding sort of way. I knew him well enough to recognise the signs. Again, as if there was something he wanted to say and couldn't find the words.

I was vain enough to imagine that, now he had moved in, he was contemplating ways of broaching the delicate subject of becoming more than a lodger. The more likely alternative – all was not well in the Edinburgh City Police.

Tentatively I mentioned the search for Sam Wild and once again he clammed up.

'Look,' I said, 'I have a major interest in this, you know.'

He gave me an odd look. 'What makes you say that?' And his lips twitched as if he was about to laugh at some secret joke.

I was furious. 'I'm the one who has been threatened, in case you have forgotten.'

'Oh that! I don't think you need take that seriously – or consider that you are in danger any longer.'

'Does that mean Sam Wild is no longer in Edinburgh?'

He shrugged, said coolly, 'Let's say that it's all in hand.'

But I wasn't prepared to accept this. Determined to have some answers I said, 'It isn't good enough, Jack. After all, you did ask my help and now you're closing the door in my face.'

A vague gesture of dismissal. Avoiding my eyes, he said, 'Let's just say there are things I can't discuss with you at the moment.'

This was Inspector Gray all over again. I was

furious. I opened my mouth to protest and as he leant forward he said sternly, 'Just leave it, will you, Rose? Believe me, I will keep you informed when the time comes. Now to more important matters, what are we having for supper?'

But Sam Wild and Jack's irritating behaviour continued to occupy my mind. Had Wild been lurking at the hospital, awaiting a chance to murder Felix? How did he know that he was showing signs of recovering? Even Elma did not know that.

It was all completely baffling, especially as my life now felt very disrupted by Jack's continued presence. He gave no indication of how long he was staying and looking after him made me feel less like a private detective and more like a housekeeper, a role I did not wish to know more about.

When I questioned him, rather pointedly I'm afraid, regarding the progress of the new housing, he said, 'Slow but sure,' adding with a mischievous grin, 'anxious to get rid of me, Rose?'

What I did not know until much later, too late, was that Jack was staying in Solomon's Tower for a very different purpose.

The trap was set and I was bait. The perfect bait to lure and capture the elusive Sam Wild.

And Jack got his wish.

CHAPTER TWENTY-FIVE

I bicycled homewards at dusk that day after visiting
Rice Villa in the hope of seeing Elma. I felt that I
should put in an appearance. After all, even with a
devoted twin brother at her side, a bereaved wife might
appreciate another female, her allegedly 'dearest friend',
at such a time.

My visit was in vain. Neither she nor Peter were
at home and I gathered from the housekeeper that the
mistress and her brother had gone into the city that
morning.

They had not yet returned and she had not been
given a time to expect them or received any instructions
regarding supper.

'There is much to do,' she added reproachfully, as if
I should be aware of the disruption the master's death
had caused.

I imagined Elma was still shocked and hysterical.
Relieved that she had Peter, I hoped she hadn't heard
the grim details that Jack had imparted concerning
Felix's last hours and the suspicion that her husband

was showing signs of recovery before he had been murdered.

I bought a loaf of bread in the Pleasance and as I remounted I was suddenly aware of a flat tyre and, to make matters worse, it had begun to rain.

Cursing loudly, for there was not a soul in sight and I still had a mile to walk, I pushed the bicycle without my rain cape which, for once, I had not replaced in the saddlebag; I would be drenched by the time I reached home.

Head down, I battled on, standing aside to get out of the way of the trotting horse cab. The driver stopped and looked down at me.

'Give you a lift, miss. Heading for Duddingston to pick up a fare.' And pointing out the obvious, my already streaming hair, 'You're getting soaked.'

I pointed helplessly to the bicycle. 'Got a puncture.'

'No trouble, lass. We'll put it on the back. Where are you heading?'

I shouted up to him, 'Solomon's Tower.'

He jumped down, seized the bicycle, attached it firmly and, helping me aboard, he said, 'Good job I was heading past your way. Don't get many fares to Duddingston. Last time was the early hours in the morning. Couple of lads, blind drunk, legless. Been to a party. One carrying the other. I gave them a hand inside, hard to decide who was worse; dropped them off by the loch. The one who could still speak said his mate needed fresh air to sober up a bit, as his wife would give him hell.'

He grinned. 'I got a good tip and nearly got hell

from my wife when she smelt the whisky fumes in the cab.'

He refused my tip, nice fellow, said he had been glad to help.

As I rushed indoors and dried my hair, I was excited, almost certain that the two drunks had been Hodge and his killer. Probably 'legless' confirmed that Hodge was already dead. And three o'clock was the time I heard a carriage on the road outside the Tower.

I could hardly wait to tell Jack, but what was waiting for me banished all thoughts of that illuminating encounter with the kindly cabbie.

It was almost dark in the kitchen. Thane, lying by the fire, looked up and wagged his tail in greeting.

Laying aside my wet cloak and lighting a lamp, I heard footsteps in the hall.

'Hello, Jack,' I called. There was no reply. He hadn't heard me.

'Jack,' I called again. 'Kettle's on. Tea in a minute.'

And after washing my hands, I seized the bread knife and began cutting slices from the new sweet-smelling loaf.

Footsteps again. I turned, and in the fire glow, I saw that the figure approaching was too tall for Jack.

In that moment I knew who it was. Who had invaded my home.

I had come face-to-face with Sam Wild.

He was walking swiftly towards me. I couldn't see him clearly but I thought fast and realised I was not completely defenceless.

I had a weapon – the bread knife in my hand.

The lamp behind him revealed a glimpse of a man's face scarred on one side, and greying tousled hair.

My heart raced. I drew a deep breath. He was just a few paces away. I raised the knife and lunged forward.

My reaction took him by surprise, but with the amazing speed learnt, no doubt, in the ring at the circus, he swerved aside and the knife aimed at the region of his heart struck his upper arm.

He yelled out. I thought he was going to fall and prepared to strike again as he stumbled, fell forward and grabbed hold of the table's edge.

I turned, screamed at Thane. Thane who should have been my protector was standing by, an interested spectator to the scene of horror.

'Do something, for God's sake, do something!' I shouted.

Sam Wild straightened up, one hand covering his arm, and looked at me.

'You always were good with a knife, Rose, me darlin'. Even better than a rifle.'

The greying hair, the face scarred on one side, but the voice. The voice was...

Danny McQuinn. My Danny!

He held out his hands, one covered in blood.

The moment I had yearned for, dreamt of these long years had come...

'Danny,' I whispered and knew no more.

CHAPTER TWENTY-SIX

I was in the armchair by the fire, the kettle singing on the hob. I stirred, opened my eyes. I had been asleep. Dear God, what a terrible nightmare.

Where was Jack? No, this wasn't Jack.

The man bending over me was my husband, Danny McQuinn, my longed-for dream come true: since my return to Edinburgh, seeing myself opening the door, Danny waiting there, holding out his arms to me, smiling.

Except that this Danny was Sam Wild, a killer.

And he was smiling, that part of the dream at least was true. He was holding out not his arms but a cup of water, a bloodied towel round his arm.

'Drink this, Rose. You've had an almighty shock.'

I drank slowly. This couldn't be happening. I would wake up properly, really wake up this time after I blinked several times (the way I knew I could rely on to banish nightmares).

But Danny remained. This tall, almost emaciated man with greying hair, the left side of his face deeply

scarred, but the right side unmarked, the dark-blue Irish
eyes, well-marked eyebrows, the gentle mouth, was my
once handsome, beloved Danny. So changed.

I felt tears welling. He stroked my hair back from
my forehead, a gesture one would give to a frightened
child, a gesture I remembered from days of terror, our
lives in turmoil and danger in Arizona.

'There now.' He sat back on his heels. 'You're all
right, my Rose. The sight of blood took you—'

'Your arm – I'm sorry.'

He shrugged. 'Just a scratch, nothing to worry
about.' Then he grinned. 'You've gone soft, my Rose.
Sure now, and I've seen you shooting down renegades
and Mexican bandits without turning a hair.'

He looked at me, smiling gently, holding my hand.
And I knew that I might have changed but that Danny
still loved me. It was all there in his eyes for the world
to see. He had lost me and now I was found again.

And suddenly the awfulness of the situation took its
grip.

What if Jack walked in any minute? Sam Wild was
a wanted man.

'You're in danger – they're out looking for you.'

He smiled. 'Oh, that fellow I've seen, the policeman.
Married now, are you?' He took my left hand.

'Of course not. That's your ring, Danny McQuinn.
The one you put on my finger more than fifteen years
ago. What makes you think I'm married?' Then I
remembered. 'You've been watching us.'

I looked towards the kitchen with its now curtained
window, remembered Thane's odd behaviour. We

should have known there was someone out there...

Danny sighed. 'Sure now, and it was very cosy the two of you looked, just like a happy married couple. I hadn't the heart to intrude.'

Thane had come over. He had his head on my lap. Danny stroked him absent-mindedly. I looked at Thane and demanded, 'And what were you doing, Thane, letting a strange man into the house? What kind of a watchdog do you think you are?'

Thane managed a reproachful look and Danny laughed.

'Thane? Is that your name, now? Sure now, the name for a Scottish noble becomes you.'

Thane looked pleased, with that almost human smile, and Danny grinned, stroking his head. 'To tell you the truth, Thane and I are friends. I've been living rough. Out on the hill there. I was resting in the rain and this dog appeared out of nowhere, gave me a friendly lick and led me to a cave.'

He took Thane's head in his hands, frowned, 'Sure now, it's a strange creature, you are, right enough.' And giving me a puzzled look, 'He seemed to know me.'

I hadn't quite worked it out yet, but I was getting the message of why Thane had deserted Jack and me and spent so much time staring out of the kitchen window.

That was only one answer. Among the many others was how on earth he knew that Sam Wild was Danny McQuinn. Unless he could recognise Danny's photograph on my dressing table, which I doubted. But nothing about Thane responded to the application of human logic.

Danny straightened his shoulders. He winced and I said, 'I'll attend to that arm of yours. I'm so sorry...'

'It can wait, I've had worse. I'm starving, Rose. Haven't had a proper meal since the soup kitchen at the convent.'

'I'll get something. Have some bread meantime.' I buttered two thick slices, and as he took them like a starving man, my heart ached with pity.

'So it was you that scared the life out of the young girl at the convent.'

He nodded. 'Thought that girl was you when I first saw her working in the vegetable garden. She looked so young, so like you – remember, when you cut short your curls for practical reasons, in our Arizona days? I see they have taken over once more in their wild golden glory.'

And he reached up, twisted a curl around his fingers, a gesture from the past, as he added, 'Undimmed by the years and very becoming still.'

As I put the hastily prepared meal of scrambled eggs and bacon before him, sliced more bread, he ate hungrily, sometimes pausing, fork in the air, to say, 'There's a lot to tell, Rose darlin'. I don't know where to begin.'

'Later,' I said. 'It can wait. Eat first, while I attend to your arm.'

As I examined and bathed what was fortunately not a deep cut, there was a lot I wanted to ask as well. I needed urgently to know the truth but the clock striking five was like the voice of doom.

It was now completely dark and outside the rain

streaming down the window cast its own note of doom.

Jack would be home in an hour. We had so little time. His arm now bandaged, as he drank a third cup of tea, I knew that Jack must not find him here.

Sam Wild was a wanted man, Jack was a policeman searching for a killer, and the fact that Sam Wild was also Danny McQuinn, his ghostly rival come to life, certainly would not endear him to Jack's heart.

One thing was growing clearer by the minute. I had to hide Danny and somehow get Jack away from the Tower.

But how? And then I thought of that old room upstairs, the secret room Jack and I had discovered years ago. The perfect temporary hiding place and, unless Jack knew Sam Wild's real identity, he would not have the slightest reason to suspect that Danny was in the Tower.

I would need to take other precautions, keep the kitchen, our usual entrance to the house, locked at all times. This I could explain by telling Jack that it felt safer, and to Elma and Peter the same safety precautions would apply, although I guessed I would see little of them until Felix's funeral was over.

Fortunately Jack did not have a key, as locking doors was a new innovation, and if asked I would tell him that there was only one ancient key of enormous dimensions in existence, and should he suggest having another made, as his stay was only temporary, it was hardly worthwhile.

The sound of a rap on the front-door knocker

echoed through the house. We both jumped. I sprang from the table, motioned Danny to hide upstairs while I went to the door.

The caller was impatient, and when I released the catch, my heart thumped. A policeman!

I recognised Constable Hoskins. Looking like a drowned rat, he was holding out a piece of paper. I gazed at it in horror.

'For you, Mrs McQuinn. From the Inspector, urgent, like. I live just along the road past Duddingston,' he pointed to his bicycle, 'so I said I'd hand it in.'

He had a sudden bout of sneezing. I felt so sorry for him and, as this was an unexpected opportunity to get some information on Felix's last hours in the hospital when Hoskins was on guard duty, I said, 'Do come in. Maybe the rain will abate while you have a cup of tea.'

I had some anxious moments but there was no sign of Danny, not a sound from upstairs as the constable gratefully followed me through to the kitchen.

As he discarded his wet cape, I took the note to the lamp.

'Sorry, won't manage this evening. Urgent police matters out of town. May be very late, will try not to disturb you. See you tomorrow. Hope you enjoy the concert.'

Concert? What concert? I had completely forgotten in the events of the last hour that I was supposed to be meeting Jack at the Assembly Rooms.

As the constable ate the buttered scone I gave him, I asked after his family and said how delightful his children were and how the inspector and I had enjoyed the picnic at Yellowcraigs.

He gave a rueful smile and said, 'I'm in bad with the inspector just now.' And obviously believing that his boss and I were on intimate terms, he said. 'Probably told you about the... er...incident at the hospital. Never live it down. Feel badly about Mrs Miles Rice and her brother too. Nice folk, thoughtful too. Never came in empty-handed, every day always something tasty.' He sighed. 'Now looks like turning into a murder enquiry.'

This was exactly the information I was hoping for. I murmured sympathetically and said, 'You didn't see anyone, then?'

He shook his head. 'No, I didn't. But one of the nurses saw a man rushing out in a great hurry. She just saw his back. Wasn't much help.'

I smiled and said nothing. It was obviously Peter whom I had met but I didn't want to muddy the waters by having the police question him.

He had returned to search for Elma's missing earring. Hoskins had been absent. Was Felix already dead? Was that why he had rushed out, to find someone?

He would not have had the slightest idea, until the police came to tell Elma, that his brother-in-law had been murdered and that he had just missed the killer by a few minutes.

There wasn't much Hoskins could add to what I already knew and, after some polite pleasantries, I looked out of the window. The rain had ceased, and thanking me, Hoskins went on his way.

Danny came cautiously downstairs. 'What was all

that about?' he said, and giving me an anxious look, 'Bad news?'

'On the contrary, it's good news. My lodger, the policeman Inspector Macmerry, isn't coming back this evening, so we have a few hours.'

'How did you meet him?'

So I told him about my new role in life as a private detective and roughly how that had come about through meeting an old school friend, hearing about a murdered servant and a husband who was behaving suspiciously.

'Lady Investigator, Discretion Guaranteed.' Danny laughed. 'I like that. Good on you – always did have the knack of solving riddles. Do you make a living out of it?'

'I've had my problems. Edinburgh society rather frowns on a lady riding a bicycle.'

That amused him too. 'You don't say! They should have seen you fighting off Indian raids as well as being the confidante of the saloon girls.' And nodding towards Thane, 'Where did you find him?'

'He found me.' I told him of our first meeting but I don't think he heard all that strange saga. Exhausted, sitting by the warm fire, he nodded off.

He looked so ill. His sleeping face was that of a stranger who bore no resemblance to the man I had loved and waited for. Only occasional glimpses of that other Danny in the sudden smile, the Irish brogue which he had never lost, a turn of his head.

I wanted to weep. I had lost him, lost my one true love. But now I had to save him from prison, or worse, the hangman's rope.

But first I had to keep him hidden until his arm healed and he got back his strength again, while I devised a method for his escape. Somehow help him flee to a place of safety, far from Edinburgh. Even if it meant never seeing him again, at least I would know he was alive.

I looked at him with compassion. Could this be the face of a murderer? I shuddered. My Danny, a killer. It seemed impossible. And yet, perhaps anything was possible of this stranger who had taken his place.

I had to think quickly. First of all, Jack's presence in the Tower must be ended. There was no possible way he could remain in the house at night sleeping in the great hall downstairs with Danny hidden overhead in the secret room.

Making sure that the back door was bolted against any unexpected visitors, Danny never stirred as I moved quietly about the kitchen, gathering lamp and cleaning materials.

Climbing the stairs, I opened the panel to the secret room with some difficulty, and once inside, covering my hair, I brushed aside the cobwebs, and choking against the dust, swept the floor clear of the debris of a hundred and fifty years.

An hour later I looked round at the results of my labours. The palliasse would have to suffice meantime as I sought out blankets and pillows from the landing cupboard. At last I looked around, straightened my back. I felt as if every bone was aching, so tired that I longed to lie down and sleep – anywhere. But hard work brought a feeling of satisfaction, a sense that there was nothing like gruelling physical activity to keep at bay the true terror of a situation.

Putting on those final touches, removing all evidence of the secret room's previous occupant, I thought that once again in its history the room was to provide refuge for another man with a price on his head. Who had used it before? A deserter from the Jacobite army at Prestonpans, or one of the Hanoverian enemy? I would never know: time was silent on that, as on so many questions posed regarding the unwritten history of Solomon's Tower...

Closing the door and making sure that the inside bolt still worked, if somewhat stiffly, I regretted the necessary absence of a fireplace. The room would be less than comfortable for more than a brief stay. Daylight would reveal all its inadequacies but in the faint light that struggled through the slit window, invisible from the outside ivy-clad wall of the Tower, it would be safe enough for Danny until I could help him escape.

Escape? I thought wryly after all these long years of dreaming of the moment we would be together again, this was to be the sad ending, which goes to prove the old adage that one should be careful about what one asks the gods to provide, seeing that it can also be answered in a way that is completely unacceptable.

And never was a moment in my life more unacceptable than this.

CHAPTER TWENTY-SEVEN

I went downstairs quietly, tiptoed into the kitchen.

Danny's head jerked round.

'I'm awake.' And yawning. 'I needed that sleep, Rose.'

'I've made up a bed for you.' And I told him about the secret room.

I expected him to be intrigued, but I could see that he was too tired to ask all the questions that its strange history involved.

'Where do you sleep, then?'

'Upstairs, just along the corridor.'

He said nothing, avoiding my eyes. I felt suddenly embarrassed. It had never occurred to me that this Danny, who wasn't at all like the husband I had lived with for those ten years of married life in Arizona, would expect me to sleep with him.

There were a lot of things that needed to be resolved before I would be able to make that decision. First and most important, I needed to hear his story of the events that had led him back to Edinburgh as a hunted man, a criminal.

My first wild hopes fled when he said, 'The police – your policeman, I expect, as well – are all out looking for me. I killed that poor guy in the bank. I didn't mean to, it was an instinctive reaction born of many years with Pinkerton's where we learnt in moments of danger to act first and think afterwards. And that was what happened. I just hit him too hard.'

'What were you doing there in the first place, robbing a bank?'

He shook his head. 'I have to go back to the beginning for that.'

'Before you do. Round about the same time as you arrived with the circus, just streets away from the bank, two girls who were friends committed suicide, hanged themselves in adjoining flats of the same tenement. At least that's what the police thought originally. A weird coincidence, but the circumstances were so bizarre that it now seems possible that they were murdered.'

'Oh, I heard about that at the circus. A suicide pact.' Pausing, he looked at me. 'Do they think I was responsible for that too?' he whispered.

I didn't answer and he said, 'Rose, now what would I be doing killing a couple of girls I've never met?'

I knew that was true, for the secret of whoever was responsible for their deaths lay with Will Sanders, Belle's grandfather.

'What about Felix Miles Rice?' I asked.

He looked bewildered, repeated the name. 'Isn't he the philanthropist I've read about – saw in a newspaper that he was in hospital with a heart attack and just died?'

'That's the man, Danny. Only there was a suspicion that it was no heart attack, that it was attempted murder. There was a police guard on his ward and when he showed signs of recovery someone came in and smothered him.'

I paused, watching his expression as I added, 'And the suspicion is that his attacker was Sam Wild.'

He stared at me. 'What are you trying to say, Rose? I don't know the man, never heard of him until what I read in the newspaper. Why on earth should I want to kill him?'

'Did you ever meet a man called Hodge?'

'Hodge?' he repeated. 'Not that I know of. Who's he?'

'He was valet to Miles Rice. And apparently he committed suicide by walking into the loch down the road here at Duddingston, just days after his master was admitted to hospital.'

Danny frowned. 'And why on earth should he do such a thing?' He frowned. 'Unless he was responsible and his guilt drove him to it.'

'That's very unlikely. I talked to him and I was pretty sure he hadn't told the police everything about Miles Rice's mysterious visitor that afternoon. I thought he was protecting someone and now I'm pretty sure it was murder. What's more, I think I have proof...'

And I told him the cabbie's tale about the two drunks.

He whistled. 'Three suicides and a murder, Rose. Deep waters you've got yourself involved in.' And shaking his head. 'None of them anything to do with me, I assure you. My only crime in Edinburgh is the accidental death of that poor guy in the bank at Newington.'

'Tell me about it.'

'I was desperate for money. I'd joined the circus in Glasgow but was told I wouldn't be paid until they had seen me in performance. That's the rule. I needed to find a place to stay, food to eat, and I had a few dollars I'd brought with me. All I wanted was to exchange them... Then I saw this bank.'

He shrugged. 'The guy behind the counter refused to give me any money for them. Very self-important, officious and suspicious, probably never seen American dollars before, said I was a stranger and how did he know they weren't forgeries. We argued. He lost his temper, came round and tried to throw me out. He grabbed hold of me. That was it. I hit him, helped myself to a few pounds, the rough equivalent of the dollars, and feeling furious, left in a hurry.'

There was a pause and I asked, 'What brought you back to Scotland?'

'To go back to the beginning. When we lost trace of each other I had a bad time. I'll spare you the details. On a secret mission for the Bureau of Indian Affairs, captured by renegades...tortured...' He looked away, his expression not wanting to remember. 'They have their own vile ways of dealing with hated white eyes. It's a long story, but when I escaped and got back to Pinkerton's, the time we agreed you should wait if I disappeared had long since elapsed.

'I still hoped you might be in Phoenix. I tracked you

down as far as the Apache reservation to be told that you were dead. Died in a fever outbreak. They even gave me the gold locket you used to wear. It had my photograph and one of your sister in it.'

I remembered that locket, lost or stolen so long ago.

'So you never knew about our baby,' I said.

'Baby? What baby?'

'Daniel, our son.' The tears welled again as they always did.

'Your son, Danny, born six months after you disappeared. We were attacked by those renegades. We took refuge in the reservation and there was a fever outbreak. But whoever told you got it wrong, it was our son who died, not me. I buried him out there in the desert. Thought you were dead too, so I came back to Edinburgh as we had agreed, if you ever disappeared without trace.'

'A son,' Danny whispered. 'We had a son after all those years.' There were tears in his eyes too when he looked at me, and I knew he was remembering all the disappointments, the pregnancies that came to nothing.

He took my hand, held it tight. 'Never mind, my darlin'. We are together again. We can have more babies.'

And even as he said the words, just looking at this new Danny who had come into my life again, I knew it would never happen. It was just part of that other dream.

There would be no marriage renewed, no babies. The future was a dark void, promising nothing but sorrow. When I made no reassuring response, perhaps

Danny realised it too. There's an old Scots proverb:
'What cannot be changed must be endured.' And it
looked as if we had been made for that, I thought
bitterly as Danny sighed and continued his tale of
disaster.

'I'd had more than enough. I was finished with the
Indian Bureau. The thought of staying in Arizona but
imagining you dead somewhere out there in the desert
became unbearable. So I got Pinkerton's to transfer me
to their New York office. All went well; then, last year,
I got into an argument with one of my colleagues, a
detective I was working with.'

Pausing, he added slowly, his eyes sad, remembering.
'A fight over a girl, Rose. Someone I had become
friendly with.'

For friendly, I read by his expression 'in love with'.
Who was I to complain? I had believed he was dead
when I took up with Jack Macmerry.

He sighed. 'She was beautiful, a showgirl. And he
was torturing her trying to get information about the
gangster we were looking for.

'I shot him, killed him and then I knew my time
with Pinkerton's was over. I had to leave and quickly,
so I stowed away on the first boat I saw weighing
anchor, heading for the River Clyde. When we landed
it was to discover that news of Sam Wild, the alias
Pinkerton's had given me for New York, had reached
the UK. I was wanted for murder.

'By a mere chance I met up with Hengel's, and what
better disguise for a wanted man than being a clown in
the circus? Especially as you know there was nothing I

couldn't do with horses. Rodeos, trick-riding, came as natural as breathing.'

As he spoke I remembered, as I should have done long since, a clue I had missed, that Danny McQuinn was a superb horseman.

'They were coming to Edinburgh. Edinburgh – what memories of the past: of you and Emily as youngsters, of being your father's sergeant.' Pausing, he smiled, shook his head. 'You were always determined to marry me; I warned you, my poor darlin' Rose, you got a bad bargain there.'

I took his hand and held it. 'No, I got what I asked for – ten years of happiness with the man I loved, the only man I had ever loved from being twelve years old, Danny. That was a long time to be faithful to a dream.'

He nodded. 'As you say, as you say. When I arrived here with the circus, I had no idea you were alive, much less living a mile down the road. Then a strange thing happened. I knew no one, I was totally among strangers and the sadness of that, of reliving those past years, bothered me. So I decided to look up the nuns at the convent, see if any of them who brought me up were still around.

'It would be great to talk to them. I didn't want to be apprehended by a policeman, just in case word of Sam Wild had reached Edinburgh, so I approached by the back road I remembered as a lad.'

He paused, staring at me. 'And there, by the grace of God, was this girl – you – at least I thought it was you. I couldn't believe it. The years hadn't changed you. I seized her hands, talked to her, called her Rose, asked, "Is it you?" She went white as a sheet, shaking, absolutely terrified. I thought she was going to faint. She obviously hadn't listened to a word—'

'She couldn't, Danny. She's a deaf mute. One of the nuns, Sister Clare, told me about this wild man who scared the young novices working in the vegetable garden. Her name is Marie Ann.'

'So you've met her.' He gave me a quizzical look. 'Haven't you noticed that she is the spitting image of you at her age? Of course, I suddenly realised, fool that I was, that my Rose was past thirty and must have changed quite a lot from the girl who followed me to America, and now there was going to be trouble. She suddenly pulled away from me and rushed inside.'

Again he shook his head. 'Trying to explain was beyond me. I fled. Then I thought I saw you sitting in the front seats at the circus. I was sure it was you this time, an older Rose. After the performance there you were again, this time talking to a policeman. As I guessed they might be looking for Sam Wild for the bank robbery, I didn't linger. I was confused. I had thought for years that you were dead, and now, I still couldn't be sure, couldn't believe my eyes...'

He sighed and touched the scar down the left side of his face.

'Where did you get that?'

'A bullet. It narrowly missed my brain, in one of our gangside encounters. I'm fine, I've got used to it, but my vision isn't as great as it used to be, as I discovered when I was part of Miss Adela's equestrienne act. No more circuses for me.'

We were both silent, sitting there in the firelight, surrounded by peace and safety. At least for the next hour or two.

I closed my eyes. Danny back. Wasn't this the miracle I had been praying for? My miracle answered, one moment out of time when I wished the world would stop turning and that we could stay like this for ever.

'What do we do now?' he asked.

He looked so ill, even the firelight couldn't change that. 'You have some ideas?' he asked hopefully.

'I'll answer that in the morning. Meanwhile we get you off to bed. It's a bit spartan,' I added apologetically.

He nodded, rose to his feet, slowly, almost painfully. Like an old man. 'Can't be worse than the floor in that hostel for down-and-outs. Staying with the clowns was too dangerous.'

'Sleep well, my darling,' I whispered, kissing that poor ruined face goodnight. Grateful that he didn't take me in his arms, for I didn't think I could have coped with the emotions that would arouse.

CHAPTER TWENTY-EIGHT

I slept badly, dozing, to suddenly awake thinking I had dreamt a dreadful nightmare, and in the next moment, knowing that it was real: that Danny McQuinn had returned, wanted by the police as a dangerous criminal, and was sleeping on the other side of the wall just a few yards away.

Once dawn broke over the hill, I abandoned any further attempts to sleep and began weaving elaborate plans, fantastic ideas of how he could escape from Edinburgh, none of which, I knew, would seem feasible reviewed in the cold light of morning.

The result of all this nocturnal planning was that when I finally fell asleep it was to be awakened by a hammering on the door.

Nine o'clock. I had overslept and the caller could only be Jack Macmerry, come for breakfast as usual.

Groaning, I flung on a robe and rushed downstairs, opened the front door.

'Sorry, you told me to keep the back door locked.'

'Of course I did, but I thought you would have been

up and about by this hour,' he said with a disapproving look at my dishevelled state, curls wild and disordered as if I had been giving hospitality to nesting birds.

I listened. There was no sound from upstairs. Thankfully Danny would remain out of sight until this visitor departed. Except, alas, that Jack was no visitor but a lodger and I was glad indeed that there had been no extra key to the Tower, or it would have been even more difficult to keep him from arriving without warning.

That had been one of my dozing nightmares. How on earth was I to keep Danny and Jack from meeting? Knowing human nature, however carefully one planned, there was bound to be a slip-up somewhere. The tenuous state of Danny's residence in the Tower certainly could not be maintained for an indefinite period.

I opened the kitchen door, let Thane out and, returning, prepared breakfast, conscious that Jack was watching me with a rather puzzled expression.

'What's wrong, Rose? You're all flustered. Something bothering you?'

I turned rapidly from the frying pan. 'Of course not, why should there be?'

'I just wondered. You seem more hassled than usual.'

'It's just oversleeping. Always upsets my day.'

Jack considered that for a moment; then, helping himself to a cup of tea, 'Well, what was the concert like? Did you enjoy it?'

'Concert?' I had forgotten all about the concert. No point in lying, he would soon find out.

'I didn't go.'

'But we had tickets. I'd reserved them – what a waste.' He sounded annoyed, and no wonder.

'I didn't want to go on my own. It's quite a distance—'

'You could have taken your bicycle, that's your usual means of transport,' he reminded me sharply.

'Not to a concert, Jack. The clothes I wear would hardly be appropriate.'

'Who cares about that, for heaven's sake? No one would have noticed...'

'In Edinburgh – at a Beethoven concert? As you know, most of the audience would be in evening dress, arriving in carriages,' I said angrily.

'You could have always asked your friend Elma to accompany you.'

'Hardly, at such short notice,' I said.

The last thing I wanted was an argument so I shrugged it aside. 'I just didn't feel like making the effort. However, something happened yesterday that will interest you...' And I told him about the cabbie and the two drunks, one of whom I suspected was Hodge, already dead.

He wasn't as excited by this story as I hoped.

'It could be true, if Hodge was murdered. But how are you going to prove it?' When I didn't answer, he said wearily, 'This is more of your circumstantial evidence. Hard evidence is what we need, without it we can prove nothing. It was dark and your cabbie could possibly have been taking two genuine drunks home.'

I was convinced my theory was right but I knew

Jack would never be convinced. Disappointed by his reaction but without further comment, I asked. 'What was your evening like?'

'Oh, the usual dull routine stuff, we had to go down and talk to someone in Peebles. However, when I was in the vicinity of home, I decided to go the extra miles and see the folks.'

He paused. 'They were asking after you, Rose.'

I hadn't seen his parents since the time of our wedding that never was, two years ago.

'I hadn't seen my father since he came through to Glasgow for the funeral.' I realised Jack meant his late wife's funeral.

'Is your mother pleased at having a new granddaughter?'

I realised that was a mistake as he visibly winced. 'She didn't say much about that. She's hardly likely to see her much. Glasgow's a fair distance away and Ma doesn't care for travelling.' Another pause. 'She was very sorry about us, always fond of you, Rose.'

I was silent. There was nothing I could think of as a suitable reply.

He helped me clear the table. 'It's their golden wedding this Friday. They both said they hoped you'd come with me.'

I put the plates into the sink. 'Jack, they're a sweet couple and I'm fond of them, but don't you see it wouldn't be fair?'

'I don't know what you mean – 'wouldn't be fair'.'

'Well, think about it. If I appear in their lives again, they'll be hoping that means we're back together and

I couldn't bear to give them false hopes, disappoint them—'

'You can only bear to disappoint me,' he interrupted with a bitter smile.

'Oh please, Jack. Let's not go into all that again, I beg of you.'

I could see that he certainly wasn't going to make it easy for me to add that I wanted him to move out.

He shuffled his feet a bit and said, 'Well, I do have one interesting piece of information. Knowing your interest in Sam Wild.'

I almost jumped when he said the words.

'What...what interest would that be?'

'Come now, Rose. Joey the Clown and all that stuff. Well, here's something for the record. You won't have forgotten all your theories about the bank robbery?' When I shook my head, he went on, 'We have at last received the results of the autopsy on the bank clerk.' He shook his head. 'They've certainly taken their time about it, but seems that the poor chap had a congenital heart defect. And that's what really killed him. He was alone in the bank, the junior clerk had gone across the road to the baker's shop. When he came back and saw the back of a man running away down the street, and found his colleague dead, he assumed that he had been murdered. And that went into his statement. But there were no marks of intent to kill, nothing that could be described as a death blow or any real violence apart from a bruise on his jaw.

'I've always had my doubts, especially as there were only a few pounds taken from the drawer behind the counter and some dollar bills scattered about. An attempted robbery, serious enough for an arrest, but that's one murder we can write off the slate.'

I could have told him what really happened but had to remain silent. I hoped the man's widow had his life insured. Jack agreed and I felt like laughing out loud, so relieved that Danny wasn't a murderer, at least not on this side of the Atlantic.

A great relief but Jack continued that he would still be guilty of attempted robbery and assault instead. Where was the evidence, the proof? Had the other assistant witnessed that he wanted to exchange dollar bills into pounds sterling and that the ensuing argument led to an exchange of blows, there would have been evidence, but he hadn't.

That was bad enough. But there was still the Pinkerton's man in New York.

And Danny McQuinn, by his own admission, was his killer.

CHAPTER TWENTY-NINE

Jack did not delay his departure. I could hardly contain my relief, almost certainly obvious to someone who knew me as well as he did. He made no comment, merely promised that he would try to be home early for supper. My heart sank at that piece of news.

I said, 'Don't promise.'

He smiled wryly for this had been the pattern of our lives together, a continuation of my early life in Sheridan Place. A list of last-minute cancellations of Pappa's presence at two small daughters' school events. As for fairs and the circus, we soon learnt to accept that Edinburgh City Police came first; his substitute on such occasions was our housekeeper Mrs Brook, or Vince, and this state of affairs appeared as quite normal, part of the vows taken at the altar by a policeman's wife.

After the door closed on Jack, Danny cautiously came downstairs. Perhaps I had expected some transformation by a night's sleep, but I was alarmed to see that he still looked so ill, worse in fact than yesterday, a troublesome cough, paler than ever, unshaven, his hair too long. A contrast, indeed, to the Danny of Pinkerton days, always clean-shaven, even imbuing rough and shabby clothes with a certain dignity. A man who had an inborn style and charm, whatever the circumstances.

I presumed he had a razor in that valise he carried and would use it when his arm hurt less. As he sat down at the table he was curious to know about Jack, so I gave him the carefully edited version of our relationship, with no hint that we had ever been lovers. Depending on what Danny had in mind, that might have been too great a blow to bear.

He listened silently and then asked, 'Do you love him, Rose?'

'What a question! He is an old and trusted friend, a widower and awaiting a new home; it is merely a convenient arrangement for him to be a temporary lodger.'

Danny gave me a shrewd look and said quietly, 'You haven't answered my question. Do you love him?'

'It is you, Danny McQuinn, I have always loved and waited for here in this house for five years.'

He gave me a mocking glance. 'Not this Danny, my darlin'. I'm a wanted man, remember. A man who has killed—'

'What nonsense! Wasn't that always a possibility of your life tracking down criminals at Pinkerton's?'

'In the line of duty, yes.' Slowly he shook his head, looked at me, almost with pity. 'But the Danny you loved and waited for was lost – lost a long time ago.'

It was so exactly like what I was thinking that I wondered if he had read my mind, that I was so transparent.

'Never had your willpower to resist temptation. After we parted, no longer with your good influence, there was gambling, getting into bad company – yes, and killing too. The rough life that living out west demanded for survival.'

He spread his hands wide. 'And now you see before you the mess it got me into. I was once a good Catholic, but I lost my God too. Haven't thought about him or even said a prayer in years. Adding up my list of transgressions, the Devil would find me a suitable candidate for hell, in fact.'

He cut short my protestations with a shake of his head, smiled wryly and said, 'So what about this admirable policeman of yours?'

I took a deep breath. 'I'm still married to you, Danny. Still your wife in the eyes of the law.'

'And so you are, my darlin'. Till death do us part,' he added sadly.

As I cleared away Jack's dishes and reset the table, I noticed him touching his bandaged arm, the knife thrust I had inflicted. I was so bitterly sorry. As if he did not have enough to bear.

'I'll have a look at that.'

'No, no. It's fine really. Later, maybe.'

He took the porridge I set before him, but before he had taken the last spoonful, his head dropped forward. He was asleep again. I touched his forehead. Did he have a fever?

I panicked. Where could I find a doctor? I knew none who would not feel it was their duty to inform the police about being called in to attend Sam Wild.

He stirred, his eyes opened, sighed. 'Sure now, you always had nice cool hands, my Rose.'

'You had better go back to bed.'

He rose from the table and, with a brief nod, slowly climbed the stairs, heavy-footed. An old man, I thought sadly. Seeing him safely into his room, I said I must go out for a while, and not to emerge — ignore all sounds downstairs.

'Don't come out until I get back.' I looked at Thane who was at our heels and now prepared to lie on guard outside Danny's secret hideout. 'Thane will take care of you.'

With two extra mouths to feed I needed more provisions and, as I bicycled down to St Leonard's, I noticed that Will Sanders' door was open.

He was home again. In answer to my call, he came out, grinning, wrist in splints but still deftly managing his crutches.

'Come in, lass, come in.' I handed him the sealed envelope. A word of thanks and I offered to make tea for us both. He accepted, watching gratefully as I buttered scones and set them out on a plate.

'Right glad to be home again, lass. Out of that awful place. Like my own fireside and my own bed and knowing what's going on — and what I'm eating.'

I made up the fire and, although he objected strongly, I tackled a pile of dishes, brushed the floor and tidied the room.

'That's enough, lass. Come and sit down. I want to talk to you. I did some serious thinking while I was in yon place and decided that I had to tell someone – about Belle.' He paused and regarded me thoughtfully. 'Something that maybe another lass might understand.'

He extracted the letter from his wallet. 'This was what I told you about. This letter from Belle. She tried to explain it all.'

And taking a deep breath, 'She wanted me to know wh-why she killed Amy and herself.'

I stared at him in disbelief. 'She killed Amy? You must be wrong.'

'No, lass, it's all written down here. This is the suicide note the police were wanting and I kept it from them. Amy and Belle were always close even when they were bairns. And when they grew up, they never were interested in lads, never wanted to get married. Watch out or the two of you'll be old maids, I used to warn them. And my Belle would say, "Why should we care about husbands when we've got each other?"'

He sighed, remembering. 'Then she said, "I could never love a man as much as I love Amy." I tried to explain to her that it was different. But I couldn't find the words about loving a man, having his bairns and so on. She didn't want to hear, just clammed up. That's how it is between us. But you're not to tell anyone. Understand?'

Will shook his head sadly. 'But I didn't understand then and I don't now. I know about love between a man and a woman, but between two lasses, that's beyond me.'

A pause, he sighed deeply. 'And then, out of the blue, this awful thing...it all went wrong. Amy met this sailor, crazy about her, wouldn't leave her alone. That was bad enough, Belle and her could have laughed about that. But worse was to come. His uncle had a sheep ranch in Australia, keen for them to settle with him, promising a great exciting new life. Amy was tempted, sick, and fed up of her dreary existence: hard work, no money and no future to show for it. She might never get an offer like this again. She was fond of the lad and decided to get married and go with him.

'My Belle was appalled, screamed and cried all night, like someone demented, heartbroken. She could talk of nothing else: this man was taking Amy out of their life together, taking her away for ever. She tried to tell Amy that she was making a big mistake, that she would find out too late that she could never be happy, not really happy with a man, or with any other living soul but herself.

'Amy wasn't to be persuaded, there were words between them, harsh words. When Belle heard that Dave was on his homeward journey and the banns were called, she was suddenly calm, said she would make it up after all.'

'It was a washing day and Amy had been doing the bedclothes so Belle went upstairs and said she'd help her, as she always did, to put them on the drying rack. But instead, she took the rope and wound it round Amy's neck and strangled her. And having killed the one person she loved above all others in the whole world, she went to her own flat, and hanged herself.'

His eyes were full of tears. He began to sob and I put an arm around his tired old shoulders. 'I found her and this note.'

He tore the envelope open. 'Here, you read it.'

'"Dear Grandpa. I killed us both. You know why. It was the only way. We'll be together always. Your loving Belle. PS. I don't want anyone else blamed."' I felt like crying too as I handed it back to him.

Folding it carefully away in his wallet, he said, 'I couldn't bear the police to read it. What if it got into the newspapers, for everyone to read about "an unnatural love" as they would call it. That was my secret and Belle's. But when I read that the police were considering that the two girls might have been murdered and were investigating possible clues – what if some innocent chap got the blame?'

'But that time in hospital gave me time to think. Knowing that I was an old man, I had to share this terrible burden. That's why I gave her letter to you. If I died, someone would know the truth.'

Like Will, I had never experienced anything other than love between man and woman, that all-consuming passion I had for Danny. But I believed I could understand the other kind. While we were in Arizona folk said that some of the legendary women of the west, like the notorious Calamity Jane, had female lovers and we knew two saloon girls in

Phoenix who were the subject of wry glances. They used to walk about with their arms around each other, cuddling and kissing. They boasted that they sold their bodies to the men out of necessity for survival, but their true and only real love was for each other.

I hurried back home, anxious about leaving Danny on his own. He was in the kitchen and didn't seem to have a fever. He said his arm was fine now. At least he was fit enough to have boiled some water, washed and shaved, which added to the feeling-better illusion.

'I'm fine now, been making myself at home.' He grinned. 'I'll be ready to retreat upstairs when the lodger returns. How much time have we?'

'About a couple of hours. We've a lot to catch up on, and just this afternoon, you'll be glad to know I've cleared Sam Wild's name in connection with another local crime.'

And because he knew of the love affair of the two saloon girls I told him Will Sanders' story of his granddaughter's suicide.

'Just as well he has that note, the evidence. I can well understand his wish to keep that information to himself. Do you remember those Phoenix girls saying what they did with men was business, but what they did with each other was pleasure? I guess most of Edinburgh folk of your acquaintance would find that hard to understand. Men and men, maybe – behind scandalous whispers and speculations. But never women and women.'

And as we talked about other Arizona days, the nostalgia of our lives together returned and I thought sadly that everything between us was like that – past, lost for ever – and I could not help feeling that there was no way forward, no future for us.

CHAPTER THIRTY

When we heard Jack's footsteps on the path outside, Danny retreated upstairs, with Thane at his heels. I realised it was dangerous if he lay down outside the secret room, so I called him down ,and when Jack gave me an enquiring look, I said, 'He's taken to sleeping on his rug upstairs.'

'Maybe he's heard someone say that two's company,' Jack replied and added sadly, 'if only it were true.'

Ignoring that, I told him of my meeting with Will Sanders.

He was not as surprised as I had expected, indeed, he seemed to have revised his earlier suspicions.

'I was always pretty sure that there wasn't anyone else involved despite the sensational press statements. They'll say anything to sell a few extra newspapers. I was always sure we weren't looking for a killer and that it was a suicide pact. And that is how the verdict went, the case has now been closed and there's no danger of opening it again or of anyone else knowing what really happened.'

He sighed. 'However, we still have Felix Miles Rice's death on our books.' To my question about anything new, he said, 'Yes, things are on the move. I don't suppose you heard while I was away that, according to the Miles Rice office in George Street, his lawyer was to call next day at Rice Villa. All they could get out of interviewing that tight-lipped gentleman was that it was for a purely personal matter, not one handled by his business interests.

'We've also had a visit from Peter Lambsworth. He came to see us anxious to make a statement that he found Felix was dead when he returned to recover the diamond earring his sister had lost on their earlier visit...that he was deeply shocked, and as there were no nurses or doctors around, and Hoskins was also absent from his post, he guessed that Felix must have just died and that they were away making arrangements.

'Lambsworth, however, was so upset that he didn't delay and rushed out to be the first to break the terrible news to his sister. He added that Mrs McQuinn of Solomon's Tower, who had been visiting at the time, could confirm this. But what was more important than explaining why he rushed out without informing any of the hospital staff was that he remembered having seen a man with a scarred face, a shifty-looking character was how he described him, hurrying down a corridor. He called out to him to stop, but the man just took to his heels and disappeared. Lambsworth thought this might be significant.'

Pausing, Jack looked at me curiously. I was confused, thinking of Danny, who to all intents and purposes fitted the description. My expression must have betrayed some anxious moments, as he asked, 'Did you see this character by any chance, Rose?'

'No. I saw no one like that.'

Jack shrugged. 'I doubt whether you would have made a note of that in any case, remembering where you were. Just as I told Lambsworth not to forget that, leaving the hospital by the reception area where accidents are admitted, a man with a scarred face might not be an improbable sight. He said he was glad about that and explained, somewhat apologetically, that being aware the police were on the lookout for a wanted man of that description, when he had informed his sister, she insisted that he should mention it to the police.

'He sounded rather cast down and disappointed that we were not taking seriously what he and his sister had thought of as an important piece of observation, apologised once again for having taken up our time and so forth.'

Knowing that the twins fancied themselves as amateur detectives, I wasn't surprised at Elma's reactions or the results. But I got the distinct impression that Jack wasn't very concerned about the mystery man with the scarred face who Peter was hinting might be Felix's killer.

I knew for sure that it could not have been Danny, who hadn't ever met Peter, Elma or her late husband. However, the alarming thought came unbidden that, if Peter was right, then perhaps there was a scarred man who might prove to be a likely suspect, as Jack continued:

'Whatever Lambsworth claimed to have seen, all the evidence points to his brother-in-law having undoubtedly been murdered, and we have absolute confidence in finding his killer, however long that takes; we will get it sorted out in the end.' And looking round he said, 'Now, where's that dog of ours? He seems to have deserted me.'

'Thane,' he called upstairs. 'Come, Thane.'

And Thane, who was proving to be a good actor, came as called, wagging his tail delightedly as he took his usual place at Jack's feet.

Jack stroked his head. 'What's come over you, lying in that cold bedroom when there's a nice fire down here with us?'

Once more I cleared away the supper dishes, always taking care to meticulously remove any extra cups or signs of Danny's presence; I knew that we were playing for time. This absurd situation of Jack and Danny living under the same roof was on a very thin wire.

They were bound to encounter one another by accident, or ill timing, sooner or later, and I did not want to consider the consequences of that meeting, for Jack would be obliged in his official role, whatever his personal feelings for my distress, to arrest Danny McQuinn as Sam Wild.

Although he was not guilty of murder, the unfortunate death of the bank clerk might well be classed as manslaughter. He would still be guilty on a charge of robbery. But, much worse, he was wanted for murder in the United States.

Whatever happened, I could see myself in a dangerous situation as an accessory for having sheltered a known criminal. Even if I didn't go to prison, that would certainly be the sad end of my career as a lady investigator.

Each passing day was of gnawing anxiety, a feeling of doom I could not shake off. A routine was established: each morning as soon as Jack departed, Danny came downstairs and I made another breakfast.

I was pleased to see that, although he still looked pale and ill, his arm was healing nicely and he was getting restless. He was not used to inactivity or solitary confinement, so I decided after much careful thought and deliberation that he should walk on the hill with Thane.

He would be quite safe: Arthur's Seat was a wild and lonely place on weekdays, only a few stray sheep grazing, and Thane would give plenty of warning, with his ability to hear the approach of anyone, scenting a human or animal well before they were in sight or sound.

My real fears were on behalf of Elma and Peter and their informal visits. Would Thane's warning system fail when he considered the two as friends made warmly welcome in the Tower?

I was expecting them imminently as I had heard nothing from Elma for a few days – obviously she was too involved in her husband's funeral arrangements. She was expecting me to be present on that sad occasion but, for several reasons, I decided to give the funeral at St Giles' Cathedral a miss. I had never met Felix and women were not expected to attend the graveside committal service. And afterwards I had no desire to return to Rice Villa or some expensive hotel marked down for elaborate refreshments and a turnout of Edinburgh society.

There was a spread in the newspapers about Miles Rice's sudden tragic death, his great loss to the community, and a lot about his beautiful heartbroken grieving widow and brother-in-law. It all sounded like a normal obituary of a well-respected Edinburgh citizen.

I wasn't surprised to learn from Jack that he and his senior colleagues had also been present at the cathedral and the cemetery. I imagined them trying hard to look inconspicuous on the faint off chance that they might have a chance encounter with Felix's killer.

Although I knew that they still had an unsolved murder on their books, a killer on the loose, it seemed a useless exercise to me. I could not imagine that creature turning up at the graveside, although I was informed, quite seriously, by Jack, that such things often happened.

'Perhaps just making sure,' he said, 'or a warped sense of taking a last look and breathing freely at last, seeing their victim has really gone for ever and will not trouble them any longer.'

The following day I encountered something very strange and sinister while making up Jack's bed in the great hall, something he usually did for himself, but that morning he had overslept and left in a hurry. I seized the opportunity to do a little tidying.

I turned my attentions to the table, its normally pristine surface scattered with discarded sheets of paper – Jack's attempts to teach himself to use the typewriting machine. He had not progressed very far: there were lists of three- and four-letter words, simple everyday ones used to make it easier to recognise the letter positions of the typewriting keys, words like 'you' and 'yours', 'two' and 'wore.'

The machine symbols QWERTYUIOP seemed odd to my way of thinking. Why not have a proper ABC? I glanced at one page of words and noticed that on the 'you' and 'yours' the letter U was missing altogether or very faint.

Very faint indeed, and tentatively I tried it out for myself on Jack's last practice sheet of paper which was still in the machine. I had to hit the letter U really hard...and then...I remembered. This was probably the result of the damage the machine sustained when I was attempting to carry it and, losing my balance, bashed against the wall.

I went suddenly cold. For that faint 'U' was the letter I had noticed was faint on the warning note I had received, informing me: 'Your turn next'.

There was only one possible conclusion. I backed away in horror as if the machine was guilty, for it had typewritten that note.

Which meant that someone had been in the Tower, used it in my absence. Of course the kitchen door had, until lately, always been left unlocked for Thane. But who was to know that? Had the writer of the note been lurking about outside somewhere just awaiting such an opportunity? That I knew was nonsense.

Was the writer, then, a joker perhaps?

I did not think so. And the only persons with legitimate access to the Tower in my absence were Jack, and Elma and Peter, who had occasionally taken shelter driven inside by the rain or awaiting my arrival. But it was absurd to imagine either of them doing such a thing, although on second thoughts, I wasn't past considering Peter might fancy himself as a joker: his sense of humour was a little warped on occasions, something that embarrassed poor Elma exceedingly.

But on the rare occasions when we had been in the great hall together, neither had shown much interest or curiosity about the typewriting machine under its leather cover, and I remembered how shocked they had been at the warning note, Elma in particular frantic for my safety.

I decided not to tell Danny. He had troubles enough of his own without having to listen to long explanations about the typewriting machine and the note, thereby giving him the extra burden of worries for my safety.

After supper with Jack that evening, I produced the note and we compared it with the words he had been practising.

'Sharp eyes!' He whistled. 'I should have spotted that!'

He listened carefully as I recalled the events of the day that the letter had been brought by the postman while I was out.

'Remember when I showed it to you, you insisted that I got curtains for the kitchen window?'

He nodded. 'A very interesting development. Who had access to the Tower that day apart from yourself?'

When I said only Elma and Peter, who had called in and were waiting for me, he asked sharply, 'Can either of them use a typewriting machine?'

I thought that highly unlikely. But as I watched him pocket the note, saying that he would add it to the file, I doubted whether it could have anything to do with the present investigation into Felix's death.

CHAPTER THIRTY-ONE

Jack was going to his parents' golden wedding and, before he left, he tried once again to persuade me to go with him.

Handing him his valise, once again I refused. 'We've gone into all the reasons, Jack. I'm sorry. Have a happy time and give them my warmest wishes.'

His departure was a blessed relief. It meant that Danny and I had a whole weekend together in safety, but each passing day saw me battling for a solution to the problem of what was to happen to Danny. We had to have a plan: obviously he couldn't stay in this area of Edinburgh, but once he was stronger perhaps he could make his way to another town, find work, get a regular job, settle down.

He smiled at that. 'Sure now, and maybe you could join me there.'

But he didn't sound very convinced about that and, frankly, neither did I. And I think he interpreted by my silence that my life was very much Edinburgh related.

'You could start up as a lady investigator in Glasgow

or Aberdeen, or we could even go south down to England. Or back across to Ireland,' he added hopefully. 'You would love Kerry.'

Again mute, I wondered what an ex-policeman, wanted for murder in the United States, had in mind as a regular job.

'What will you do?' I asked.

He said vaguely he could turn his hand to most things. Building was one of them. And he was strong enough for labouring work.

I doubted that. Although he had been so at one time my general impression was that Danny of today was a sick man who, for the moment, seemed content to remain almost, but not quite, a prisoner in Solomon's Tower with its secret room.

And then, when I least expected it, a visitor, the most welcome visitor in the whole world.

I heard a carriage coming along the road, we listened. It stopped and Danny quickly retreated upstairs.

I opened the door cautiously.

'Vince!'

Was this the miracle I had been praying for? I thought as, laughing, he swung me off my feet as usual.

He followed me into the kitchen. 'Oh, Vince, I am so glad that it's you. You have no idea...'

He made a face. 'Only very briefly, I'm afraid. Matter of hours. This time you have the royal train to *thank*. Bit of trouble, some problems on the way back from London. Damned engine broke down just short of Waverley Station, fortunately. Got the engineers looking at it. They reckon it isn't serious, a couple of hours will do it. But I couldn't miss the chance—'

'Vince,' I interrupted, 'Danny is back.'

'Danny!' He stared at me as if I'd gone mad.

'Yes, Vince. Danny is alive. He's here – upstairs.'

Vince looked utterly bewildered, he opened his mouth to speak, closed it again, and repeated, 'Danny – here?'

So I told him as briefly as I could the events that had led to Danny's return, including the circus.

Vince shook his head as if he couldn't take it in. 'Where is he now?'

'I'll get him.' I called and Danny appeared.

He came slowly downstairs. I glanced at Vince. I could see from his expression that he was shocked by Danny's changed appearance.

I watched them together, these two who had not met for many years. Danny was overjoyed to see Vince again, teased him about that expanded waistline, the good living, slapped him on the shoulder.

When at last I got a word in edgeways, I mentioned the complications regarding Jack also staying in the Tower.

'As a lodger,' I added hastily as my stepbrother gave me a hard look. Sitting around the table, he cleared his throat and said, 'A very difficult situation indeed.' However, his frowning glances in Danny's direction indicated that Dr Vince was more concerned regarding this particular patient's health.

He asked a number of casual questions which Danny fielded with a smile. 'Sure now, and you're the doctor, I forgot. But don't worry about me, I'm fine. Getting plenty of rest.'

I could see Vince wasn't satisfied with this and he said, 'Well, as I'm here, I'd like a look at that arm. Not really my present category, but I know enough about knife stabbings in an academic way from my student days in medical college here. And I've picked up quite a bit on gunshot wounds from occasional accidents during the shooting season at Balmoral. Just a general check up, eh, Danny. Junior physician to Her Majesty's household – what a chance. Something you can boast about to your mates. Would cost a fortune in Harley Street.'

His tone was mocking to Danny but a swift glance in my direction said plainly, 'No woman present.'

While I was putting supper together the two men retreated. When they returned half an hour later I thought I detected a false heartiness in Danny, and Vince seemed more than a little preoccupied.

I looked at them both. 'Arm all right?'

'Of course, you were a great nurse,' Danny said smoothly. 'Wasn't she, Vince?'

Vince nodded, a quick smile intended for reassurance, as he flicked open his pocket watch. I guessed he was now more concerned about the train waiting in Waverley station than his new patient.

All too soon we heard the approach of a carriage. The two men embraced and I went out alone with Vince.

'Tell me the truth,' I said. 'I want to know what's wrong.'

Vince stopped with his hand on the carriage door. 'It is not good news, Rose. Those headaches, affected vision, Danny knows the score. All that circus work must have been the final straw.' He shook his head. 'Well, you've asked for truth and you must prepare yourself.'

That deep sigh was from the heart. 'Danny is going to die.'

'Oh, dear God, no. When?'

'It could be tomorrow, or next week or next month.'

I think I already knew that. I was speechless, just wanted to cry.

Vince took my arm and said, 'I could take him back with me, put him in the cottage hospital at Ballater, but it won't prolong his life. He wants to stay here with you. I must go.'

He leant out of the carriage window. 'He asked me not to tell you but this is too grave a secret to keep from you. He will never leave Edinburgh, Rose. You're strong, you've coped with and survived many disasters together and I suggest you get rid of one of your complications by telling Jack the truth. I don't know how he'll respond, but I have faith in Jack. He's a good man, hardly likely to take Danny off to jail or have him shipped back for trial in America.'

We kissed goodbye and, standing by the gate, miserable and stunned, I watched the carriage disappear. I needed breathing space before I faced Danny.

He called my name and came to the door. 'Everything all right?'

'We always remember last-minute things. We don't see each other very often,' I added lamely as we went inside.

'Great seeing Vince again after all these years,' said Danny. 'Gee whiz, how prosperous he looks. Life has been kind to him...'

And on and on he went, while I sat there watching him, aware of that dazed fixed smile on my face, knowing how little time we had, our future sealed by Vince's verdict.

We got through the rest of the day somehow.

I wished now that Jack would return so that I could share my misery with someone. Any caring friend would do.

I almost got my wish when, next day, the Rice carriage rolled up the hill. Danny fled as Elma emerged.

She hugged me, full of apologies for not coming earlier, but of course I understood why.

She gave me a reproachful look, however, and added, 'You're not looking well, Rose. Have you been ill – is that why you didn't come?'

I knew she was referring to the funeral so I muttered something about a head cold – a lie, of course.

As we sat down at the table for the inevitable cup of tea, she sighed.

'This is so nice. Seems ages since I saw you. How's your nice lodger?' she added with an impish smile.

'Away to his parents in Peebles for a couple of days.'

'You will miss him,' she said archly and sighed. 'Peter and I have missed you. Anything exciting to report about our investigations?'

I could hardly say, Yes, as a matter of fact Sam

Wild, also known as Joey the Clown, our prime suspect, is hiding upstairs at this moment. Instead I said, 'Well, I have solved one of our intriguing little mysteries.'

Her eyes widened. 'You have?'

'Yes, that threatening note, warning me, remember?'

She frowned as if remembering was an effort, hardly surprising when so much had happened since, and I continued, 'As a matter of fact, I've discovered where it was written.'

'You have?' She looked amazed.

'Yes. Jack, my lodger, has been practising on the typewriting machine...' And I explained about the faulty letter 'U' and how it matched up with the same letter on the warning note.

Puzzled now, she shook her head. 'And so...'

'Well, don't you see what this means?'

'See what?' she said dully.

I laughed. 'So much for your powers of detection, Elma. Don't you see that it proves one thing for certain.' I paused and when she made no comment, just staring at me, quite expressionless, I added patiently, 'It proves that the warning note was written on the typewriting machine in the great hall.'

'But that's impossible!' she said shrilly. 'How could anyone—?'

I interrupted, 'It means that it could only have been written here in this Tower – unless there are hundreds of machines across Edinburgh with the same faulty letter. Which is extremely doubtful.'

Again I waited for some response, but there was none. She was painfully slow on the uptake. 'Don't you see? Someone came into the Tower when I was out and printed the warning note.'

'But it was posted in Edinburgh.' She remembered that. 'Surely the person who you say printed the note would have just left it here for you to find.'

I smiled indulgently. 'There's a very good reason for that, Elma. The writer, our chief suspect, the killer, was very crafty: by carrying it away and posting it in Edinburgh, he hoped that it could not be traced back to him.'

She was looking at me considering. 'Have you still got the note, Rose? I'd like to see it and so would Peter.'

And even as she said the words some piece of the puzzle clicked into place at the back of my mind.

'I haven't got it any longer. I showed it to Jack and he took it away with him.'

'To the police station, you mean?'

'Yes, he thought it might be important evidence.'

She was silent for a moment. 'You realise what this means, Rose. I'm sure it has occurred to you that you are in even more danger than you thought. That somehow this man Sam Wild, who we believe was responsible for poor Felix's death, was always near at hand – at the circus as Joey the Clown, of course.' She sounded quite excited now, as she added, 'That's it. He'd been lurking about nearby, watching your movements, waiting for just such an opportunity.'

I tried not to laugh at her solemn and completely irrational explanation when she went on triumphantly, 'And this, dear Rose, ties up with the other reason I came to see you. If your investigation hasn't progressed, then Peter and I have some very exciting clues to add. You'll never guess who was at the funeral,' she added triumphantly.

I shook my head. I hadn't the least idea.

Leaning forward she whispered, 'Sam Wild was there.'

'Sam Wild?'

'Yes! We both saw him, beside one of the trees near the graveside.'

'Were you sure about that?'

'Absolutely certain. He was near enough for us to see his scarred face.'

'Why didn't you do something about it?'

'How could we...make a fuss at such a time?' She sounded wounded, irritated by my response, which was not what she had hoped for.

'Inspector Macmerry, my lodger Jack, was there and some of his colleagues, on the lookout for just such an incident – that the killer might put in an appearance,' I said.

'Well, we didn't see them,' she said shortly.

'A pity indeed. But at least you can tell the police what you saw and that Felix's murderer is still lurking about somewhere.'

She stood up to leave. I wanted her to go. I had a lot of thinking to do, for unless there was another man with a scarred face, an innocent spectator at Felix's funeral, then she and Peter were wildly mistaken.

And since Sam Wild or Danny had never left the Tower, the story was either a remarkable feat of imagination or a complete invention.

And the question I now asked myself was...why?

CHAPTER THIRTY-TWO

I felt rather ill after the revelations of Elma's visit and decided to tell Danny. After all, he had been a detective.

He listened carefully and at the end he said, 'I realise you are reluctant to face the truth but there is only one answer to that note. And that is, Elma and Peter were the only ones who came into the Tower, apart from Jack and yourself. I think we can discount the possibility of a stranger entering; although you left the kitchen door unlocked, Thane would have seen any stranger off.'

Pausing, he looked at Thane. 'He is your clue, Rose. He would never admit anyone, unless he knew they were friends of yours, namely Elma and Peter.'

'I'm sure it wasn't Elma. She wouldn't have known how to use a typewriting machine.'

'Probably not, but Peter most likely did.'

And once I had started, there were other things lined up against Peter. I told Danny how I had met Peter rushing out of the hospital and afterwards had heard that Felix had been murdered.

'Jack tells me that Peter went into the station and described the scene. His awful shock at finding his brother-in-law dead...'

'A means of diverting suspicion from himself,' said Danny.

'There was more. The man with the scarred face he saw disappearing down the hospital corridor was the same one who appeared at the funeral.'

I looked at Danny. 'The elusive Sam Wild again.'

'Not only elusive but capable of being in two places at the same time.'

Danny sat back in his chair. 'It seems that Peter or, I regret to say, Elma too—'

I shook my head. 'No. I agree about Peter. But Elma, I can't imagine: she has always been such a friend.'

Danny was silent, considering. 'How did you meet in the first place?'

So I told him about her spraining her ankle on the hill and how Thane led me to her. How she was grateful for her rescue and took me to the circus.

'That sounds normal enough.'

'Frankly I was rather surprised that she suddenly wanted very much to be my friend, especially as I felt she must have many friends in her own social circle.'

Danny sighed. 'And so – I put it to you as gently as possible – flattered as you were, you did not consider there was a purpose behind this sudden friendship. What happened next?'

'She took me to the theatre.' And then I remembered. 'Danny, there was a man who met her outside while I was in the carriage. True, there were only street lamps, but when we met in Edinburgh I was sure it was Peter. She insisted that the man at the theatre exit was just an acquaintance of long ago and that it could not possibly have been Peter who was in London at that time. I must confess, I was never convinced about that either.'

'If you were right, then Peter Lambsworth was in Edinburgh at the time of her husband's attack.'

And that led me to Hodge, Miles Rice's devoted valet, and my meeting with him.

'The one who walked into the loch at Duddingston?' said Danny.

'The same. Except that I was sure that he had been killed first.'

'And you thought that he was protecting someone. That someone could have been the mysterious visitor.'

Danny stopped and we both looked at each other, the same thought in both our minds. Who else but Peter?

'Where was Elma when her husband was attacked?'

I was relieved to say that it couldn't have been Elma. 'We were having tea together in Jenners.'

'And where was Peter?' Danny demanded sharply.

'Still in London, according to Elma. He arrived back in Edinburgh a few days later.'

'That's when you met. But if he was the man at the theatre and already somewhere in Edinburgh, then it could have all been arranged, with you providing an alibi for Elma while he killed Felix.'

I then said what I was reluctant even to think. 'You believe they were both in it together.'

'I'm afraid so, or Elma is very much under her

brother's thumb. So let's take it a step further. What was the reason Felix had to die? That's an easy one.' Pausing, he added grimly, 'Money! The same reason wives have been getting rid of wealthy husbands through the ages. And the lovely Widow Miles Rice will do very nicely.'

Danny thought for a moment. 'Consider the police guard at his bedside. They were suspicious and wanted to be there if he recovered, so that he could tell them who had attacked him.'

And if that person was Peter, then that was the reason for murdering him. Danny was right about him, but Elma? No, I couldn't accept Elma's part in it, our friendship a sham, a ruse for an alibi.

'She was so anxious about him. Peter and she went in every day, so angry that the police would never allow them to be alone with him.'

'And a very good reason for that,' Danny said grimly.

I shook my head. 'She was so unhappy, she just adored him.'

But even as I said the words I remembered Vince implying that adoration on either side was not the general impression at Balmoral.

Danny said slowly, 'I think we have our villain. Brother Peter.'

'And that story about Elma's missing earring,' I said reluctantly, 'something they had dreamt up when Peter met me as he was rushing out of the hospital. No wonder he was so scared, knowing that I might mention it when I learnt that Felix had just died – had been murdered.'

'All carefully planned,' said Danny. 'And a lot of money for them to enjoy together once they got rid of Felix.'

'I'm not absolutely convinced about that. Jack has hinted that Miles Rice might be on the brink of bankruptcy.'

'If that's the case,' said Danny, 'then there has to be some other reason. If Felix recovered, then he might name his attacker.'

'The reason for the police guard and for the valet's so-called suicide.'

But we were getting nowhere. If only Jack were back from Peebles, I was sure he could fill in some of the gaps in the puzzle that Danny and I were so tortuously trying to solve, without all the missing pieces.

The sound of a shot outside, quite close on the hill.

We looked at each other. 'Someone out shooting rabbits,' I decided. 'We're getting quite overrun.'

'Bit near the house, Thane will be pleased. A free meal.'

We jumped at the sound of a loud banging on the kitchen door. I hoped it was Jack home early, but as a precaution Danny once more retreated.

I opened the door. Peter, the last person I wanted to see.

He didn't wait, as politeness usually demanded, to be invited in.

'Why on earth was the door locked?'

He pushed past me into the kitchen. I smelt gunpowder. Surely *he* hadn't been shooting rabbits on the hill? He looked around as if to make sure that we were alone.

'I decided to keep it locked, after that warning note, remember?'

He gave me a mocking glance. He knew what I was talking about and for the first time I was scared. I felt as if the air was still full of our recent speculations about him.

'The warning note, yes, of course.' He smiled.

My patience was wearing thin. 'What do you want, Peter?'

'Oh, just to clear up one or two small matters.'

'Where is Elma?'

'Let's not worry about Elma at the moment. We have other matters to attend to.' And so saying he put his hand in his jacket pocket, withdrew a revolver and placed it on the kitchen table.

I stared at it. 'What on earth is that for? You need a rifle for rabbits.'

'Rabbits!' He laughed. 'As a matter of fact, I have just shot your dog.'

I gasped, unable to take that in. A bad joke. Then... that shot...

Oh no, dear God, not Thane.

'You monster!' I screamed. I lunged forward for the gun. I would kill him for that. But I wasn't quick enough.

He seized my hand in a cruel grip. 'Had to kill him. He went for me out there. Never cared much for him, anyway, and Rufus didn't like him either.'

I tried to wrestle my hand away. He held tighter. I was helpless.

The gun now pointed at me.

'Afraid you will have to leave this lovely Tower,

Rose. You have another destination – heaven or hell, I don't care either way.'

'Where is Elma?'

I heard the rumble of a carriage outside. Jack, I prayed, let it be Jack.

'Oh, that's Elma now.' Light footsteps going past the window. He called her name and she came in, stood at the door, taking in the scene, looking at me.

This was Elma, the friend I had trusted. 'You, too,' I whispered. 'And your twin?'

Peter shook his head. 'No, Rose you are mistaken. I'd like you to meet my wife.'

Your wife. And the last fragment of the puzzle fell into place. The reason why Felix had to die. Elma, a bigamist, could never inherit any money. She could go to jail.

He raised the gun, pointed it at my heart.

'Peter,' she said, 'must you? I don't want her hurt.'

'Shut up, she won't feel a thing. Just bang, bang – and it will be over.' As he spoke, his eyes never left me. The eyes of a killer. 'She has to go, she knows far too much, our dear lady investigator.'

I said nothing. All I wanted was to get that gun. And kill him – for Thane.

He laughed. 'Well, let's tell her some more, shall we? She isn't going to tell anyone now – ever.' He smiled, he was enjoying this.

'That warning note, well, it was my idea. But the missing diamond earring, a piece of ingenuity. My wife's an excellent actress, you know, and she has a great imagination.'

He paused. 'The stage was set. All I had to do was stay around after our usual visit until one of my wife's delicious cakes that poor Hoskins appreciated so much took effect – just a little something in it, not to kill, but to give his bowels a very nasty turn. I'd located an empty small ward where I could patiently wait.

'Then, at last, Hoskins rushed out. That was the moment I was waiting for.' A grim smile. 'The deed done, I did not expect to meet Miss Busybody on my way out. And she could ruin everything. But by the time they find her we'll be on our way to France. There's a ship at Leith.'

I looked at Elma, one last plea, calm as I could. For all she had done, I still believed that she could save me. 'You were my friend. Are you going to let him do this?'

She looked at me and I knew the answer. The way I'd seen her so many times in Jenners considering a garment, a piece of material, a choice that was to be rejected.

She shrugged, and Peter smiled. 'She's my wife, she'll do anything I ask, anything. If I handed her this gun and said, kill her, she would do as I asked. Wouldn't you, my love? Look away, if you don't want to see.'

Elma turned her head, but she made no move. And I knew it was true.

I heard the gun click. And at that moment, a whirlwind entered the kitchen. It was Danny. I had never seen anyone move at such speed. His feet seemed hardly to touch the ground.

Peter and Elma were taken by surprise. Danny leapt forward, pushed me aside.

He was bigger than Peter, but the gun was cocked.

I heard the shot. Danny staggered, and as we both fell, Peter laughed, levelled the gun.

We were both to die. But this time the shot came from the door. Peter whirled round, he'd been hit and he yelled. As he fell, Elma, screaming, rushed to him, tried to wrest the gun from his hand.

The room was full of people. Jack and Inspector Gray, as well as uniformed policemen and Hoskins...

I was on the floor beside Danny, holding him in my arms.

I saw Peter being led out, wounded, a last glimpse of Elma screaming obscenities at his side.

Jack came forward. 'Rose. Rose...'

There was blood all over me. Danny's blood.

'I'm not hurt.'

Jack knelt down, tried to take the weight of Danny from me.

Danny's eyelids flickered open. He looked at me. 'Sure now, it's a good place for a man to die – in a lovely woman's arms.'

'Danny, Danny, don't...don't leave me.' I whispered as there flashed through my mind, in that timeless moment, the many times we had faced death together. As well as that dream of mine that one day I would open the door of Solomon's Tower and Danny would be standing there, smiling, his arms outstretched to hold me. Only it was I who held him. And he was dying.

Jack helped me support him. His eyes were closing again, like a weary old man.

'Look after her, Jack,' he whispered. 'Do that for me.'

He coughed. There was blood on his lips. His eyes closed, this time for ever.

I sobbed, held on to him. Unwilling to let him go.

Jack said, 'The ambulance is here...'

I looked up, sudden hope in my heart. Maybe?

They were carrying him away. I held on to his hand. 'No, please, no.'

Jack shook his head, put an arm around me. I buried my head in the region of his chest as high as I could reach, mourning for Danny. For Thane.

In the now silent Tower, we were alone.

EPILOGUE

Jack took over. Vince came from Balmoral and they saw Danny laid to rest, as Sam Wild.

'Someday the truth will out,' Jack said. 'Meantime we stick with the belief that Danny died in Arizona.' Perhaps that was the truth.

The Lambsworths had been under investigation by the Edinburgh City Police since Felix Miles Rice's obituary fell by chance into the hands of an old acquaintance of theirs now living in Glasgow. They had swindled him out of several thousand pounds in their London days. He had an account to settle and an interesting tale to tell.

Elma Lamb and Peter Worth had met a decade earlier, thespians in a small local company. They discovered that they shared the same birthday and as both were fair, blue-eyed, fellow actors they laughingly christened themselves 'the twins'. They fell in love, married, and took the name Lambsworth.

On tour with a Shakespearean company, by chance Felix Miles Rice came to a performance. Enchanted by

Elma, he fell in love and, unaware that she was already married, he proposed – a wealthy man with much to offer. Peter, weary of touring and bad digs, decided that Elma should accept. She did so and by the time they had moved to Edinburgh, Peter had worked out a plan.

Both were aware that, if Felix found out about his bigamous marriage, the consequences would be disastrous. They had to get rid of him. As his widow Elma stood to inherit everything.

Peter had thought out the details meticulously. Among Elma's friends she had learnt of a lady investigator, Rose McQuinn, and cultivating her friendship would provide the perfect alibi for Peter's plan. He had left it too late. Felix was suspicious of their relationship. One step ahead, someone in the London branch of his firm discovered that Elma Miles Rice's twin was in fact her husband.

So Felix had made an appointment with his lawyer for the next day to cut Elma out of his will. But proud and successful and with a belief in his own infallibility, and wishing to avoid a public scandal at all costs, he could not resist the temptation to let this miserable little swindler know the truth; it was his undoing, for Peter meant to kill him.

Unfortunately for him, he was seen in the garden by Hodge who, loyal to his mistress and her brother, could not bring himself to voice the suspicions which cost him his life. So he had to be disposed of by Peter, carried in a hiring cab, the one I encountered the day that Danny arrived at Solomon's Tower.

*   *   *

Jack honoured Danny's last wish, a promise to be there when I needed him. I knew that marriage would be included, if that was what I wanted.

I discovered that Jack was a better actor than I gave him credit for. One day he said, 'How you managed to keep us both in the house without meeting was quite an achievement.' He gave me a quizzical grin. 'I guessed that the secret room had a new tenant.'

'You knew?'

He nodded. 'Almost from the beginning. I knew from my visit to New York that Danny McQuinn, your heart's darling, was also Sam Wild. I just wondered how long I could keep that from you and from the Edinburgh City Police.'

'And risk everything – including your career, if they found out.'

'That too.' He shook his head and said warily, 'Then, at my folks' golden wedding, I had thought you would be safe in the house with Danny to protect you but something was wrong. I had one of my weird moments. You were in terrible danger. It's happened before.'

I knew it had, although Jack was always reluctant to admit that he might have a psychic side to his nature, defying all logic.

'I'm grateful,' I said.

He grinned. 'I don't want you to regard it as an excuse for a happy ending.'

'The jury's still out on that one.' I laughed. 'But it will be taken into consideration.'

Jack and I are close, but not lovers. Crimes solved, cases closed, explanations found.

All except one.

Over and over I have relived that moment of agony when Danny had died in my arms. No words for my bitter grief overflowing. For Danny. For Thane.

I had lost them both.

Jack had held me, let me weep. But there was no comfort on earth in that scene of desolation and heartbreak, no one could help me. I was alone.

But not quite alone. I looked down. My hand was wet.

It was being licked.

Thane!

'Oh, Thane,' I put my arms around his neck and cried, 'That vile beast said he had killed you.'

Jack said, 'He certainly killed something. There's a dead sheep at the bottom of your garden. We almost fell over it.'

Life goes on, but there is this one tantalising mystery still unsolved. Maybe it never will be.